TOO LATE

"Too Late," by B. Hayden Hawley. ISBN 978-1-951985-34-9 (softcover); 978-1-951985-35-6 (eBook).

Published 2020 by Virtualbookworm.com Publishing Inc., P.O. Box 9949, College Station, TX 77842, US.

This is a story tracking the progressive destruction of three lives. Like quicksand, once the process begins, nothing can put it in reverse.

Aline Kranick is an ambitious young writer working for one of New York City's most prestigious news magazines. Afraid of being laid off due to exhaustion, she comes up with the idea of combining a vacation with an assignment. Her plan takes her to an inconspicuous coastal town in Maine where she is witness to events having a domino effect, leading to her disillusionment and poor decision-making alternatives.

Aline follows her course of action without hesitation, to a tragic ending for everyone involved, including her best friend and lover.

Refusing to face the truth in order to exist in her world of pragmatic reality, she has only one choice left and she takes it, at the risk of losing everything that has taken her a lifetime to achieve.

I wish to thank the following individuals and organizations for their time, responsiveness, interest and support at the time that I contacted them.

Col. Kenneth Moore, P.A., Chief Investigator,
Medical Examiner's Office, St. Johns-Putnam-Flagler Counties, St. Augustine, FL

Lt. Art May, Deputy Sector Commander,
Operations Division, St. Johns County,
Sheriff's Office, St. Augustine, FL

Steve McCauslin, Department of Public Relations,
Maine State Police, Augusta, ME

Mr. Shuttleworth, Maine Historic Preservation
Commission, Augusta, ME

Maine State Library
State Cultural Building, Augusta, ME

Connecticut Department of Public Health
Hartford, Connecticut

Kennebec Valley Chamber of Commerce, Augusta, ME

Boston Police Headquarters, Boston, MA

Concord Trailways, Rockland, ME

Greyhound, South Station, Boston & Stamford, CT

And special recognition and appreciation to my editor,
Beth Mansbridge of Mansbridge Editing & Transcription,
St. Augustine, FL

"Some horrible thing-violence- always hits you in nature.

Doing a tempera called "River Cove," I lay for hours watching the tide creep like little fingers up over the shells dried in the sun. What horrified me was that no power could stop it . . ."

Andrew Wyeth
Life May 7, 1965

TOO LATE

by

B. Hayden Hawley

1.

MORE THAN TWO WEEKS HAD PASSED since it happened, but the memory of it was still fresh. His head collapsing like an overripe pumpkin, left out in the sun too long.

Most of it wasn't difficult to do. People seemed to want to help in the completion of the goal. Finding a ride to the bus station didn't take much effort, either. Looking lost and defenseless always worked. People took on a superior air when they helped those in need. Lending a helping hand made them feel good about themselves. Some of them even offered to donate money.

The last leg of the journey brought back the sadness. A sense of relief would come only when it was over. And it would soon be over.

After crossing the Maine border, it would take another two and one half hours to get to Cape Warren. Anyway, what worked in Norwalk would work in Rockland. It was successful because no one expected it.

Especially him. He always left himself in such a vulnerable position—trusting, open-door policy, preoccupied.

Walking on the uneven ground in the dark was the most difficult part. The small pocket flashlight was a help. So close, so close to finishing it.

As anticipated, the front door was unlocked. Why not? No one would have any interest in following that difficult road to its destination. It was an obstacle course.

The weapon of choice was in plain view, always had been. And he was also in plain view, just exactly where he should be.

He turned around when he felt the first vibrations. But by then it didn't matter. He couldn't do anything to stop it.

The screaming was the worse part, bone-chilling and desperate. "STOP! What are you doing!"

The louder he screamed, the more violent the vibrations became. "Please STOP! For God's sake!" The screaming fueled the attack, made it more satisfying to achieve.

"PLEASE! DON'T DO THIS! I BEG OF YOU!"

It didn't take very long to destroy him. There was plenty time to get out of the way. When he fell, flailing his arms and legs, he resembled someone trying to learn how to swim.

"AH-h-h-h-h!"

In actuality, it was rather pitiful. The sound of him hitting the ground was gruesome—heavy and wet. But there was no doubt about it, he was dead. No pulse. Those eyes of his remaining open, staring blankly into nothingness. Staring at what *he* had never experienced, an empty void. Somehow, it now seemed appropriate.

Every aspect of the plan was turning out as forecasted. And that quiet, friendly place allowed it to happen, and become unknowingly, the silent ally. Nothing like this ever occurred there. Not there. Not to anyone's knowledge. Walking away would be so conclusive.

2.

BUT THIS WAS NEW YORK CITY. Here and only here could this happen. For first- and last-chance people, it was always the top choice in an attempt to succeed. They hoped this city held all the answers—they knew it represented the challenges. Most of them were young, some not so young, but with a little luck they might be able to make it in New York.

Back home, nobody cared who they wanted to be or what they wanted to accomplish. Outstanding opportunities to show off their talents were nonexistent where they came from.

New York was different. No one knew them and no one noticed them, but that didn't matter because here everyone at least had an opportunity to make it. They could start fresh and build a whole new future out of their gray lives.

And besides, most New Yorkers didn't even come from New York. They had escaped from Lanson Falls, Vermont, or West Harmon, Ohio, or Ionia, Nebraska, or maybe Crayton Point, North Carolina. If you asked them where they came from, they'd tell you without blinking an eye that they came from New York.

Once in a while they might return home for a short visit. But they wouldn't mention it to their associates. And of course, before long, it would always be, "Well, I really have to get back to *the city*." It would be easy to leave because that always sounded much more important than whatever they were doing in Ionia.

The holidays were different. They succumbed to the security of old friends and Mom's cooking. Then, they would brag about going home: "I'm going home for Christmas," or better yet, the cosmopolitan: "I'm going home for the holidays." What they were actually saying was, "I have a place to go, do you?"

So New York absorbed these homely, expectant achievers who loved this big city and now, being New Yorkers, were living the dream of success.

Aline Kranick was one of these New Yorkers: single, impatient, and six years out of college, who had taken the City and her job by the teeth and was already exhausted by it all. She labored as a reporter on the staff of a pulp magazine which featured articles on celebrities in theatre and the arts. Being the youngest in her department, she had overworked herself in order to prove that her sheer stamina could meet the incessant deadlines. Working late nights and weekends was her usual routine. The more she accomplished, the more she wanted to do. It was eating her up.

Her tireless energy and driving determination had taken their toll. One bout with mononucleosis had almost hospitalized her and she was constantly fighting off numerous colds and sinus infections. Her rundown condition targeted her for the viruses that made the rounds throughout the office.

Aline lived in an anxious state of mind, fearing a layoff or forced leave of absence because of her poor health. In New York there was always the threat sitting on your shoulder that another overachiever was waiting for the opportunity to take away your job.

Her editor-in-chief had his eye on her. She knew he was concerned about her and this only caused her to work harder.

She needed to come up with a solution. And then, one Sunday afternoon, while skimming the *New York Times*, it struck her—why not take the initiative before all these misgivings became a fact. Turn it around.

In the *Arts* section, next to the list of exhibitions, was an article on a new one-man show on Madison Avenue that caught her attention. An American landscape artist, a Mr. Thomas J. Elcock, was retiring and this show recognized his extensive body of work. He'd already been published and some of his art was to be on permanent exhibition at the Metropolitan Museum of Art after the exhibition closed.

One of his paintings had been chosen for a commemorative stamp by the U.S. Post Office series on American artists. His work was now in constant demand in the New York area and his earlier canvases were already considered collectors' items.

Aline put down the paper and slipped into deep introspection. The Arts section of the paper had always appealed to her. She had taken some art courses in college and it was a hard decision for her to choose between a career in art or creative writing. Her father finally convinced her that the latter offered more potential as a career. However, the unfulfilled yearning to be a commercial artist or graphic designer occasionally pestered her.

What if she requested that the magazine allow her to take off a few weeks—no—give her an assignment—to interview Elcock at his studio in Maine. Anything with any significance in life needed procedure. Develop a feature article for an upcoming issue. She recalled a discussion at the last staff meeting that revealed the usual lack of ideas for the months following fall and the holidays. The time frame of October through December always bombarded the writers with an overflow of concepts to choose from. January or February would be the perfect slot for an article on the Maine painter.

First thing Monday morning she would present her idea. The more she thought about it, the more its pure logic presented itself as the catalyst for her undertaking.

She cut the article out of the paper. Seeing the exhibition today was imperative, and the gallery closed in three hours.

3.

TIME WAS CRUCIAL. Aline quickly changed into a pair of black slacks, bright red turtleneck sweater and tweed jacket. She rushed down to the lobby to grab a cab. Her doorman whistled for one and almost immediately, a Checker pulled up. Still grasping the newspaper article, she jumped into the back seat, leaning forward to give the cabbie directions. Then she sank back, trying to catch her breath.

She pulled a small black comb and compact out of the zippered pocket in her purse and looked at herself. There wasn't time to apply cosmetics, but her youth and good looks would make up for that. Good hygiene had protected her fair complexion from the destructive qualities of the city's dirty air. She briskly combed out her short, dark hair and brushed on some blush. Clear gray eyes looked back at her, reflecting her eagerness and determination.

In fifteen minutes, they were there. She paid the driver and stepped out of the cab, facing the front of the gallery. All the doors stood wide open. The place was packed with people, mostly dressed in black, some gathered in small groups on the front steps. When she entered the exhibit, the din of loud conversation met her with full impact. On a small table to the right of the entrance, lay an abundance of literature regarding the show and she started to collect samples, in duplicate, of anything that seemed relevant: pamphlets describing the shipbuilding industry, the Maine coast, and a brief history of some of the more renowned sailing vessels that had made their mark in navigational lore. This material would be invaluable as backup to support the urgency of her proposal.

She bought an exhibition catalog and this was to be added to it a reprint of an article in *ArtToday*, containing a descriptive background of Elcock's education and a synopsis of his career. The overall impression was that Elcock chose this career more as a way of life than as a business.

The exhibition rooms were stark white, with high ceilings and indirect track lighting. Displayed before her were the largest canvases she had ever seen. Seascapes and landscapes covered the gallery walls, but the most overpowering works depicted sailing ships dramatically battling the sea and the New England weather.

At first, Aline stood rooted in one spot in the center of the room, trying to concentrate on the paintings, but so many patrons crowded around them that it was difficult to get close to them for viewing. She nudged her way toward the front line. Before her was the culmination of a lifetime of experience and talent, as well as a total devotion to subject matter. Quite clearly, the man was very familiar with the sea and loved his association with it.

With some difficulty, she worked her way around the galleries. She took a little notebook out of her jacket pocket and started to jot down notes.

About four-thirty, people began to drift out of the exhibitions. The city had taught Aline to appreciate the absence of crowds. She relished the renewed spaciousness of her surroundings and stepped back from the art, seeing it in a whole new perspective.

Studying the labels made her realize that this man's career as a painter spanned for over thirty years. The quality of his earlier work stood apart from that of the seascapes completed within the past ten years. A notable difference was in his choice of color. The later paintings used more somber tones, less yellows and reds, which dominated most of his early oils. Sunrises and sunsets had been replaced by stormy scenes or the reflection of light on water observed at dusk.

At ten minutes to five the gallery guard blew his whistle and asked the remaining patrons to leave the building. Aline started inching toward the front door, still poring over the canvases with appreciation as she moved along.

Out on the street again, she stood near the curb, looking off into the distance, but focusing on nothing. Something about this whole experience frightened her a little. A gnawing in her subconscious told her that this was predestined. She felt drawn into this assignment by some force, some power she couldn't control.

"Cab, miss?"

The cab driver's voice jolted her back to reality. His Checker was idling right in front of her and she didn't even hear it approach.

"Yes please."

As they drove away, she kept looking out the back window at the gallery until it disappeared.

When the taxi arrived at her building, she was pleased to see that the doorman wasn't at his usual post; she didn't want to deal with the usual small talk right now. All she cared about was to be alone in her apartment with her thoughts.

The lobby was empty. Within seconds, she was focused on the elevator buttons, impatient to get to her apartment. At last she reached her floor and quickly gained entry into her apartment. The timers had already turned on the lamps and the mellow lamplight was welcoming to her.

After her shower, she put on a robe, retiring to the sofa with a cup of cappuccino. She lay in the soft light, trying to sort out her feelings about what she planned to do about this encounter.

A feature article on Thomas Elcock was a bit offbeat for her since she usually covered off-Broadway reviews or new plays. The potential assignment challenged her merely because its concept was so unparalleled.

Starting out as a proofreader could never be enough to quell her ambition. Submitting samples of her creative writing to the head of the department was an aggressive move on her part. But it paid off. After two trial months working as a contributing reporter, she was permanently promoted to that position, an advance she cherished.

Aline was optimistic about receiving approval. Elcock was presently a notable social item in New York. The prominence of his show would be conclusive.

4.

MONDAY MORNING. The door to Marty Rosen's office was always open. As editor-in-chief, he learned a long time ago that open communication with his staff was not only his first priority, but the key to his control. It kept the production of the magazine flowing and guaranteed that decisions were joint efforts which produced more intelligent and effective results. He was always there for them, to help them with any struggles concerning story outline, subject matter and the magazine's code of ethics and deadlines.

Aline always worked successfully with him and prospered by his experience and recommendations. The articles that she produced, with his assistance, always reflected the state of excellence required of the magazine. His guidance, invaluable in teaching her about technique, was the keystone to developing her individual style of writing. Her admiration for him as a professional, a superior and a friend was overwhelming. She was never afraid to go to him for direction, whether it be related to business or personal matters.

As she approached his office, Aline could see him bent over the paperwork on his desk. Even though his hair was thinning, he still looked very young for a man in his mid thirties. He was promoted very quickly, from assistant editor to his present position in only six years. His leadership qualities, intelligence, diligence and drive impressed everyone who met him. He hated sensationalism and strove to give the magazine a tasteful identity. He worked his staff hard, yet he was fair and he more than appreciated their individual efforts and contributions.

As she approached his desk, he looked up. The expression of his dark brown eyes softened as he noted Aline's intense demeanor.

"What's up? You look pretty serious." He motioned for her to take a seat next to his desk.

"I need to talk to you about an idea I have."

He leaned back in his worn-out leather chair and pushed himself away from the desk, and said, "I'm right in the middle of something, but I always have time to hear you out. Shoot."

"I'm asking you for permission to go to Maine on assignment. The *Times* had an article about a fascinating artist, Mr. Thomas J. Elcock. He has a one-man show on Madison. He's retiring and I'd like to go up there before they break down the show and interview him for the January issue. Here's some literature on his work. I went to the gallery yesterday and I was amazed by what I saw. His work is absolutely incredible!" She spread out the pamphlets and papers on his desk.

"Yeah, I've heard of him," he said while rummaging through the literature. "My wife showed me this article. She's going over there today. I should get over there myself on one of my lunch hours to check it out, so I can relate to her. What made you decide on this proposition?"

Aline was ready. She knew it was necessary that she present this project as an assignment, not as a leave of absence. "Basically, I guess it's my interest in art. It was hard for me decide a long time ago whether it was going to be the brush or the pen. Anyway, this man is hot right now. He's getting a lot of exposure. I figure he's not interested in the talk show circuit, but he may be receptive to being published again, especially if we reproduce some of his work. With your approval, I'll make an effort to find out today if he'd be interested."

As always, Marty was listening to her with an open mind. His hands were resting on his chest. After what seemed like more than a few seconds, he said, "Let me think about this. I have to check the work load to see if I have you lined up for anything more demanding between now and the January deadline. In the meantime, try to find out whether your idea is going to fly with Elcock. If he won't go for it, there isn't any point in pursuing it further. I think your idea has validity. Everyone loves art—or almost everyone. My wife has been hounding me to take her to the show. She read about this guy in *ArtToday*. By the way, did you know that she takes art lessons at City College? I wish my workload gave me more time to get involved."

"I never knew that Judy was interested in art. She never mentioned anything about it. What's her interest?"

"Right now, ceramics and drawing. Next semester she wants to take oils. She never seems to have any time for herself, what with taking care of the kids and her parents. We have to carve out some quality time for her. Her mother sits for us when Judy's in school." His gaze fell again to the papers on his desk.

Aline was acquainted with Judy and their six-year-old girl and five-year-old boy. She'd attended last year's Christmas party at their spacious two-story brownstone in Queens. They were obviously very happy together after eight years of marriage.

Marty looked up and asked, "What are you working on now?"

"I just finished that article about Anthony Hopkins for December. Currently, my desk is clear."

"O.K. Let me know how this develops. I'm going out to lunch with one of my old college buddies who's in New York on business, but I will be back later this afternoon if you need to talk to me. We'll try to make a decision as soon as you have more information. Are you sure that you're up for this if I give you the green light? You look tired."

She readjusted her sitting position to the edge of the chair and smiled as she assured him that she was physically prepared to take the trip. "I'll be fine. Getting away for a bit wouldn't hurt," she added in a casual tone of voice.

"How much time do you think you'll need to complete this project, if it all falls into place?"

"Two to three weeks should be adequate. I'll be sending you rough drafts as I write the story. I'd like your input, as usual."

"You have to be more specific, Aline. What about budget? I'll need a breakdown of your expenses. You're aware, of course, that any project of this nature which involves leaving the office, has to be approved by my boss. I'll need lots of details to satisfy his analytical mind."

"1 understand, Marty. My work's cut out for me today. I'll have a typed proposal, including a budget and work schedule, on your desk by five o'clock."

"Well, I doubt if we'll be able to finalize everything in two working days, but I'll take all that you have to offer into consideration before I make the final presentation."

He pulled himself up to his desk. The meeting had ended.

Aline sprang up. "OK, talk to you later." She walked briskly out of the office. He was giving her an opening to survive.

5.

ALINE CLEARED HER DESK so she could get organized. The shared space with four other reporters represented a cluster of desks, file cabinets, computer stations and other office equipment. The noise level was unbearable at times, with the telephones ringing, copy machines humming, and voices overlapping. Learning to concentrate through this racket had developed into an invaluable occupational skill.

A new deadline. She loved it. Working under pressure was her forte. Many facts would have to be gathered in record time if this idea was to come even close to reality.

The first step was to contact Elcock. It was urgent that she present the project to him in a manner that he would accept. If he didn't support the idea, she must accept defeat.

The gallery would have Elcock's telephone number in Maine. If the director refused to give it to her, she would think of a way to persuade him to volunteer it. Maybe giving the gallery some free publicity or a credit line for the show would help soften the expected resistance to the request.

She planned to stay in Boston overnight before arriving in Maine on Friday. Once in Cape Warren, she would look for a room to rent in a private home in order to economize as well as guarantee some semblance of solitude and quiet.

It was time to call the gallery. The phone rang for a long time, but finally someone picked up.

"May I help you?"

"Good morning, my name is Aline Kranick. I'm a reporter for *East Side/West Side* magazine. Is the gallery director available?"

"Speaking. Roger Golding here. What can I do for you?"

"My magazine would like to print a feature article on Mr. Elcock in our January issue. It's imperative that I contact him. Could you assist me in locating him?"

Silence. Her heart sank.

Finally Golding responded, "Aren't you being a bit presumptuous? The gallery is hardly in a position to give out such private information. We are committed to protecting the confidentiality of our artists."

In a low, soothing voice, Aline responded, "Mr. Golding, I understand your position completely. Before I continue, I want you to know that you've done an exquisite presentation with the exhibition design. The article I'm writing is dedicated to Mr. Elcock's life and work. However, a significant portion of it will be an expression of praise for your gallery. You and your colleagues deserve high accolades for offering to the public an opportunity to appreciate the superlative quality and content of his creative ability in the most exquisite setting possible." She waited while his ego inflated. He'd probably take the bait.

He cooed, "Thank you for your support. I'm sure that my colleagues will be pleased to hear of your approval."

"Everyone I know has seen the exhibition. Most of my friends have seen it two or three times."

"Well, this is a bit irregular, but I suppose I could give you his number—on one condition, though."

"Yes?"

“Don’t ever let him become aware of your source of information. I have an important position to uphold here.”

“I, personally, am making you a promise that I shall never divulge my source.”

After she hung up, she let out a sigh. It was after ten-thirty, not too early to call Elcock. She retrieved a legal pad and some pencils on her desk and dialed his number. After three rings, he answered the phone.

“Hello. Thomas Elcock speaking.”

The sound of his voice surged through her nervous system. She answered him, her voice trembling. “Mr. Elcock, my name is Aline Kranick. I work for *East Side/West Side* magazine in New York. We were hoping to write an article about you for our January issue. I’m a reporter for the magazine and after seeing your show, I felt that our readers would be very appreciative to be introduced to you and your lifetime of artistic achievement and commitment.”

“How did you like the show?”

Her confidence flooded back. “Mere words can’t express how much it meant to me. I have never seen such power and magnitude reflected in any art, until witnessing your work,” she wanted to sound sincere, but not effusive.

“Well, thank you. It can’t match the spiritual vitality of the great works of Picasso or Delacroix, but I share their passion.”

“I saw the show this weekend and plan to go back when and if the crowds subside.”

“I’m glad you enjoyed it. According to the papers, it’s getting a favorable response. It may be held over.”

Her heart jumped. She hadn’t expected such a receptive response, and it stirred her enthusiasm. “How would you feel about being interviewed by me? The magazine would pay for your time and publication rights. There is a standard agreement for you to sign which protects you from being published without your consent by any service other than *East Side/West Side*. I could mail you a copy for your review." She tapped her pencil on the desk while waiting for him to answer.

"Do you want to reproduce my work?"

"Yes, but only with your permission. And you alone would choose the artwork that would accompany the text."

"Well, I do have to think about this. There are some phone calls I have to make. I will call you back later today and give you my decision."

It wasn't a "no." All she could do was wait. "That would be fine, Mr. Elcock. I look forward to your call." She gave him her home number as well as her office number.

To keep her mind off his return call, she started to contact Boston hotels and car rental offices in the city. Marty would have all his figures by the end of the day.

Thinking back on the conversation with Elcock, she felt fairly successful. He seemed agreeable only to a small degree, but at least he was pleasant to talk to.

By late afternoon Aline proceeded to print out the proposal for Marty's review. Somehow the neatly organized numbers on the sheet of white paper had a pristine look of thoroughness. All it needed was the stamp of approval. He wasn't back from lunch when she went to drop off a copy. She placed it on his chair so he couldn't overlook it. If she left it on his desk, it would certainly melt into the clutter of papers that constantly surrounded him.

Returning to her desk, she waited for Elcock's call, avoiding conversation with her co-workers. They knew something was happening and kept looking at Aline, trying to break the ice. She avoided their eye contact.

At twelve minutes to five, the call came. It startled her and she let it ring three times before picking up.

"Aline Kranick."

“Hi, it’s Thomas Elcock. When can we get together?”

Everyone around her was also waiting for the call and now they were all staring at her. She shielded her eyes for concentration.

She was almost choking on her excitement. “Anytime at your convenience, Mr. Elcock.”

“How about a week from today, next Monday. I’ll send you a map of how to get to my house once you’re settled in town. I live in Cape Warren, about three and a half hours north of Boston.

“That would be perfect. I will call you after I arrive and we can set up a schedule.”

“All right. There aren’t any hotels in Cape Warren, you know.”

“Actually, hotels are too noisy. A rooming house would be a more suitable choice. It would offer a quiet place to work.”

“Well, we have plenty of those in town, young lady.”

They talked for a few more minutes and then said good-bye. He told her to have a safe trip. After she hung up the phone, Aline folded her arms on top of her desk and rested her forehead on them. She didn’t want the whole office to see how elated she was.

Marty was in his office, talking on the phone, as usual. She started moving in that direction, struggling to suppress her excitement. He hung up the telephone when he saw her approaching. She could read the expression on his face. It was time to prepare for Maine.

6.

TUESDAY. TODAY AND ALL DAY TOMORROW would have to be committed to completing a list of time-consuming tasks before Aline left New York. Updating her existing production schedules wouldn't be too labor-intensive, but making notes in the piles of folders and papers stacked on her desk would be. She couldn't file them away, give them away or throw them away, so she made them look neater by arranging them in the order of accomplishment and potential future use.

The afternoon was dragging on and her fellow workers occasionally would stop by to wish her a productive trip and ask her questions about the assignment. As expected, someone suggested that the editors take her out for a few drinks after work. She showed her appreciation by accepting their invitation. Most of the people in the office were personal friends and the limited socializing that she had time for was spent in their company, either going to the theater, taking in a movie or an exhibition, or simply sharing dinner.

At five-fifteen they assembled around her, holding their coats and discussing with her the options offered in the immediate neighborhood. Finally a decision was made and they turned off the lights and computers, locked the doors, and headed for the elevators.

They left their office building on Madison Avenue, walking a short distance to a nearby café. Once inside, they selected a large corner table for five and started pulling out chairs and folding their coats on the empty table next to theirs. Marty had gone home earlier in the afternoon. He didn't drink, avoided bars, and said his good-byes to her before he left. Aline also felt he didn't want to handle her departure surrounded by other employees. Privacy was essential to him and his relationship to his staff.

Ed McNeal and Jim Hardy were both young men, her age, college graduates and occasional escorts. Martha Wilson, who lived in Connecticut with her mother, was in her early forties and had been with the magazine for ten years. Aline often turned to Martha for advice, especially when she felt that she couldn't handle an emotional situation by herself. Martha liked Aline very much and always felt flattered when she was invited to join this small group of younger colleagues for these impromptu gatherings. Aline and Martha often dined together when they both worked late and sometimes they would spend Sundays at Aline's apartment, sharing brunch and reading the papers. Martha would usually stay over and go to work with Aline in the morning. She loved to stay in the city overnight and looked forward to spending these Sundays with her only true friend. Sometimes the two of them would go to a movie in the evening if the lines didn't look too long.

Betty Harrison rounded off the little group. She was an inspiration to Aline. She lived in Manhattan on the Upper East Side, was married to a theater director, had two girls in college in New England, was a gourmet cook, and could conquer the world if she could fit it into her schedule. Unlike Martha, she combined the drive of youth and the competitiveness of Ed and Jim to stimulate her. She was very social and always invited her coworkers to the frequent dinner parties held by her and her husband. You'd cancel another appointment to attend one of their parties. The food was fabulous and the guests consisted mainly of actors, playwrights, painters, directors, photographers, all of whom were active in the theater and the arts, fascinating to talk to and fun to party with.

After everyone sat down and ordered their drinks, the conversation naturally turned to serious shop talk. Jim finally decided to tell a few jokes which were interrupted often with laughter and the feeling of intimacy that only close friends can share. Aline wanted to tell them that she was going to miss them, but she hesitated, knowing full well it would cause a chain reaction of rebuttal and sarcastic remarks. She elected to say nothing.

It was after seven-thirty when they left the bar, the wind pulling at their hair and coats. Martha and Betty said their good-nights, wished Aline well and headed for the subway. Ed and Jim, however, hesitated to leave Aline, each vying for the opportunity to ask her out for dinner. Each man was too shy to ask her in front of the other. She sensed the awkwardness of the situation and decided to make the logical decision of saying goodnight to both of them at once. Before either of them could say anything, she hailed a cab and gave the driver directions as she climbed into the back seat. Once seated, she lowered the window and blew a kiss to them. As the cab drove away, she waved out the back window. Neither one of them was moving as she drove out of sight. She would have to make a point of calling each of them from Maine, once she was settled there.

She leaned back in the seclusiveness of the back seat and thought about leaving New York and her friends, suddenly realizing she must get away from all of it for a while. When she returned, she knew she would be fulfilled again with renewed energy and productivity. This was the right move for her at this time in her career.

The cab stopped in front of her building on 3rdAve. and E.68th St. The new doorman, William, was waiting out front and greeting her as he opened the cab's door to help her out. She barely acknowledged him as she entered the building..

An empty elevator awaited her in the lobby. She was relieved that the usual entourage of leashed dogs, straining for their walks, was missing.

As she unlocked her door, a sense of relief filled her—home at last. She couldn't wait to hang up her coat and change out of her work clothes. She put on her bathrobe and slippers and went into the kitchen to prepare a light supper.

The studio apartment was neat and compact. Simple but functional contemporary furniture characterizing a room decorated in neutrals with black and white accessories. An off-white tweed sofa bed, two soft, black leather reading chairs, a glass and chrome coffee table, and modular cast-iron bookcases made up the living/sleeping area. At the far end of the living room, a wall of books served as a room-divider. A round dining room table and two chairs were placed in front of an expansive plate glass window and balcony overlooking Manhattan. From the sixth floor in this neighborhood, the view was less than spectacular. Brick and gray stone buildings, air conditioning units, stained copper-green rooftops, and old water towers made up the landscape.

The kitchen had a dishwasher and an oversized refrigerator, usually empty. New Yorkers ate out most of the time. Aline never took the time to shop for groceries, cook, or entertain. Once in a while, she would invite Ed or Jim over to share take-out before going to a movie or a play. Besides, groceries in the city were overpriced and the local produce was usually poor in quality. Living alone, there wasn't much motivation to cook. Even Betty complained about shopping in New York. She and her husband tried to make an adventure out of it, scouting everywhere for farmers' markets and Jersey produce in order to find the perfect ingredients for their recipes.

Aline sat at the dining room table, sipping her soup and staring out the window. She wasn't very hungry because there was too much on her mind. What to pack, who to call to water her plants, how much money to take, were all questions racing through her mind. And more importantly, how would her mother react when Aline told her about going away for three weeks?

It seemed like too much decision-making at this particular moment. There was time to go over it step by step, so it could wait until tomorrow.

Suddenly, the urge to go right away was overpowering. No packing, no calls, just go. But life didn't function along those lines. Fate was handing her an existence dictated by structure. She was following a procedure already set up for her.

7.

EARLY THURSDAY AFTERNOON, the 2nd of October, Aline started loading the rented four-wheel drive for the trip north. She didn't own her own car since in New York it was more of a liability than an asset. The idea was to travel light. All she really needed were fall clothes, her laptop, iPod, camera and a few pairs of sunglasses. A briefcase stuffed with legal pads and writing materials sufficed for office supplies.

It was almost one o'clock when she was finally ready to leave. She sat in the unfamiliar vehicle, examining all the buttons and their functions, waiting for the engine to warm up. The four to five hour trip to Boston promised to be restful, but uneventful. After ten minutes, she pulled away from the curb and was on her way.

It was a clear, sunny day bragging a cobalt-blue sky. Autumn skies were always the most spectacular. She cracked the window, breathing deeply. The crisp, invigorating air added to her excitement and expectation. It would keep her alert, especially when she was on the interstate.

After driving for an hour she finally reached Route I-95 north. The drone of the engine and the straight highway were monotonous, but pacifying, helping her unwind from the last few hectic days.

She passed the "Welcome to Connecticut" sign, and was surrounded by bursts of color from the wooded areas on both sides of the road. Huge blotchy masses of yellows, oranges, burgundies and reds faded gently into subtle combinations or crashed head-on in contrast against the dark green pines. The patches seemed to be slowly devouring each other—a startling and almost violent sight—in their last desperate statement.

The dramatic scenery absorbed much of her attention until she arrived at the outskirts of Boston around five forty-five. One of the Cambridge hotels had been recommended to her. It guaranteed a full view of Boston and the Charles River from every room. Driving over the Longfellow Bridge, she spotted it in the distance. As a landmark, it was unique, located on the edge of the water and offering recreational areas with benches and picnic tables.

The parking lot was full but she finally found a space close to the hotel entrance. Carrying her overnight bag containing a change of clothes and the basic essentials, she approached the lobby. A sharp wind whipped through her hair and refreshed her even though it smelled of the river, penetrating and industrial.

The hotel was crowded with people strolling around looking for something meaningful to do. Most likely, they were conventioneers who would end up in the gift shop, buying something they really didn't want or need.

Aline checked in and went directly to her room on the seventh floor. As promised, the window offered a breathtaking view. Boston's night lights danced on the water's surface in pinpoints of pinks, blues, whites, and pale yellows. The beauty of it froze her there for a few moments.

Finally, she pushed off her shoes, turned on some lamps and flopped on the huge bed. She closed her eyes, finding it hard to believe. She was actually here and all of this was in fact happening. A hot shower and a change of clothes would revive her. She was looking forward to lingering over a seafood dinner on her first evening in New England. The long drive from New York guaranteed a healthy appetite.

The top-floor main dining room afforded its patrons a spectacular panoramic view of the city. The bar area was occupied mostly by traveling salesmen, who eyed her as she passed them. They were probably seeking some kind of relief from the lonely night ahead.

The maitre d' indicated there would be no wait for a table and pointed to one on the far side of the room, overlooking the river. Following after him, she felt very lucky at this turn of events. He left her to examine the menu, which remained closed on her plate. The view of the river captivated her, its surface alive and moving. Blue-black silhouettes of buildings blending with the sparkling lights and then plunging into the depths. The constant motion of the waves was mesmerizing.

When a waiter appeared, she ordered a glass of house wine and asking him to come back in a few minutes for her dinner order. Rushed through the meal wouldn't be appropriate tonight. Tonight was special—the beginning of an adventure she was creating solely for herself under the guise of an assignment. This was a moment of accomplishment and she wanted to relish every moment of it.

After dinner was ordered, she started glancing at her surroundings. The noisy clatter of dishes, the mixture of many voices coming from nearby tables, and soft background music, were all stimulating to her and made her feel as though she was caught up in the flow of life.

Most of the patrons chose to take a long walk along the edge of the Charles River to close out the evening. This was appealing to Aline. In New York, this would have been prohibitive. Manhattan was too dangerous at night. But Boston was different, especially on this side of the river. Most of the Cambridge population was academic and the streets were usually filled with students from Radcliff, Harvard and M.I.T., jogging, shopping, going to coffee houses and restaurants, or crossing their campuses. There were more colleges and universities in Boston than in any other city in the United States.

Before going out, she returned to her room for a light coat and a pair of gloves. This working vacation demanded a good portion of her winter wardrobe. New England became very cold early in the season.

Leaving the hotel, she turned up the collar of her coat to protect her neck from the invading night air. Other hotel residents were also out walking and some were sitting on the wooden benches facing the water.

She strolled along, strategizing her trip to Maine and her first meeting with Thomas Elcock. It would save time now, formalizing in her mind some relevant questions to ask, questions leading to the facts and revealing the most appealing aspects of his personality and artistic disposition.

But, fatigue was blocking this effort and her mind kept drifting away. Resting her forearms on the railing, she looked deeply into the dark water. It kept moving urgently against the stone retaining wall with murky hostility, resenting its restraint. So much energy and nowhere to go. Its constant struggle, seemingly aimless.

Biting wind cut to her bones. Looking around, it was apparent to her that she was alone on the river. It was now after nine-thirty. Deciding to turn in and get a good night's sleep was all there was left to do this night. Tomorrow would be a full day, one of the most important ones she would ever experience.

8.

FRIDAY MORNING. The eight-thirty wake-up call. Ten hours of sleep consuming her, roughly figuring the time she dozed off. The drive from New York taking more out of her than she realized. Thanking the operator, she hung up and went back to sleep. When she woke up, it was now nine forty-five and she was behind schedule.

Quickly exiting her room, Aline decided to have a light breakfast before checking out. Turning off the lights after a brief scan of her surroundings, she walked to the elevators.

Three men and their wives stood looking at her as she arrived to join them. The husbands had plastic name tags pinned to their jackets, their spouses showing off gaudy corsages. They were all acting quite self-conscious.

Aline was the first one exiting when they reached the ground floor. A sign indicating the direction of the restaurant caught her eye and she followed it.

The coffee shop was nearly deserted. A few businessmen dallying over their last cups of coffee while skimming through the morning papers. Waitresses clustered near the entrance to the kitchen, joking with each other and talking about their kids. The morning rush was over and it was their turn to relax a little and ignore the customers. After surveying the situation, Aline decided to sit at the counter to save time. Finally one of the waitresses came over, taking her order of coffee and English muffins.

After breakfast she went directly to the front desk, waiting in line to check out. The wall clock above the clerk's head read ten-thirty.

At last, the hotel was releasing her to the fresh air and the parking area.

As soon as she was in the car, she placed a map of New England on the passenger's seat next to her, studying it for easy reference.

Traffic was surprisingly light leaving Boston. She hoped to make up the valuable time lost at the hotel as soon as she was outside the city limits.

The roads were dry and the day was bright and cloudless. She calculated that she should reach Cape Warren between two-thirty and three o'clock, depending on how many stops she made. It was important to take her time and reserve her energy. After reaching her destination, she would find a place to stay.

Elcock was thoughtful enough to mail her a map with directions spelled out in detail. The weekend would afford her plenty of time to take a dry run to find his house before their first interview. The anticipation began to build in her mind as she saw the skyline of Boston fade away in her rear-view mirror.

9.

THE LANDSCAPE STARTED CHANGING as she drove north. Pine forests gently replacing the oaks and maples. The environment starting to take on a more austere appearance after crossing into the state of Maine.

Aline researched as much information as she could about the New England coastal region. The population of Cape Warren was somewhere between six and nine thousand people. Years ago, the fishing industry afforded these residents a profitable way of life, but overfishing and pollution resulted in a serious depletion of their economy and many people decided to relocate to larger urban areas to find work and better security for their families.

It was two-fifty when she reached the edge of town. Not a soul could be seen anywhere. However, as she drew closer to the center, residents started to appear, puttering about in their yards or walking along the side streets. School was out, and children were playing with their friends in their front yards. Unlike the city, the street corners were devoid of groups of teenagers, jostling each other, eating slices of pizza and smoking cigarettes.

Cape Warren's plainness bespoke more of heedful modesty than a lack of character. The old clapboard houses lining the streets, were small and simple in design, like two-dimensional shapes cut out of craft paper.

They stood out boldly against the dark backdrop of tall evergreens and rocky cliffs. And even though they took on the appearance of being empty, it was obvious that people were living in them.

Aline's social background didn't include spending time with New Englanders. Their attitude toward life was unfamiliar to her. She sensed they upheld a delicate balance here. It had to do with tradition, heredity and respect.

She found herself driving very slowly, as if her inner being was honoring it.

In spite of the apparent absence of signage, a logical configuration of Main Street eventually presented itself. A two-story, wood-framed house was the post office. It appeared very formal, unlike the general store which stood opposite. Like most rural general stores, this one was a multicolored, confusing maze of annexes and extensions added onto the existing architecture over the last fifteen years. Doors and windows were obvious afterthoughts, and the overall impression was one of haphazard slapstick.

These two structures were the foundation of the downtown area. Aline also noticed a seafood diner and a small stone courthouse at one end of the street. The police department and the fire department were positioned behind the courthouse as if nothing unusual ever happened in Cape Warren. A hairpin turn ran behind the courthouse and continued along the waterfront. Small slips jutted out perpendicular to the seawall. A few yachts and several lobster boats were moored at the slips.

Even though Cape Warren was a coastal town with an abundance of natural beauty, it didn't exactly offer the type of facilities stimulating the birth of a resort. There was no hotel and the only motels were found in neighboring communities. The water and the land mass never really warmed up, even by the middle of July, and that alone contributed largely to the relative unpopularity of the place. There were few summer residents here. However, it was scenic, and people driving through would usually stop to take photographs of the harbor. These sightseeing motorists allowed a few mom-and-pop corner stores and the gas station to eke out a living.

Aline parked in front of one of the docks and walked toward the end of it, bracing herself against the wind and glancing into the boats tied up alongside. They strained at their moorings. The collection of rusty machinery, cables, nets, blocks, barrels, lines and winches made the fishing procedure appear to be a very complicated science. A combined stench of tar, salt, dead fish, and diesel oil was overpowering. At the end of the wharf, the horizon stretched out in a flat blue-gray band that extended beyond infinity. It pulled her toward it, out of her state of consciousness.

For a brief moment, she was possessed by it. Slowly, she returned to her more immediate needs, dinner and finding a place to spend the night. The diner near the docking area was the simplest solution. It didn't look like it would hold many customers by its outer appearance. However, upon entering, Aline was surprised at the number of people packed into the place, filling it to maximum capacity. She stood in disbelief, looking for a table. A man sitting at the counter had just paid his bill and when he stood up to leave he spotted her.

"You can have my seat, miss. I'm just leaving."

"Thank you very much," she said, smiling.

The restaurant windows were steaming up from body heat, and the loud dishwasher in the back. Grills smoked up the atmosphere, creating a thick haze which hovered near the tin ceiling.

Aline ordered pot roast, the special-of-the-day and coffee. Homemade pies lined the aluminum shelving over the grill opposite her. They looked gigantic by New York standards. The portions here were overly generous and the food was hearty. Her waitress kept refilling her cup as soon as it was half empty. In New York, she would have to pay extra for a second cup. But this wasn't New York.

After eating, she lingered over her third cup of coffee. Capt'n Zack's diner was busy, noisy and crowded, but it made her feel accepted.

Reluctantly she stood up, preparing to leave. Soon it would be dusk and she didn't want to be driving around in the dark in an unfamiliar area. The best plan of action was to simply drive around the neighborhoods that appealed to her and look for a guest house. Finding a place to live was a challenge for her; it represented more stability toward achieving her goal, giving her concept the credibility it needed for her to continue. She would call Elcock tomorrow.

10.

ALINE WAS GETTING PRESSED FOR TIME. She paid her bill, deciding to go back to a section of town she passed earlier where the streets were wide and lined with huge shade trees. Judging by the size of the houses there, large families must have occupied them in the past.

Fifteen minutes later, she was driving through a residential section that fit this description, searching for a sign in a front window indicating a room for rent. Most of the homes in this neighborhood were shuttered and well-attended. Some were crowned with widows' walks. These housed the families of sea captains or seamen and their sense of historical significance gave them an aura of dignity.

Two thirds of the way down a street labeled Mitchell Street, she noticed a white clap-board Victorian with dark green shutters. It looked freshly painted and the landscaping was neatly pruned. On a weathered light post next to the driveway hung a tiny hand-lettered sign, ROOMS. The house drew her to it and without a moment of hesitation, Aline pulled up in front and turned off the ignition.

A neat flagstone path led to an expansive wraparound porch with a high wooden railing. Two large oak doors with beveled glass inserts, curtained from within, made up the front entrance. The oval glass was etched into a graceful floral design. Aline studied it for a few seconds before twisting the brass doorbell.

The sound was shrill and resounded loudly in the crisp October evening. Within a matter of seconds, footsteps responded. One of the doors opened and standing within the dim foyer was a stately woman of imposing height, maybe in her mid seventies, white hair severely pulled back from her face into a French twist. She wore rimless glasses over light green eyes, and her milky skin hinted a lack of exposure to the sun or harsh winds which usually put a flush into the cheeks of those who live through the trying New England weather.

"May I help you?" she said in a reserved tone.

"Good evening, my name is Aline Kranick. I'm looking for a room to rent."

"Please step inside."

The two women moved into the front hall.

"My name is Mrs. Prentis. What brings you to Cape Warren?"

"I'm from New York, Mrs. Prentis. I work for F.A. Morse Publications as a reporter for *East Side/West Side* magazine. The magazine has assigned me to write an article for the coming year and I'm going to combine the work with some vacation time."

"Things are pretty quiet around here in October. Most of the tourists pass through here during the summer months. How many nights would you need a room?"

"I'll need to stay for at least two weeks, maybe longer. I could use some extra time to relax before returning to work."

"How long have you worked in New York?"

Aline realized she was being carefully screened and many more questions were needed to be answered satisfactorily before any decision was made in regards to her staying here. "Almost five years. I started working as soon as I graduated from college."

"What college was that?"

"Skidmore College."

"I never heard of it."

"It's in Saratoga Springs, New York."

"Are you married?"

"No, I'm not." Aline handed Mrs. Prentis her business card. She put herself into Mrs. Prentis' position. Letting a complete stranger into your home does require some caution, especially in this day and age.

Aline continued, "Would you like to see some references?"

Without looking at the card, Mrs. Prentis replied, "I don't think that's necessary. I think I may have something for you. It's a nice room upstairs at the back of the house, very private. Would you like to see it?"

"Yes I would." Aline started feeling more relaxed.

Somehow, moving out of the foyer eased the situation for both of them. Aline followed Mrs. Prentis up a wide set of stairs and then down a long hallway. At the end of the hall they entered a bright yellow room. All the trim and wooden furniture was painted with white enamel, including an antique iron double bed. The room was spacious, with an old oak writing desk on the right hand wall, as if her arrival was expected. Just beyond the desk was a closet. A massive dresser with glass pulls, a full-length mirror, and an overstuffed reading chair with an ottoman filled the remaining space. Next to the chair was a wrought-iron floor lamp with a worn shade. Two windows on the wall opposite the bed faced the house next door. A single window on the back wall of the room overlooked an enormous back yard hosting a maze of bare clotheslines. At the end of the driveway stood the garage with two sets of doors. Dark curtains behind its glass windows obstructed a view of the building's interior.

Aline turned her attention back to the room. It was old-fashioned, but clean and lived-in comfortable. The oversized windows would give her plenty of light to read and write. It was exactly what she was looking for.

"Well, what do you think?" Mrs. Prentis stood in the doorway waiting for a response, her hands thrust into the deep pockets of her plaid housedress.

"This is just perfect. I'd like to rent it."

"Glad it suits you. The bath is two doors down on the left. You're lucky that you won't have to share it with anyone because you're the only one on the floor."

Back on the first floor, they discussed the rent and easily agreed on one hundred dollars a week. Aline paid her for two weeks in cash and Mrs. Prentis handed her a receipt.

"I'll be working late most of the time. I hope it won't disturb you."

"I seldom ever hear any noise when I'm renting upstairs. I'm a little hard of hearing. Besides, I on1y come up here to clean and change the linens."

"Please let me know if any noise I make bothers you."

"There's only one rule you have to abide by in my home. I don't allow cooking or smoking in the rooms. Fire regulations, you know. However, I will allow you to share the kitchen facilities. We can work out some kind of an arrangement. Do you smoke?"

"I quit six years ago."

"Good for you. Have you had your supper?"

"Yes ma'am, I have. The diner down by the waterfront has very good food. I stopped there earlier."

"Please call me Cora. We might as well be on a first-name basis since we're going to be living together for a while."

Aline was impressed by Cora's straightforward approach. All those rumors about New Englanders being standoffish, tight-lipped and suspicious somehow didn't apply to this woman. Her landlady was more than accommodating, and Aline felt they would develop a satisfactory relationship.

"Let me know if you need anything." Cora's words interrupted her thoughts. "Towels are in the second drawer of your dresser. I'll leave the house key right here on the hall table. Yours has a red ribbon on it. Please don't lose it."

"Don't worry, I won't. I'm going to put it on my key chain right now, ribbon and all. Well, I better unpack my car while I still have some energy."

"You can park at the end of the driveway, in front of the left-hand set of garage doors. If you're not going out again, I'll lock up the house early tonight."

"I need to rest. I just want to take a shower and turn in early."

"All right, Aline. I'll leave the kitchen night light on. The empty cupboard to the right of the sink is for your groceries. We'll share the fridge."

"Will I see you for coffee in the morning?"

"I'm afraid not. I'll be up and out of the house long before you wake up. I'm a tea drinker myself, but I'll leave coffee on the stove for you. Please always check the burners before you go out."

"It sounds like you're one of those early risers I envy so much."

"Yes, I am. I'm usually up by quarter to six."

"I would give anything to have a work ethic like yours."

"I have a very busy day tomorrow. Besides taking care of this big house, I do volunteer work at our clinic in Alliston and work part-time at the courthouse."

Aline listened intently. She was wondering where all Cora's stamina came from.

The landlady gave her a quick smile and said, "I'll leave you alone now to finish up. We'll probably see each other tomorrow. I hope you sleep well." Cora departed to the back of the house.

“Thank you for everything,” Aline called out to her.

After the SUV was emptied and all her belongings were brought upstairs, Aline collapsed on top of the bed. She didn’t move for a long time. A feeling of satisfaction overcame her. The day was ending on a very positive note. She was pleased with Cora Prentis, her room and this house.

11.

When she woke up Saturday morning, it took Aline a few seconds to realize where she was. Sleep was involuntary here. The morning sun was beating against the shades, determined to flood the room with bright daylight.

This was pure escape. The transformation from New York to Cape Warren was very abrupt and could be difficult to adjust to. But here she was, lying in bed, staring at her new venue.

Reality finally prodded her to look at her watch. It was ten thirty-five. She felt a little guilty about not being up early on her first morning on Mitchell Street. She dressed in jeans and a sweatshirt and hurried downstairs to the kitchen.

A crisp note, folded like a miniature starched tent, was waiting for her in the middle of the table: "Knew you'd probably want to sleep late. Juice and mix for scrambled eggs in the fridge. Coffee on stove. Have a good day."

Aline scrambled some eggs and made toast. As she ate her breakfast, she began glancing around the room. It was immaculate and neat. Everything was whitewashed, including the furniture and beadboard cupboards. The walls were completely devoid of color or decoration, reflecting a feeling of composure in its honest display of simplicity and order. Mrs. Prentis's personality was disclosed in her daily routine. The concise compactness of the living habits of one who'd been alone for a long time was very evident. A used tea bag in a glass on the sink, a lonely cup and saucer turned upside down in an otherwise empty dish drain, a calendar over the light switch with no notes scribbled on it, no dates circled. No one to see?

At first, this was a little sad, but at the same time very self-assured, worry-free and uncomplicated.

Aline wondered if this way of life, this consummation of Cora's existence was also to be *her* future. And if it were to be her fate as well, she wondered if she could handle it with as much grace and confidence as her landlady had displayed.

After the dishes were washed and put away, it was time to plan the day. More time could certainly be spent exploring the territory and the town. A dry run to Mr. Elcock's house would eliminate any uneasiness concerning the first interview on Monday morning. The map he sent her was simple and left little room for error.

She was eager to get started. Making sure that the front door was securely locked, she walked to the end of the driveway to retrieve her vehicle. Once inside, she began to study Elcock's map again. Second-guessing directions on the highway was not acceptable in her rule book on travel.

Leaving town, she noticed that the houses were becoming swallowed up by the wooded areas. The scenery was comprised of a few deserted farms and unplanted acres of land.

She timed the trip to Elcock's access road, about twenty minutes, just as his directions indicated. The sign to his studio was nailed to an old pine tree and after spotting it, she turned around to go back. Now, she wouldn't get lost.

On the way back, the sun was illuminating everything it touched, glinting off the surface of the sea in the distance. She drove toward it. There was a large parking lot near the edge of the harbor and she chose a space in the section designated for tours. A few people were strolling along the waterfront, others were taking pictures. Some chose to sit near the water's edge, reading newspapers or pamphlets.

She started walking along, losing her identity and it was pleasing to her. All responsibility was gone at this moment and the aimless drifting along on this warm autumn day represented irresponsibility. There was no role to play and no pressure to endure. She let the flow of the walkers pull her along, going into the shops they entered, looking into the same windows, and letting them control her movements and influence her direction. This occurrence gave her a sense of freedom and abandon.

Eventually, she stopped to buy a hot cocoa and a local paper and went outside to sit. She held the thick paper cup tightly with both hands, inhaling the aroma, the hot liquid sending up steamy clouds of condensation.

Buying the local paper every week was an educated way to keep abreast of what was happening in and around Cape Warren. As she expected, most of the space was devoted to advertising. However, there was also promotional news on community theater productions, a calendar of events and articles celebrating the occupational achievements of the recent crop of high school graduates. Aline drew a circle around the date of the next town meeting. Maybe she would go to one while she was living here. Learning about the town's concerns and priorities was now important to her. She wanted to show the general interest that any citizen would naturally demonstrate.

Being independent was, and always had been, one of Aline's strongest characteristics. Basically, she was a loner with a very limited and selective social life. This was the price she paid in order to evolve into a successful career woman. But everything in life was a tradeoff, one way or another. At least New York presented it to her as such and she accepted it as *status quo.*

She put the paper down, watching the strollers walk by. Here she was again in the midst of many people, even though, realistically, she was totally alone. It didn't really matter where she was. . .New York, Cape Warren. She was always fully a part of it, yet truly outside of it. Her lifestyle put her into this situation most of the time. It was second nature to her.

12.

THE WEEKEND WAS PASSING QUICKLY. Saturday was spent putting her room in order, organizing her desk and window-shopping in downtown Cape Warren.

Now it was already Sunday, Aline's favorite day of the week. In New York, she usually spent it in her pajamas buried under a mound of all the papers. Her friends were always criticizing her for allowing them to be piled everywhere. The stacks grew taller and more cumbersome as the days went by. She made a mental note to end this lazy habit in Maine.

The answering machine would handle the calls, because she wouldn't pick up the phone. Sometimes she invited Martha over to join her for brunch.

Today, she would spend most of her time in her room, figuring out her strategy for the upcoming weeks and specifying the goals to be reached, day by day.

It was important to utilize very precisely the time allotted with Elcock. The content of each interview should be carefully outlined. The interviews were to be part of a fact-finding mission, not a social opportunity.

Earlier, she went downstairs to retrieve something to eat. Cora was nowhere to be seen. Maybe she was at church, but a Bible was still lying on the front hall table. She could go out later for dinner. Coffee and toast would do for now. Tomorrow, after the interview, she would go shopping for a few groceries.

She worked on through the afternoon, stretching out on the bed, her back resting against the pillows, working on her laptop. Late into the afternoon, she decided to take a nap. The bedspread would suffice as a blanket.

It was almost dark outside when she awoke. The small electric clock on her nightstand indicated six forty-five. Her nap was almost two hours.

Retrieving a clean towel from the dresser, she walked down the hall toward the bathroom. As she passed the staircase, she noticed the front hall light was on. Cora must be home, but the house was quiet, the stillness intimidating. It was as if she was the sole occupant here. There was no Sunday dinner cooking, no radio playing and no television blaring in the background. Only silence creeping up the stairs, snuffing out everything in its path. Aline found this vacuum unusual and unexpected.

She showered as fast as she could, got dressed and descended the front stairs to the foyer. A night light was on in the kitchen.

When she left the house, she closed the front door as quietly as possible, almost afraid of disturbing this hushed aura which wrapped itself around the whole property.

She stood on the front walk and looked up toward the house next door. The lights were still on in her room, casting golden shadows on the neighbor's property, reassuring her. There were still signs of life for her to cling to.

13.

MONDAY MORNING. The first full week of October. By eight o'clock, Aline's breakfast was over. In her possession was Elcock's note confirming the first visit. She decided to head out to his place around nine, allowing herself enough time to review her notes and tidy up her room.

She checked the kitchen, turning off the lights and making sure the burners on the stove were cold and the table clear of her dishes.

Cora was already gone for the day. But, Aline was concentrating on the interview with Elcock and gave it no further consideration. Gathering her purse and briefcase, she departed.

The day was windy and heavily overcast, but she felt optimistic in spite of the dreary weather. The start of any new assignment gave her renewed vigor and this one was exceptional.

Dry leaves covered the front walk and crunched under her feet as she walked to her car. She started the engine and sat waiting for the defrosting system to erase the condensation on the glass. Within a few minutes it was clear and she slowly backed down the driveway. At last she was on her way. The morning mist carried a sharp chill, and she was grateful to be dressed in corduroy pants, wool jacket and heavy sweater.

Driving along, she tried to memorize certain obvious landmarks that would help her recall the route later: an antique shop displaying a red rooster on its sign, a decomposing barn, its roof caved in and a rusting, blue car with no doors, parked on the lawn like some decrepit trophy. All of this became indelible, imprinting her memory.

The macadam road ended as soon as she reached the approach to Elcock's studio, turning into a narrow dirt track worsening as she progressed toward her destination. Slowing down, she avoided the most obvious bumps and potholes. Thunderstorms and their flash floods from previous summers left behind deep gouges and ruts in the soft, sandy soil exposing cable-like, twisted roots of the towering deep-green pines. Thick and tall, the treetops made it difficult for light to reach the forest floor. Under this canopy, the air was raw and saturated with nature's musty perfume of decaying leaves, pine needles and woodland debris. The dark, sensuous atmosphere with its clammy embrace seemed to threaten her.

Gradually the trees began to open up to an elevated clearing. Even with the engine running, she could hear breakers thundering into the rocks below like a series of explosions.

The studio was built two and one half stories high and faced the water, salt air turning the cedar shingles to a satin patina of silver-gray. Even the wooden shutters were sea-stained, bathing the whole structure in monotones, a drab blotch huddled against the black woods overwhelming its presence.

She approached the front door which opened long before she reached it. Obviously, he was watching and waiting for her arrival. A tall, large-framed man with masses of snow-white hair and full beard filled the doorway poised to greet her.

"Hi. Thomas Elcock. You must be Miss Kranick. Come in, come in." She shook his extended hand. It was rough and strong, indicating years of physical labor.

She entered the house, smoothing down her windblown hair and returning his broad smile.

"Hello, I'm Aline. I'm so pleased to have the opportunity to meet you."

"Well, Aline, thank you. I appreciate that. How 'bout some coffee?"

"That would be wonderful. Your map was very well drawn. I didn't have any trouble finding your road."

"Well, that's encouraging. I am an artist, as you are well aware of."

They both laughed. He was going to be fun to work with. She liked his personality immediately and felt grateful to be working with someone who was as good-natured and easy to communicate with. He was already meeting her half way.

"Cream and sugar?"

"Just milk, thank you."

He left her to prepare their coffee. When he was gone, she observed the room. Unlike the approach to the house, it seemed to contain all existing light, bright and diffused, softening everything it touched. The lofty ceiling contained four skylights and the wall facing the ocean was mostly plate glass, giving the old house a contemporary look. The interior was integrated more intimately with his wooded property by bringing it indoors.

Mr. Elcock reappeared with stoneware coffee mugs which he placed on a small nail keg positioned between two huge wooden captain's chairs. He gestured for her to sit down and stood facing her, offering her a choice of muffins overflowing a large basket held in his right hand.

"Oh, thank you. They look delicious."

"They're blueberry. I made them specially for this occasion."

His hospitality couldn't be refused. He placed a large one in a paper napkin next to her coffee, then chose one for himself and sat down. He was looking at her with an honest openness in his expression which she wasn't used to. She, in turn, was observing him at close range.

Thomas Elcock had massive arms and hands. His unruly hair and bushy eyebrows seemed out of place to his soft-spoken and gentle manner. In a denim shirt and overalls, he looked like a man who was always ready for work.

"If you want to take off your jacket, I'll hang it up for you. You still looked chilled. I can start a fire, if you like. The wood-burning stove over there really heats this place up, a bit too much for my liking. I used to fire it up for my wife when she complained about the house getting drafty."

As she removed her jacket, Aline looked around the house for evidence of a woman's touch. No sign of anyone having shared this living space. No dried flower arrangements, no pictures, no curtains or knickknacks were visible. No nonsense. Her reporter instincts guarded her against asking questions about his wife. He was going to have to volunteer that information.

He sensed her caution. "My wife died over twenty years ago. Her name was Louise. She was very ill with Alzheimer's disease. In those days they really didn't know too much about the condition. She suffered quite a lot and I did too, watching her deteriorate. This was the only place where she could get any rest."

"I'm very sorry to hear that. You must miss her very much."

"Yes, I do. When she was healthy, we enjoyed many activities together. She loved to hike through the woods and go on short excursions with me when I had errands to run out of town—any excuse to get out of the house."

Aline nodded her head.

Elcock added, "Because of her condition, death was probably the kindest solution for her. I was so thankful that her torment finally ended."

In spite of the subject matter, Aline didn't feel awkward with him. She felt certain he would not allow her to back herself into a corner. She respected him for that. They talked for almost two more hours, concentrating mostly on his house, which he was responsible for building himself. He explained to her how much he loved Maine. Once in a while there was another reference to his wife. He spoke of her with tenderness and affection.

She listened to him intently, not caring to take any notes. That would be her homework. When the time came to close the interview for the day, she didn't want to leave. They decided ahead of time not to extend the visits past noon. In this way, her work would not interfere with Elcock's lunch plans or afternoons designated for painting. She waited for the right time in the conversation to make the break. It came when he stood up to offer her more coffee.

"Thank you, but I think I better be going. I've certainly enjoyed our first meeting. It's been very rewarding for me to have made your acquaintance at last."

"The pleasure is all mine. Would you like to see my studio before you leave?"

"Let's save the studio for tomorrow morning, as soon as I arrive. "

"All right, I will abide by your rules," he said with a chuckle. "Tomorrow morning it is."

They said their farewells and she assured him she would be back the next day at approximately the same time.

Driving back through the woods, she noticed, even though it was already noon, the atmosphere here was the same as before. And her reaction to it was also the same.

At last the SUV broke out of the woods and a sense of calm—or was it escape—began to replace her feelings of foreboding. The sun was struggling to break through the brooding sky, a good omen. Her first day with Elcock was fulfilling.

Returning to Cape Warren, she wanted to stop and buy food for the house, including a bag of roasted peanuts, her weakness. For a small town, it appeared to be quite busy, and finding a parking space took longer than she expected.

The general store was a classic. Piles of work shirts, blankets, linens, fabric rolls and boxes were placed over large display tables. Hanging from the ceiling and walls were fishing rods, creels, hunting gear, rubber boots, tents, lanterns, camping equipment and extension cords of all lengths and colors. The place was a jungle of hardware, housewares, sporting goods, and foodstuffs, all crowded together on shelves reaching to the ceiling which appeared to be ready to collapse under the weight of all the merchandise suspended from it.

A short, thin man wearing bifocals and a leather apron over his wool clothing came up to her. "Afternoon, miss. Need some help?"

"Yes, please." She gave the clerk an oral list of the items she wanted to purchase.

He impressed her with his speed and efficiency in finding them. Before leaving the store, she thanked him profusely. The afternoon weather was improving since early morning, and she was looking forward to working in her room as soon as she returned to Mitchell Street. Her assignment now was a dynamic reality, born of her own creativity and determination. *Her baby.*

14.

TUESDAY BROKE COPPER-YELLOW WITH SUNSHINE as she headed for Elcock's place. The drive proving exhilarating, she began to find herself completely absorbed by the beauty all around her. Shaggy and primitive, the scenery was startling in its candor. Because she was now familiar with the route, the trip seemed much shorter than before.

Nearing Elcock's house, the menacing feeling still crept over her. He stood waiting for her and somehow his pleasant demeanor didn't fit in here.

He waved and called out, "Good morning. Your coffee is ready. I just put it out."

Walking toward him, she asked him, "Besides being a perfect host, a baker and a famous artist, do you have any other hidden talents?"

He smiled as he stepped back to allow her to enter. After taking her coat, they sat for a while. This soft transition into the interview was valuable for both of them and gave Aline a chance to sense his mood and channel the questioning accordingly.

He turned to her. "Where do we begin today?"

"You wanted to show me your studio."

"Yes, I remember. There's no heat back there so you may want to keep your coat on. I have an extra jacket you can put around your shoulders. I work better when the studio is on the cool side. It energizes me."

He went over to the front door and pulled down a heavy windbreaker folded on a high shelf. Accepting it without a word, she put her arms through the sleeves as he held it for her. It was much too big for her, but it didn't matter because it would protect her.

"Just follow me."

He started walking back in the direction of the kitchen with her trailing behind him. She was wondering, *How many people have ever been invited to share this with him?* The appearance of the small kitchen indicated to her the lack of importance for meals. All the countertops were clear of dishes and cooking utensils. Pots and pans hung in a row from the ceiling beams on large hooks. They were arranged according to size. *As with many creative people*, she thought, *eating is an inconvenience when he is working.*

They entered an expansive room with a cathedral ceiling. The roof was comprised of skylights and a wide glass supporting wall which faced the sea. Cloth shades on pulleys, in modular units, covered the windows and skylights. They could be maneuvered to adjust the light to any desired intensity.

He used a gigantic easel, large enough to accommodate the immense size of his canvases. An elevated wooden framework was erected in front of the easel so he could reach any part of the painting he wished to work on. It rose to the top of the vaulted ceiling in case in became necessary to undo a snag in the pulley ropes.

Wooden planks, placed end-to-end on the supports, created a walkway for him to move freely back and forth in front of his work. Portable taborets on coasters held pots of brushes, his palette and tubes of oil paint. They could be conveniently positioned anywhere he desired on the walkway.

A painting was in progress. Even in the beginning stages of this work of art, there emerged from it a sense of power, of vitality, of undisciplined force, unlike anything Aline, with all her Manhattan living, had ever experienced. She couldn't move. Being transfixed, she almost eliminated the presence of the man standing behind her. Nothing else in this atmosphere seemed to exist except the birth of this artwork which only she was being allowed to witness.

Elcock had been talking to her, but she didn't respond. When he tapped her on the shoulder, she spun around.

"Oh! I'm sorry. I guess I was preoccupied."

"Are you cold?"

" . . . Cold? Oh, no. Thank you." She turned and was spellbound by the painting once again.

The artist explained, "I've designed storage areas beyond in the right-hand wall for a large majority of my work when I'm not on exhibition. It's climate-controlled. The canvases must be rolled up in order to hold all of them. Reframing them is the only difficult aspect of exhibiting. Most museums have a staff available to do the framing for a show. It is an extremely and demanding aspect of exhibition design. I can not do it alone."

She was desperately attempting to get back into the conversation. "Now that you've retired, one of our more prestigious art museums will probably desire to add some of your paintings as an acquisition to their permanent collection."

"You flatter me."

"Not really. I think the extraordinary quality of your work is self-evident. Considering the opinions of curators who make these kinds of recommendations to the Board of Trustees, I know for a fact the competition is going to be fierce in regard to procuring any part of your total collection."

"You sound like you've been talking to some knowledgeable sources."

"I've done my homework," she said simply. She wasn't in a position as yet to disclose any confidential information, but her discussion with a few acquaintances working at the Metropolitan Museum of Art backed up her theory. According to the museum scuttlebutt, Elcock's work was going to be sought after, both in Boston and New York.

Elcock was touched by her confidence in him. He wasn't used to such blatant attention from the media. His initial apprehension was a fear of any published article about him and his work falling short of his expectations. However, Aline's professionalism gained her his respect and contributed to eliminating most of his doubts.

"Shall we go back to the living room? I think you've suffered back here long enough."

He didn't want to press her for more information. Not now. They would be spending a considerable amount of time together and he felt she would eventually tell him everything she could in regards to his future in the art community.

She followed him back through the kitchen into the front of the house. They took off their coats. He said, "I think we need something to warm us up."

While she waited for him to retrieve the coffee, she was thinking about the information just disclosed to him. Maybe she said too much. She didn't mean to end their conversation so abruptly, but it was best to move on and not dwell on it. Anyway, everything she said was true. She didn't really regret asserting herself. It was important for him to realize his worth.

When he returned, he put down her steaming coffee and sat holding his mug in his big hands, gazing past her.

Aline was ready with her pen and notebook. "Why don't you spend the rest of this morning by telling me about how you learned so much about ships and why they became, in time, your favorite subjects."

"Well, I really started as a landscape painter. When the weather was good, I used to go down to the harbor and draw the horizon line with the town growing out of it. There was a certain peninsula of land with a crazy old house stuck out on the end of it. I concentrated on that view for a long time. Then one morning, a big clipper ship was anchored right in front of my peninsula, blocking my familiar point of land. I was very enthralled by its presence, to say the least."

"How long did it remain there?"

"Almost two weeks. The crew was caulking and repairing the rigging. Maybe the lines were tangled together due to a storm. Some of the canvas was damaged because I saw them replacing some sail."

"Did you ever think of trying to board her?"

"Actually, it was one of my first impulses. I did a lot of waving, but I didn't get any reaction."

"Maybe they didn't see you."

"I think you're right. Anyway, they were too busy and couldn't take the time to contact me."

"Was that the only time you ever saw a ship anchored there?"

"Yes. After it left, it was necessary to go down to the shipyards to find other subjects to paint. Sometimes one experience is all I you need to inspire you enough to want to continue in the same train of thought. I made many sketches of the ship while it was anchored there. I still have those drawings around here somewhere. Let me see if I can find them for you to look at."

He went over to a large walk-in storage closet and dragged out a dusty, old trunk. It was covered with dried out black leather and wooden strapping. The top if it showed the most wear. The leathery straps turned powdery when his hands touched them.

When he lifted the lid, an aroma of moldy confinement escaped. He searched carefully through dozens of tattered aged sheets of drawing papers. Near the bottom he found a large brown package. The tape sealing it closed was disintegrating with age.

"Here they are. I thought they were in here."

Aline dropped to her knees, close to the trunk. "How old are these?" she asked, afraid to handle anything he was offering her.

"Must be over thirty years old, I'd say."

Looking at him with a doubtful expression, she said, "Maybe I better let you handle them."

"Nonsense. Please don't be afraid to look at them."

With shaking hands, she slowly pulled out the drawings. They were drawn in charcoal, in bold aggressive strokes. They were so exquisite, she didn't want to let go of them. "I can't believe how beautiful these are. Why did you turn to oils when this technique is so extraordinary?"

Elcock answered her, rubbing his beard with his right hand. "I wanted color to express my feelings about my subject matter. The color added emotion. Charcoal alone didn't offer the dimension I wanted."

Aline, suddenly realizing it was already past twelve said, "Look at the time! Would you rather I postponed the next interview for a few days? I'm taking up the most important part of your work day."

"No, this was the agreement. Tomorrow's all right with me if it fits into your schedule. Besides, I'm not supposed to be on my feet for this amount of time. The doctor wants me to limit my painting to five hours a day. Painting is exhausting work. I don't have the physical strength I had when I was younger."

They agreed to meet again the following day at the usual time. She drove out from under the black sunless forest, wondering if she would ever overcome it.

15.

For the rest of the week, Aline spent mornings at the studio with Elcock and afternoons writing in her room. He reassured her he wasn't tired, but she was always searching for signs of weariness, both physical and mental.

He was always standing at the front door to receive her. Looking forward to sharing the mornings with him, got her in the habit of waking long before her alarm clock was due to go off. She sensed he was equally enjoying her company. Sometimes she wondered if he ever felt lonely, living such a secluded life out in that godforsaken woods of his, but this was one question she would never ask him.

As the first week was coming to a close, she realized she was accumulating more than enough material for the article. Over the weekend she planned to edit her notes and set a goal for herself for the following week. Five more days should be more than sufficient time to complete the editorial. Maybe she should shorten the interview time or see him for only three more sessions. It was hard to decide. She was certain the completion of her work was close at hand.

The content of her material was not extraordinary. From the beginning, he told her he considered himself a very average man and he wanted her to depict him as such. She, on the other hand, felt he was exceptional, if not for himself, at least for his artistic contribution to society. If she did portray him as a humble contributor, it was her responsibility to at least convey his most obvious and overwhelming characteristics. His work was a reflection of himself in its boldness and grand scale. Elcock represented an enthusiasm for life which was still youthful and never cynical. Without overstating the glory of the old sailing days, he gave them respectability, a tribute they deserved. And he, in return, deserved the same honors.

He loved nature—seemed part of nature—and faced the future with incomprehensible courage. Most importantly, he wasn't afraid of death.

Perhaps his early history held the key. He was born on a farm here in Cape Warren during a raging snowstorm. His parents were hard-working folks, making a meager living raising dairy cows and selling milk and cream to a local creamery. Of five sons, all born on the farm, two died of scarlet fever at the ages of two and four. The other children survived illness and the Maine winters, one to become a merchant seaman and the other to crew on the boats of a fishing fleet up the coast. Unfortunately, there was little communication between the brothers. When their parents passed away, the farm was sold to one of the neighbors. Christmas was sometimes the exception when a long letter or photo of one of the grandchildren was exchanged. Thomas and Louise Elcock were childless.

He was honest and direct in his approach to life. His later years seemed to be the most fulfilling for him, artistically.

His work took on a historical quality and became extremely marketable, especially to museums. He studied the origins, logs and history of every clipper ship, packet boat, ketch, and trading vessel that ever plowed the Maine coast. He knew when they were built, who built them, where they were launched and when they died, either lost at sea in the fury of a Northeaster or crushed along some rocky shoreline in a squall. Only a few of these travelers survived. His ships represented the very meaning of his existence. The grace and power with which they defied and battled the sea on his canvas were in reality a reflection of his own soul.

16.

FRIDAY MORNING'S SESSION WITH ELCOCK rounded off the first week on a very positive note. Each day with him was to be more productive than the previous one. He shared with her the full process: how he chose his subject matter, why he was attracted to it, and how he started his preliminary research for his roughs. His studio was very organized; the work areas for the progressive stages of creating a painting were very specific and separate from each other.

He showed her his huge drawing board and the art supplies used in producing the initial layouts. Acrylic paint was used for the beginning sketches because the paint dried quickly and he could rework certain areas in a matter of minutes. Oils took two days to dry and he didn't want to wait long intervals in between stages of development. Also, the large roll of paper he used for the layouts would soak up too much oil. Acrylics were cleaner and odorless for the roughs, but oils were used for the final painting.

After completing the final sketch, he would make a 35mm slide of it and then project it onto the prepared canvas. He would ascend the scaffolding and trace off in charcoal the final drawing in proportion to the final dimensions. The whole process was fastidious.

Again, the time to say goodbye arrived too soon for Aline's liking. And he, in return, was reluctant to let her go. They stood by her vehicle as she wished him a productive weekend. He lingered near her car for a few more minutes and she found it difficult to depart from his company.

Once the car was running, she lowered the window, and reminded him it was her turn to bring something special to have with their coffee. He agreed and gave her a little wave as he turned toward the house. She sat and watched until he was inside.

Driving home, she thought about New York. Her life there seemed a million light years away. After living in Cape Warren for a week, this was the first time she even thought about going back home. Somehow the city didn't seem very important right now. Her assignment and Thomas J. Elcock preempted everything else. This article was going to be her best piece of reporting.

Maybe tonight she would go to a movie or start reading one of the books collecting dust on her desk. They remained unopened, but she fully intended to read them.

When she reached Mitchell Street, she parked the SUV at the back of the driveway. She probably wasn't going to go out again. She let herself into the house, and looked for signs of Mrs. Prentis. No one home. She went upstairs to her room and shut the door.

Now would be an excellent time to call Marty at the office. She was rather appalled with herself for not calling him sooner. He was probably wondering how she was progressing.

Marty usually did not go out for lunch, so her success ratio of contacting him at this time of day was very high. She called *East Side/West Side* on her cell phone. Sandy, the receptionist, recognized her voice immediately and was excited to hear from her. Aline spent a few minutes telling about Maine before being connected to Marty's office. He picked up immediately.

"Hey, kiddo, nice to hear from you. How are you?"

He sounded very confident. He knew how self-sufficient she was about everything.

Aline wanted to sound upbeat. "Hi, I couldn't be better. I've found a beautiful old house, a Victorian, to stay in and a terrific landlady to match. Today is the completion of my first week of interviews with Elcock. He couldn't be more cooperative or accessible. He gives me everything I need and then some. I'm delighted."

"Sounds good. How do you feel?"

Again, her health. She was disappointed—his concern for her condition overshadowing his interest in anything else. She tried to disguise her reaction. "I've never felt better in my whole life. I sleep late on weekends, go to bed early and I'm eating like a pig. It must be this clean Maine air."

Marty seemed satisfied. "You sound wonderful. Just be sure you take the sufficient time you need to get the job done right. Don't worry about rushing back to the city. I've got your next assignments on hold. They will do for the February or March issues."

She wanted him to shut up. Why did she bother calling him? He was insulting her by his overbearing concern for her well-being. He sounded patronizing and she, at the same time, was aware she was over-reacting.

"So, Aline, give me an idea of your work time-line for the remainder of your stay."

"I plan to stay up here for two more weeks, one more week of interviewing and another to wrap it up. I need a week to pull the material together and complete my presentation. The peace and quiet here will be the perfect setting to get it done. I'll edit it back in New York. Would you like to see a rough draft of what I complete this weekend? I can probably find a fax machine. Structure comes first, then style and description in the final hard copy."

"Oh, you don't need to do that. I have complete faith in your capabilities. We'll have plenty of time to go over it together when you return. Keep up the good work and call me anytime you want. You can call me at home if you like. My wife loves talking with you."

She could have written the script concerning his response. She answered him flatly, "Thanks, Marty. I appreciate it. Well, I know you're busy. I'll let you go. Got a pencil?" She gave him Cora's telephone number even though she knew he would never call. He sounded like he was humoring her. Only time would tell regarding how much genuine interest he was investing in her accomplishment.

Now it was comforting to be alone in the house. She refused to get teary. If she caved in now, it would simply be an indication of Marty's anxiety becoming fact.

She changed into a pair of jeans and her favorite sweatshirt and went down the hall to wash her face hard under cold water. It would make her feel better. After scrubbing her face, she looked at herself in the bathroom mirror. There were red rims around her eyes. Her emotions were out of control. She had to get a grip on herself.

Regarding Elcock and his art, her colleagues in New York could never know the importance of the work she was involved in unless they, themselves, could live it. This wasn't just about this man or the significance of his work. It was about Maine and the essence of the people who had lived here their whole lives. They were nourished by the sea. It was in their blood, they didn't just live near it.

17.

LATE SATURDAY MORNING, Aline eventually woke up. She read late into the night, and falling asleep with a book still in her hands. She lay there, too snug to move. The yellow and white room. Somehow, she didn't ever want to leave it. There was a certain aura about this room, giving her a sense of order and calmness which was new to her. It was an oasis in this seemingly empty house. This morning she felt luxurious and lazy as she slowly rolled over to glance at the clock. Ten forty-five—so what?

Gradually she pulled herself together, walking over to the window to see what the day was offering. Another glorious, bright blue, cloudless sky. It felt great to be alive. The work could wait until tomorrow.

A hot shower and a generous home-cooked meal at the diner was the only way to go. Maybe breakfast was over there but, she decided to give it a try. Besides, there was the whole day ahead of her to do whatever she pleased whenever she pleased.

After dressing, she went downstairs to look for her landlady. As usual, there wasn't a sound in the house. Cora must be running errands. A cup and saucer sat on the kitchen table, the usual signal indicating coffee was made for her to indulge in. Aline hadn't seen Cora for a whole week. For an older woman, she certainly was exceptionally active. Maybe they would touch base with each other over this weekend.

Aline turned off the coffeepot and placed her cup back in the drain. Putting on her jacket, she grabbed her bag and locked up the house. She was counting on seeing Cora later.

Cape Warren, like any other town, was very busy on Saturday. The diner parking lot was full, but she found a space across the street. Inside it was hot, noisy and full of chatter, the way she experienced it the first time she ate here.

She decided to wait for a table and luckily one opened up for her right away.

A cheerful young woman, close to Aline's age, approached the table as soon as Aline was seated. The blue plastic name tag on her uniform read "Terri." She poured a cup of coffee for Aline before taking the order.

Aline smiled at her, "Are you still serving breakfast, Terri?"

"Til noon, on Saturdays only."

"My name is Aline Kranick."

"Terri Shea."

"I'm a reporter for a New York magazine, doing an article on one of your residents."

"Impressive. I didn't realize any of us was newsworthy."

"Thomas J. Elcock is."

"Ah, but of course! Everyone who lives here has heard about him."

Terri took the breakfast order and left to take care of other customers. Aline noticed there was no wedding band on Terri's left hand, but that didn't mean anything these days.

It wasn't long before Aline's meal was placed in front of her. She was direct, "Terri, are you single?"

The waitress nodded. "Yes, why?"

"I'm new in town and I was wondering if you would be interested in showing me around. What do you do for excitement?"

"We can't compare to the "Big Apple", but we do have a few singles clubs outside town. I usually go out Friday nights."

"I'm also looking for a shopping area where I can find a few special gifts for my friends back in New York."

Terri looked off for an instant. "It's pretty quiet around here at this time of year. A lot of the shops shut down for the winter. If you go west on Route 1, there's a village square featuring a variety of shops. It's about five miles from the center of town, heading in the opposite direction of the courthouse. You'll see signs for the square long before you get there."

"Thanks. That sounds uncomplicated. If I decide to go out for dinner tonight, can you recommend a good seafood restaurant?"

"Most people go to *Harborview* when they go out to eat. It's sort of a resort hotel in the summer, but it's open all year long. The place stays pretty active until after New Years. By that time, all the boats are out of the water, the college kids are back to school and everyone is hunkering down, getting ready for the snow to fly."

"It sounds ideal."

"Don't mind me for saying so, but you're really off the beaten track. Do you miss the city?"

"Not one bit. The longer I'm here, the more I like it."

Terri raised her eyebrows in disbelief. She smiled and said, "Look, your breakfast is getting cold. I'll draw a map for you and bring it with the check. See you in a bit."

"You've been a big help. Thanks again." Aline began eating, savoring every bite. Why couldn't she find this communication level in the city? Maybe she didn't try hard enough to find it. No one cared to relate to anyone but themselves. Too much distrust and too much fear made it difficult for most New Yorkers to share. Too bad.

Aline finished breakfast and Terri returned with the check and the directions to the restaurant and village shopping drawn on the back of a paper placemat. She also listed the names of some of her favorite shops. Terri left Aline with great expectations for accomplishing the goals set out for the remainder of the day.

Before leaving the diner, they exchanged numbers and made tentative plans to get together the following week. At last there was someone her age to relate to on a social level.

Terri's map was well drawn and Aline didn't have any trouble finding the village square. Inside the entrance was an immense parking lot, only partially filled. She parked and walked along a brick path leading to the various stores. It was a pedestrians-only compound. Narrow cobblestone streets, dotted with benches and small greens, radiated from the central square. Ducks were swimming on the many ponds scattered over the premises. It was a beautiful day to wander along the footpaths. She chose a bench near one of the ponds to watch the shoppers and the children feeding the ducks.

Aline spent the afternoon shopping and looking for gifts. She made some discoveries of local crafts, unique to New England; homemade honey and jams, knit throws, carved wooden sea birds, and watercolors of lighthouses. She searched for a small gift for Cora to show her how much she appreciated her hospitality. Cora loved tea and Aline had found a packet of imported English blends, beautifully wrapped in colorful cellophane. This would be perfect.

By four-thirty, her feet were starting to ache and she decided to call it quits. Besides, she couldn't carry any more shopping bags. There was plenty of time to rest and prepare for dinner.

Half an hour later, she was turning down the driveway on Mitchell Street. She stopped the SUV next to the front walk in order to unload all her purchases and put them on the porch.

The front door was open. Cora must be home. It took several trips to unload the shopping bags and deposit them inside the foyer. She returned to her car and continued down the driveway. Cora was working in the back yard, raking leaves. Full rose blossoms lay in a large pile on the ground near the trash barrels. Aline walked over to her.

"Cora! Hi. The yard looks great. I can't believe the amount of leaves you've gathered. Would you mind if I chose a few of those blossoms for my room?"

"Help yourself. Most of them have passed, but you can have as many as you want. There are a few that still have some life in them." The leaves were heaped into many piles, spreading themselves over the entire yard. Cora stopped raking, leaning both hands on top of the rake handle, focusing her attention on Aline.

"Where have you been? I haven't seen you in days."

"I know. We've both been so occupied. Today, I went shopping. I found a little something for you."

"You didn't have to do that." Aline knew that she was going to say those exact words.

"I just want to thank you for making me feel welcome in your home."

Cora accepted the gift bag, pulling out one of the colorful packets of tea and turning it over slowly as she examined it. Evidently, the delicate wrapping made a pleasing impression on her..

"Why, thank you, what a nice thought. Well, I guess I've done enough yard work for today. Time to go inside. I'll put this rake away later."

Aline started to walk back to the house with her.

"A waitress at the diner told me about a village square with lots of specialty shops. I found some very unusual things."

They entered the house.

"By the looks of all those bundles, you did quite well. It's very nice there. I haven't visited it for a long time. Would you like a cup of tea? I think I'll open your gift."

"Oh, no thank you. I drank coffee earlier. But I'll take a rain check."

"I forgot that you prefer coffee."

"I started to drink coffee when I began my job in New York, probably because it was convenient. There was always a fresh pot of it available in the staff break room. We usually worked late and we literally lived on the awful stuff. No one ever took the time to brew a pot of tea."

Cora listened intently. "What are your plans for to-night?"

"I'm going to *Harborview* for dinner. It was recom-mended to me and I'd like to try it. Would you care to join me?"

"I've made plans for tonight, but thank you for ask-ing. Why don't we plan to have supper together some night next week? You can spend some time telling me about the project you're involved with."

"I'd like that very much."

"Good. Let me know what day is best for you.. Wednesdays are always open for me."

"Next Wednesday is fine."

Setting up a dinner date with Cora was gratifying to Aline. It indicated they were finally going to begin spending some time together. She was beginning to connect with the people around her.

18.

SATURDAY NIGHT. The wind was picking up. Aline looked forward to her evening out. She needed a change of pace. Terri's directions to the restaurant looked effortless to follow. The only major concern was the unfamiliarity of the narrow roads winding along the coast. Driving through this area in stormy weather or in a fog presented itself as a frightening thought, but even the same route on a clear night was equally intimidating. In daylight, the ride to the restaurant should take approximately forty minutes. Tonight, allowing extra time for caution, she added on another fifteen minutes to reach her destination.

This evening was going to be considered a reward for putting in such a productive work week. Things were running smoothly and she assumed they would continue to do so. Accordingly, perhaps her stay in Cape Warren would not be as extensive as was originally planned. Only the end of the forthcoming week would determine the time needed to complete her work. The thought of leaving sooner than expected saddened her a little.

But, she couldn't let these thoughts deter her from the responsibility of keeping her eyes on the road ahead. As she drove toward the restaurant, she recognized some of the signposts Mrs. Prentis had mentioned. After awhile, she clicked on the radio and found a station with soft music. Somehow it helped ease some of the tension created by traveling through this unknown terrain.

The two-lane highway stretched into a looming emptiness. Occasionally there would appear in the headlights a closed gas station or small general store. She didn't see any homes near the edge of the highway. Now and then, within her field of limited vision, a narrow dirt driveway would run off perpendicular to the road and dissolve into the night. There was no other traffic.

At last, the high beams began to pick up outlines of buildings emerging out of the blackness. A few pinpricks of light could be seen in the distance. Civilization! After cresting a slight hill, she could see some neon signs and yellow windows glowing in the night. The restaurant sat on the edge of a grassy bluff, with its almost empty parking lot to the left of the entrance. About a dozen cars were scattered near the front door. Two soft spotlights lit up the entry.

Most of the building was shrouded in deep shadows. Aline parked close to the front door. The restaurant was low, cedar-shingled and protected by dense shrubbery which was being whipped into a frenzy by the insistent, frantic wind. The windows effused a warmth, cozy and inviting. She couldn't wait to go inside and escape the blustery night.

When she entered the main reception area from outside, she was struck by the strong aromas of seafood dishes being prepared. The reservation desk was deserted. Beyond this, people were sitting at the bar on the left side of the entrance. On the right was a sitting area with small tables and upholstered wingback chairs. They were placed in front of a heartth which was nursing a dying fire. It wasn't crowded, but there were enough patrons dispersed throughout the adjoining rooms to give the seating areas a sense of congeniality. French doors glassed in a sun porch for dining.

The dining room was set up against the far wall, next to the picture windows. A view of the ocean could be seen during the day. Beamed ceilings, old polished tables and bright reflective tones of amber glass and brass gave the rooms a special glow. Ships' running lights and lithographs of whaling scenes were tastefully displayed throughout. Terri's choice was perfect.

After a few moments, a well-dressed middle-aged woman appeared from the dining room. She smiled slightly as her dark eyes made contact with Aline's.

"Good evening. Dinner for one?"

"Yes."

"Are you new to this area? I haven't seen you here before."

"Yes, I'm visiting. Your restaurant was recommended to me by an acquaintance of mine in Cape Warren."

"Cape Warren is a lovely town. I know it well. I have family living there. By the way, my name is Dorothy Grant."

"It's nice to meet you. My name is Aline Kranick. I'm here on business."

"Where are you staying, Aline? There are no hotels in Cape Warren."

"I'm staying with Cora Prentis. Do you happen to know her?"

A shadow passed over the woman's eyes. It was only fleeting, but Aline caught it.

"Why no, I'm afraid I don't . . . the name doesn't seem to ring a bell."

Aline suddenly wanted to change the conversation. "I love the decor. There's something about New England and the sea that is spellbinding. I live in New York and we really don't seem to take the time to appreciate where we live."

She asked her hostess to bring her a glass of wine to enjoy in front of the fire before sitting down to dinner. Dorothy agreed and left to summon a waiter while Aline settled into a chair facing the bar. She pushed back deeply into the armchair, to relax and reflect on the events of the past week.

She thought about the pace here. There was a lack of deadlines, stress, late hours and eating bad food on the fly, completely opposite from New York. Her life in Cape Warren was a logical regime, on her own schedule. She woke up at the same time every day, drove to Elcock's, interviewed him on schedule, enjoyed a cooperative client, left his house at the same time, spent the afternoons writing and editing in her room, ate her meals on a regular basis, and went to bed at a reasonable hour. In New York, none of these aspects were constant. Actually, they were always inconsistent.

This trip already was accomplishing its intention. It was forcing her to unwind. She was beginning to take the time to pull her life together, taking back the control that was eluding her.

As she sat pondering these thoughts, she didn't notice the young man sitting at the bar, staring at her. He liked the way she looked. She didn't look like she came from the Cape Warren vicinity. Her clothes, her fair complexion and chic haircut were all city. He was intrigued. He wanted to meet her.

He began walking toward her. Within seconds, he was standing in front of her, looking directly at her.

He didn't hesitate, "Hi, do you mind if I join you? If you're waiting for someone, you can ask me to leave."

"I'm not waiting for anyone. I guess it would be all right if you sat here for a while." She was tongue-tied. His shameless aggressiveness was throwing her off.

She liked his over-all appearance. He was tall and wore a pin-striped gray suit and white shirt, open at the neck. Even though it was Saturday, he was dressed as though he had just come home from work. He was lean with dark brown hair. He was acting very sure of himself.

"My name is Michael Williams. I'm a loan officer for the Shawmut Bank in Belfast. I worked in town this morning and then ran some errands. On my way home, I thought I'd drop in for a beer." He was sitting in the armchair on her right.

"I'm Aline Kranick. I'm a reporter for *East Side/West Side* magazine in New York. I'm writing a cover story on Thomas J. Elcock for our January issue and it brought me to Maine, where he lives." She decided not to offer him her hand in a greeting. Instead she sipped her wine.

"Yes, I've read about him in the paper. He's an amazing artist. How do you like Maine? It must seem pretty low-key compared to New York."

She was examining his face as she spoke; it was open, reliable. Aline sighed, "I'm getting rather tired of this reaction from the people I talk to. It annoys me. I was just thinking how much I've enjoyed myself since I arrived in Cape Warren. Being here is giving me a chance to re-evaluate myself."

"I didn't mean to offend you, Aline. How long have you lived in New York?"

"It's going on six years. My home town is in New Jersey. I go home to visit once in a while, usually at Christmastime."

"I hope that you don't mind me infringing on your privacy. I don't normally spend my evenings hanging around bars. After working six days a week, I just want to go home and hit the couch."

She was being cautious, but didn't want to be rude.

"Would you like to join me for dinner? Eating alone isn't much fun." The invitation was responding to his impulsiveness.

"I graciously accept. Let me know when you're ready and I'll ask Dorothy to select a table for us."

"Why don't you do it now. I'll join you in the dining room in a few minutes. I want to wash my hands."

Walking to the ladies' room, her mind was racing. She couldn't believe she was doing this—having dinner with a perfect stranger. Her mother would be appalled.

While she was washing her hands, she looked at her reflection in the mirror. Her skin was tight and polished. The city pallor was gone. Her complexion wasn't sallow anymore; she didn't even need makeup. She still was good-looking in spite of all the New York stress. A large proportion of her salary was spent on wardrobe. Working habits helped to keep her weight down and she always tried to keep herself looking presentable. In New York, being well-groomed was the first step to becoming successful.

Returning to the dining room, she noticed the absence of most of the clientele. She and Michael would almost have the whole room to themselves. The lights were dim and the atmosphere was softly intimate. Michael was studying the menu. He stood up when he saw her walking toward their table and pulled out her chair. For a casual meeting, he was being very attentive.

Maybe he wanted her to realize the big city wasn't the only place on the planet where one could find decorum. Returning to his seat, he handed her the other menu.

"Thank you. What strikes your fancy, Michael?"

"Steak or veal. I'm not too crazy about fish."

"Everything looks good to me."

They ordered their dinners and Michael chose a bottle of Chardonnay with the advice of the wine steward.

The conversation continued on a fairly mundane level, mostly concerning their jobs and problems coping with difficult co-workers. They both seemed at ease, genuinely enjoying each other's company. But Aline didn't want to go into too much detail concerning her project. She decided to steer the conversation in other directions and tell him about her parents.

After listening to her, Michael revealed that he was an only child, born and raised in this area of Maine. He graduated from Colby College, majoring in business administration. He did tell her he was single. She also discovered he was two years older than she was.

Time slipped away and soon they were ordering coffee, both of them wondering what the next move would be. The evening was turning out to be an extremely pleasant encounter, for both of them.

They sat peacefully sharing a brief silence while they drank their coffee. The vast blank void beyond the window swallowed up any hint of life.

Neither of them looked at their watches. Aline didn't have any idea where they stood in space or time, but sooner or later, she knew she would have to initiate the termination of their meeting.

She decided to make her move and stood up, placing her handbag under her left arm. "I have really enjoyed your company, Michael. I've met very few people since my arrival and my work takes up almost all of my time."

He started turning on the charm and she was attempting a defense against it, but it wasn't working. "I do have to return to the city. Someone will be after my job if I don't return on schedule. I can't believe I've already been here one week."

"How much more time are you planning to spend in Maine?"

"One more week is certain, perhaps two."

"When can I see you again?"

"I'm not sure. I still have deadlines to meet and the completion of this assignment is a commitment I intend to keep."

He noticed she had become very guarded and he didn't want to spoil this beginning by becoming too pushy. Her move.

She didn't want to hurt his feelings, so she added, "I'm sure that I can see you again before I leave. Where can I contact you?"

He pulled out a packet of business cards from his inside coat pocket and wrote down some telephone numbers, handing her a card.

Aline tucked the card in her bag. "I'll give you a call toward the end of next week. By then, I'll have a more realistic idea of when we can get together."

"That would be great." He waved over the waiter and slipped him his credit card before she could say or do anything. He said, "Tonight is my treat. You made my evening very special."

"Thank you. Next time it's on the magazine."

When they reached the coat room, the large oak clock over the fireplace showed the time to be around nine fifty-eight.

Dorothy bid them good night. "We hope to see you again soon."

When they left the restaurant, a sharp wind was waiting for them and fussed at them as Michael accompanied Aline to her vehicle. He opened the door for her as soon as it was unlocked.

He was stalling for time. "How long a drive do you have to get back home?"

"Oh, about forty minutes. The radio will keep me alert."

"Drive carefully. Hope to talk to you soon." He backed away from her, waving as he turned to walk to his own car.

She waited until his headlights were turned on before pulling out of the parking lot, lightly honking her horn.

On the way home, she reflected on the circumstances which led to the introduction of Michael into her life. Romance or the possibility of a romance never could enter into the overall plan. This was totally spontaneous and she must figure out how she was going to resolve it.

She was unprepared for all or any of it. And she didn't have time for it. It was too close to the end of the assignment to get involved with someone whom she would never see again once she returned to New York.

She was disappointed in herself for promising to call him, especially knowing he was wanting it so much.

Maintaining this friendship on a strictly occasional level was important to the success of her trip. She couldn't afford to allow Michael to take up too much of her time. The control was in her hands and she made a promise to herself to keep the events involving him in sharp perspective. He probably would accept this, but she still couldn't let him have the advantage in their brief get-together. Tomorrow would be soon enough to re-consider how to handle Michael.

Week number two was at hand and her impatience for it to begin was maddening for her. She wanted to uphold the initial energy of the first week and considered introducing a few fresh concepts to Elcock to hold his interest. Perhaps one or two field trips would be appropriate, especially one to the site he told her about, the point of land where he first viewed the ship. It changed his life so dramatically, a major keystone in his career. She was anxious to see his reaction if she suggested this idea to him.

19.

MONDAY MORNING. The second week of October. Today would mark a new beginning for her. The ultimate goal for her and Elcock was to start thinking out creative concepts simultaneously, reaching an exclusive communication level which was unique between two people.

He was excited about showing Aline the point of land where he used to go to paint his old house. He even suggested taking his pickup truck because he knew the area better than she did and she would have the opportunity to observe the scenery and enjoy the ride.

Elcock put a fresh thermos on the front seat of the truck and they left the woods. He showed her his enthusiasm by talking incessantly as they drove down the back roads leading to the waterfront. She tried to memorize the direction in which they were going, just in case she attempted to try to find her way back here later.

After half an hour, Elcock slowed down considerably, turning down a sandy opening heavily overgrown with bushes and dry weeds.

"I haven't been here for a long time. I think I'm the only one in this town who uses this approach."

Dry bushes scraped against the side of the truck in protest. Aline could hardly make out the definition of the road because of the thick undergrowth. She doubted the possibility of anyone visiting here recently or otherwise.

Finally they broke out of the scrub oak onto a beachy plateau overlooking the water. In the distance, she could identify the point of land, but she didn't see the old house.

Elcock turned to her. "It looks like my subject matter has succumbed to Mother Nature. It's probably in ruins out there."

Aline removed her camera from its case. "I'm disappointed. I wanted to study it with my own eyes."

"Why don't we go and take a look."

"Are you sure? You might also be disappointed. I don't want to put you in a situation which might upset you."

"Don't worry yourself about that. I guess I'm just naturally curious. This brings back a lot of memories."

"When was the last time you were out here?"

"I can't remember," Elcock said, "but it's been over twenty years. I never wanted to return to this area in all that time, but now I do."

She wondered about his lack of interest in visiting this location. But it really didn't matter—this was exhilarating! They were sharing the adventure *together*. He probably never showed this place to anyone. She felt privileged to be in his company under such personal circumstances.

"Mr. Elcock, let's get out and walk over to your point of reference."

"O.K. How about some coffee, first."

She quickly put her camera aside. "Sounds great. Here, let me pour it for us."

They decided to take their coffee with them as they stepped down from the truck and pushed through the thick shrubs. After a few minutes they reached the spot where he used to set up his easel. Elcock stomped down as many of the weeds as he could to clear a patch for them to stand on.

Thoughtfully, they stood there, gazing in the direction of the house, deep in their individual meditation. Neither of them spoke a word for a long time. The wind made loud, raspy cries as it forced its way through imbedded clumps of the matted and tangled grasses.

They didn't want to speak or move, consumed by the trance taking hold of them. The feeling was intense.

Aline was first to break the silence. "The beauty of this area is still a complete surprise to me. I never appreciated winter before, to this degree. The palette of colors at this time of the year is so much more intriguing, has so much more depth than the other seasons. I guess we go through most of our lives without really observing anything."

There was no response from Elcock. He was still staring out over the horizon. He hadn't been listening.

After a few more minutes, he turned toward her and looked through her. She felt uncomfortable, like she was intruding into his private world. She asked, "Do you want to continue?"

"Yes. Why don't we leave now. It's rather windy out here." His tone of voice was mechanical.

They made their way back to the truck and climbed up into the protection of the cab, glad to be out of the wind. He started the engine and backed up to a place where it was easier to turn around. Slowly, they turned back down the wild path to the road.

"How long do you think it will take to get there?" Aline asked.

"Oh, it shouldn't take more than half an hour." He was quiet now. A million thoughts must be careening through his consciousness. She decided to refrain from talking.

His change of mood concerned her more than she wanted to admit. When they first started out he was elated and now he was almost somber. Maybe too many memories were flooding back to a reality where he didn't care to be. All she could do was wait, trusting her faith in the rest of the day ending on a positive note.

After twenty minutes, he turned the truck down a sandy driveway, a wooden gate barring its entry. When the truck came to a stop in front of the gate, Elcock got out, walking over to where the latch was tied to a pine by a shredded piece of rope. He untied the rope and swung open the gate.

Aline was surprised by this aggressive behavior, but she made no comment and accepted it. He got back into the truck and drove on, at half-speed, even though there was little undergrowth to slow down their progress. They continued on for about ten minutes and ended up in a clearing on the entrance to the peninsula.

He stopped the truck and sat, with the engine running, looking over the area where the house had once stood. Finally, he turned off the ignition.

"Looks like my hunch was right," were his first words in over twenty minutes.

They left the truck and carefully started moving toward the tip of land jutting out into the harbor. It was soft earth and walking was a lot easier than before. Soon they came upon a weedy area with large, rectangular stones poking up out of the wild vegetation. Obviously, this was what remained of the foundation, the foundation of *his* house.

They found old bleached timbers buried under chunks of debris: a few shutters which were falling apart, broken glass, an old rusty tea pot, pieces of white railing, parts of chairs, smashed mirrors, and bits and pieces of flowered china. Anything of the value was long gone, picked over by souvenir hunters. The remains resembled the shambles of the existence of some family, of some connecting lives. No one cared about them anymore.

They combed through the ruins for a while and then decided to leave. The mood here was becoming morose and she thought about whether the effort of coming here was defeating their initial intent. She couldn't tell by his demeanor, one way or the other. He wasn't giving her any clues.

On the way home, she prayed he would say something productive to ease her anxiety.

Then Elcock stated in a soft voice, "Sometimes we shouldn't go back to certain events in our past. Nothing remains the same in life. Finding my old house in such disrepair was a bit depressing for me. I hate decay."

"Do you regret returning here?"

"Yes. I don't want to ever come back."

She didn't care to comment on his thoughts. Right now she just wanted to go home.

20.

TUESDAY MORNING. Sooner or later, the magic was going to come to an end. Aline counted four more days to share with Elcock, but this morning she didn't look forward to seeing him. The memory of yesterday was still unsettling. In a way, she blamed him for allowing a disturbing situation happen, especially since he seemed distressed at facing what he feared he might see. It didn't make sense.

She went downstairs to make herself a cup of coffee. Cora was nowhere to be seen and now Aline preferred having the space to herself. Both women cherished their independence. Aline took her coffee upstairs and sat at her desk, wondering how the day would unfold. Perhaps another field trip would counteract Monday.

He often referred to the shipyard where he found most of the stimulation for his paintings. She decided to suggest it; there was nothing to lose.

Aline knew her feelings would definitely affect his feelings and she would remain optimistic. She was ultimately responsible for the end result and could not risk sabotaging herself now.

However, doubt filled the back of her mind as she wondered how his mood would be today. She wanted to get over it and move on. Today would be much better. She just knew it.

The day started the same as every other day. He was waiting for her, expectation written all over his face.

"Hi there. How's it going?"

"Just fine. This vehicle knows its way here by heart, without me even guiding it!"

Elcock said, "You look tired."

"I stayed up too late last night reading one of the many books I brought with me. Sometimes they're hard to put down." She was lying and he knew it.

"Well, what do you have in store for us today?"

"What would you say if I asked you to take me on a tour of the shipyard, Mr. Elcock? I would love to see it and I'd like to take some pictures of the area for reference reasons."

"Your suggestion is all right with me, but I want you to know it's not very pleasant down there during the off-season. Also, you're not dressed properly. Do you have a cap to wear? If not, you can have one of mine."

"I have some winter clothes in the back of my car that should be sufficient."

"O.K. Let me get my coat."

He disappeared to gather his cold-weather gear. Soon he was back, dressed for the outdoors and they locked up the house. He waited for her in his truck while she went to get her warmer coat.

Within a couple minutes she climbed into the truck. He turned on the heater and they waited together for the dampness to evaporate from the interior.

"The shipyard is pretty inactive this time of year, but I think you'll find it interesting enough. We can go into the machine shop. I know they'll be working in there and I can introduce you to some of the men I've befriended over the years. They're used to me hanging around. I think they enjoy talking to an artist. What I do for a living is so different from the kind of work they're involved with. I'm kind of a novelty to them, I think."

She liked the sound of words he was saying. It was like a breakthrough, to erase Monday's outing.

The shipyard was up the coast, about forty minutes north of Cape Warren. In the distance they could see the huge cranes and smokestacks standing hard against the ashen winter sky. Thin streams of steam continuously spewed from the black stacks, harsh industry against a picturesque backdrop.

The main gates were swung open and they parked the truck near one of the buildings with a promise of work being done within its boundaries. Sparks from welding guns illuminated the windows in shades of blue-purple and fluorescent white. Hissing and clanking sounds accompanied the work in progress. A wide door, lit by spotlights, opened into a massive bay holding two steel-hulled vessels in dry dock. As they entered the building, their lungs were filled with acrid, scorched air which stung their nasal passages.

Men in protective hoods perched precariously on two-story-high framing, oblivious to the presence of visitors. Aline was astounded by the immensity of the structure. She felt very inconspicuous in proportion to the gigantic building and the ships hovering above her.

An old, dirty clock over the entrance indicated that it was almost ten o'clock. Gray metal cases holding time cards revealed the count of at least a dozen men working in and around the vessels at this particular time.

Elcock bent down to speak softly in her ear. "They can't hear us, but it's almost time for their morning break and they'll be climbing down for it shortly. There's an office where they go to get something hot to drink. We can wait for them there. I haven't seen them for a while."

They worked their way to the left side of the bay, being careful to avoid the electrical cables and lines which snaked over much of the floor space.

As he led the way, Elcock looked back at her, and said, "We really should be wearing hardhats, but they are too hot for me. The foreman is around here somewhere. He won't be very pleased to see me showing you around without a bucket. Once inside the office, we'll be all right."

Again she felt their closeness. They were a team. She cherished this above all else and wanted to preserve it at all costs.

Just as they were entering the brightly lit office, a loud buzzer sounded. One by one, the workers began to enter the room. Their faces were sweaty and covered with smudges of black grease and soot. The whites of their bloodshot eyes stood out in contrast to the dirt which covered their faces.

One of them recognized Elcock immediately and broke into a broad grin. "Hey, Tom! Where have you been keeping yourself?"

"Chester, good to see you. I'd like you to meet a friend of mine. Aline Kranick, this is Chester Burns."

"Pleased to meet you, Aline. What's a pretty girl like you doing in a place like this?"

The old line brought a round of laughter from the men in the room which was suddenly very crowded. She laughed along with them. She was out of place here, but felt secure with their friendliness and gusto.

Aline answered, "Would you believe I'm writing an article about your friend Tom for my magazine?"

They looked up from their coffee cups with quizzical expressions. "Old Tom? What's so special about *him*? All he is, is a big nuisance around Lincoln County!"

Again the room filled with laughter. They were having some fun with their friend and she was glad to be included in their fun. For a moment, she wondered if they were aware of his notoriety, but on second thought, she knew in her heart they were knowledgeable as to his prominence.

She still held their attention, so she said, “I think Mr. Elcock is very special indeed and I’m going to make sure the whole world knows it by the time I’m finished.”

“Ohh, Mr. Elcock, is it? Well, pardon me. Mr. Elcock, would you care for a cup of coffee?”

The appearance of the plant foreman in the doorway ended the charade, but no one could shake off their smiles.

“Hi, Tom,” the foreman said, “I haven’t seen you around here for quite a spell. Who’s the young lady?”

Elcock introduced Aline to Bill Furgeson and explained briefly why they were visiting the plant. He seemed pleased about her interest in seeing the shipyard. “Be sure to wear hardhats if you wander near the work areas. They are clearly marked. Safety is a top priority around here.”

“We’ll be very careful. I wanted Aline to meet Chester and his associates. She would like to take some pictures, if that’s OK with you, Bill. Maybe you could escort her around for about twenty minutes so that I can catch up with my pals. We haven’t seen each other in a long time. I want to hear some new stories.”

Bill liked the idea of showing Aline around the facility. It made him feel important. Female visitors were a rare exception. She agreed to be back in about fifteen minutes and followed Furgeson out the door, camera in hand. With his guidance, she wouldn’t waste a lot of time looking for the specific subjects to photograph on her list. The plant was dimly lit with the torches turned off. A close-up of the men welding would be saved for the last shot.

Struggling to adjust her hardhat, Bill gave her some help. Clouds of frosty vapor emitted from their mouths when they spoke to each other. The atmosphere was raw and damp, chilling her bones. Bill rushed her along so she could take as many photos as possible in the time allotted. After she finished, they returned to the office, where they were greeted by the men. She eagerly accepted a steaming Styrofoam cup of coffee from one of Tom's friends.

Elcock was glad to see her safe return. "Did you get your shots?" he asked.

"Yes, thanks to Bill's expertise."

Break was over and they prepared to go back to work. It was also time for Aline and Elcock to leave. On the way out, she took the last picture.

Driving home, Elcock chatted about his time spent at the shipyard and noted that the disappearance of the schooners was caused by them being replaced by steel hulls. He, himself, was a witness to the transition and expressed to her his gratitude at having been fortunate enough to document a part of history in his art. There was a deep sense of self-worth in his words and it filled her with joy to hear him talk about himself with such significance.

21.

TUESDAY AFTERNOON. They were having an incredible day together, full of energy. When they were back on the highway, Elcock said, "I'd like to take you to lunch."

Aline replied, "What a nice surprise." His eyes sparkled. She was wondering about his intentions.

"I'm taking you to meet one of my fondest friends," he explained. "He's a sail maker and he does beautiful work, mostly custom-made sails for yachtsmen. He refuses to retire. Reminds me of myself to a certain extent. Sometimes he's asked to draw up a total design, including the choice of colors for the entire vessel. He's an expert on racing boats. Many sailors confer with him for advice and most of the time, he ends up making all the sails for a particular boat."

She was intrigued. "I would like to meet him very much."

"I hope he's home. He should be. Hates to leave his loft."

They drove back in the direction of Cape Warren, retracing their steps. Forty-five minutes later, Elcock turned off the main road, in the direction of the coast, south of his studio.

Elcock continued, "I'd call him to let him know I'm on the way, but he doesn't have a phone. Likes his solitude. The local police department checks in on him once in a while to make sure everything's all right. Our postmaster gave him one of the old mail trucks when it was taken out of commission. Otherwise he wouldn't have any means of taking care of himself."

After half an hour Aline noticed that the scrub pine was becoming shorter and shorter, a sure sign that they were nearing the shoreline. Up ahead, on a hill, she could see an old, weather-beaten barn. A lot of shingles were missing and the roof was sagging. It didn't look very stable.

Elcock drove up to the front door and beeped the horn lightly. After a few minutes, an elderly man, dressed in a dark blue jumpsuit, came out of the barn and approached the driver's side of the truck. He rapped on the glass, waiting for Elcock to roll down the window.

"Hey, you old fart, it's about time you came to see me."

"Hank, watch your language. I have a lady with me."

"Sorry, ma'am, didn't see you sittin' there. Please accept my apologies." Elcock always visited him solo and Hank wasn't prepared to see anyone with him.

"Hank Swenson, I'd like you to meet Aline Kranick. She's visiting me from New York."

He gave Elcock a funny look. "Now, why would anyone come all the way from New York to visit you?"

"If you join us for lunch, I'll tell you all about it."

"You know I never go out. We can eat here, if you don't mind."

Elcock didn't want to argue with him. He was too stubborn. Besides, he knew it was hopeless to get him to a restaurant. "Fine with us, if that's what you prefer. Are you sure you don't want to get out of here for a spell? It's my treat."

"I just went shopping, so there's plenty to eat here."

Without another word, Aline and Elcock got out of the truck and followed Hank back to the barn. He seemed content to have some company and show off his space.

Aline was impressed by the spaciousness of the interior architecture. It was similar, on a smaller scale, to the bay at the shipyard. The poor condition of the exterior was no clue as to the state of the interior. Heavy beams crisscrossed the high ceiling, holding the ponderous amounts of canvas, cascading down almost to the first floor level. There was evidence of much work in various stages of completion. Material hung everywhere, turning the habitat into a cloth maze. It reminded Aline of when she was a little girl, in her backyard, running through her mother's wet laundry. It flapped recklessly in the wind, striving to free itself from the lines to which it was anchored.

Hank guided them through the white forest, a huge surrealistic painting which was constantly changing.

A small room at the far end of the first floor represented the makeshift kitchen. Under an expansive picture window was a large table, pushed up against the wall, overlooking the marsh grass and sea beyond. Their host made them cold cut sandwiches and poured hot coffee into oversized, chipped mugs.

They sat down, facing the marsh, Aline placing herself between the two men. The three of them ate lunch quietly together like they had known each other for a long time. She felt their approval; she was sharing an identity with these incredibly gifted artisans which was almost magical to her.

Swenson told his sea stories until it started to get dark. Seamen and sail makers ran in his family for past generations. When Elcock was painting the big ships, Swenson was crewing on them. An injury at sea forced him to study other options as far as making a living was concerned. He settled on sail making and now he was considered one of the finest craftsman in his field. The quality of his work was well documented and sought after. Many articles had been written about him in yachting magazines. Now he was in the advantageous position of picking and choosing only the work that interested him.

To Aline, he was a less-refined version of Thomas Elcock: same build, same height, same bushy white hair, but a little less polished. He was outspoken and unyielding. Like Elcock, he was virtually a loner and was particular about whom he chose to spend his time with. But, in spite of this isolation, he was an excellent conversationalist.

Elcock had heard most of the stories more than once, but he still enjoyed hearing them again, and took exceptional pleasure in watching Aline's reactions to them. He tried to make an effort to visit Hank at least once a month. They more or less depended on each other. The years were slipping by and they always called on each other in times of crisis.

At last there was a lull in the story-telling and it was time to depart. Aline asked Hank if she could take his picture before she left. He agreed only under the condition that both he and Elcock were in the pose, an appropriate ending for an outstanding day.

Elcock and Aline finally said good-night, and left for home, laughing and recounting the afternoon, the stories and their good fortune in finding Hank in such a receptive mood.

It was dark when they reached Elcock's studio. She told him how much she enjoyed the day and suggested they resume tomorrow at a later time, around ten-thirty. She explained about the errands she needed to run, but in reality, she wanted Wednesday to be a shorter day because of the seven hour day just spent with him. He agreed to the idea and went into the house giving her a little farewell wave as he opened his front door.

For the first time since she arrived, she entered the woods feeling totally content. Its overbearing disposition wasn't intimidating to her.

Her thoughts were with Elcock. Today he almost made her feel as though she was becoming a part of him. His creative drive, his appreciation of the Cape Warren area, and the few acquaintances who were a part of his limited social life were now part of her life as well.

22.

WEDNESDAY, ONLY THREE MORE DAYS. Three more days and the beginning of closure. The second week was building to an emotional climax, especially the relationship with Elcock.

Instead of their interview time spiraling downward in irrelevance, it was doing just the opposite. By the end of week two, she was aspiring to reaching an uncommon level of understanding and empathy with him.

These thoughts made her feel heady, even a bit grandiose. Maybe she was becoming too impressed with herself. There was one aspect she always must keep in mind, however. The main thrust of her writing was to concentrate solely on Elcock. The article couldn't become a sounding board for her personal thoughts. The issue was about him, not her.

The morning dawned gray and turbulent. She dressed in layers she could peel off in case they were going indoors. Downstairs, the coffee would be waiting for her and today she couldn't wait to get to it .

On the kitchen table stood another one of Cora's communiqués, "Don't forget tonight." To the point.

Aline wasn't going to forget about her dinner date with her landlady. The idea of spending some time with Cora presented itself as a practical idea. Aline didn't want to appear unsociable. Besides, this house was now her home away from home. She wrote a brief postscript on the bottom of Cora's note. "Be home early. Looking forward to tonight."

As she left the house, the wind caught hold of her. Spiraling masses of dry leaves were swirling all over the yard and down the street in endless rivers of erratic, crispy movement. The air was damp and it smelled like rain was on the way. Walking was difficult and she leaned forward with her head down, closing her eyes against the assault of the leaves, hitting her face like small, stinging projectiles.

Once inside the SUV, she started brushing out her hair and wiping her watery eyes. The piles of leaves previously raked by Cora earlier in the week were scattered all over the backyard, giving the property an unkempt appearance.

Broken branches and twigs were strewn along the side of the street. She hoped the weather would hold for a while and not ruin the day and the potential plans laying ahead of her.

By the time she reached the base of Elcock's road, the sky looked frightening. The pine trees moved frantically overhead as she picked up speed. She parked closer than usual to his house and made a mad dash for his front door.

His receptive countenance greeted her, "Looks like we're in for a nor'easter."

"It's very blustery out there. There are branches down all over the place," she answered as she stepped past him."

He gave a snort. "It hasn't even started yet. You've never experienced one of our famous New England winter storms, have you?"

"No, I haven't. I hear they're pretty awesome."

"You've been here for almost two weeks and I haven't even shown you the ocean. Don't take off your coat. You'll also need a hat and scarf. Here, take one of mine."

He handed her the wool items and she bundled up, following his lead out through the back entrance. A heavy oak door opened out to a narrow deck and catwalk leading to an observation area on top of an elevation of land overlooking the sea.

The coastal storm was much more ferocious here than in town. It snarled through the treetops with an exaggerated sound made even more terrifying when combined with the pounding surf below. Elcock and Aline were shouting to each other, but the deafening crescendo drowned out their voices. There was no point in attempting to talk to each other.

They fought their way along the catwalk, clinging to the sturdy handrail with all their might. He kept looking back to be sure she wasn't in trouble. She pulled the scarf up over her face, leaving just enough space to see where she was going. Droplets of salt water blurred her vision. Elcock's bulk in front of her acted like a shield against the violent forces surrounding her.

When they reached the platform, they held each other for support, squinting at the tumult below. The sea was in a rage, black and violent. It smashed relentlessly against the rocks, throwing up immense sprays of foam and brine. Anything in its path was certainly doomed.

Even though her mouth was covered, she could hardly breathe. She was gasping for air, possessed by total fear.

They knew they would not be able to stay out here much longer. Pieces of lumber and other wreckage could be seen surfacing with each new swell. The storm was bombarding the land mass, causing considerable damage, even in its early stages.

Elcock tugged at her coat, pointing toward the house. Grateful to leave, she led the way back, grasping the wet railing. The wind was now at their backs and it was easier to move, but just as risky. Every time a blast hit them, it pushed them forward, challenging their balance.

At last they reached the back door and threw themselves inside.

"Looks like we're really in for it! Are you all right, Aline?"

"Yes, just a little shaken. I've never seen or felt any force like this before!"

"I took an awful chance letting you go out there, but I wanted you to see for yourself the power of the sea. It helps you to realize the daring of the men who make a living working it."

She didn't want him to feel guilty. It had been her decision. "I wouldn't have followed you if I thought it was going to be life threatening. Don't worry, I trust you."

He accepted her answer, but didn't care to discuss it further. He poured them hot coffee and they sat gulping it down, trying to regain their composure. She was shuddering and kept her coat on.

After a few minutes, Elcock got up and paced around the room in a restless state. "We usually get the worse storms at this time of year. If the sailboats aren't out of the water by the first week in November, their owners are just asking for trouble."

She was still too cold to answer him, so she simply nodded every time he said anything.

"We can spend the rest of the morning here if you wish. The only other thing I wanted you to see before you left was a maritime museum on the outskirts of Camden. It houses early American art pertaining to the days of the great ships. The museum's permanent collection features paintings, wood carvings, scrimshaw, portraits, dolls, and ships' rigging salvaged from some of the famed shipwrecks. The new wing concentrates on whaling and a model ship exhibition. I particularly want you to see this."

Aline wasn't very enthusiastic about the idea of going out again, but she decided to accommodate him today and because of this, she conceded. "The field trip sounds fascinating to me. Let's go."

"The rain hasn't started yet, so we better leave right away. Later, we can stop to get something to eat if we're hungry."

They locked up and moved toward his truck parked next to her vehicle. Once inside, he started the engine and they sat for a while.

Aline asked, "How far away is the gallery? I don't want to get back too late."

"It's not far, maybe an hour at most. We will be back long before dark. Bad weather doesn't seem to keep people at home much in Cape Warren. It's part of our life here during this time of year."

She chuckled at him and answered in an unconcerned tone, "I guess I'm not as brave as you are."

Elcock turned on the radio for a weather update. The prognosis was not good; they knew they would have to carefully keep track of the developing conditions. Loose bark and leafy matter littered the roads, but the pickup was not affected much by any of it. Aline felt fortunate she was not driving. After an hour, billboards for the whaling museum began to appear. They would reach their destination well before noon.

According to the radio, the rain wasn't due until later in the afternoon. Aline assumed that her plans with Cora would not change because of the circumstances caused by the storm.

While absorbed with her thoughts, she didn't notice their arrival at the museum. The main portion of the complex was contained in a deserted brick building renovated to exhibit a collection of sailing paraphernalia. Old sails and rigging dangled from wire cables suspended from the roof. In spite of the oiled wood and brass polish, the interior smelled stale to Aline, after coming in from the moist salt air.

The building's nineteenth century construction and architecture gave it a bond with the material it housed.

Huge glass cases lined the walls, filled with handmade artifacts dating back over one hundred and fifty years. Aline was most fascinated by the excerpts from the sailing logs, sailors' diaries and scrimshaw. Some of the framed pages were enlarged and coordinated with the objects shown next to them.

Elcock was most interested in showing her the whaling exhibits and didn't want to get involved with the other displays. She sensed he was becoming anxious and followed him into the new wing. Here the plastered walls were painted an antique cream color. Spotlights mounted on the ceilings highlighted objects of particular interest like harpoons, narwhal tusks and ships' tackle. He especially wanted to show her the paintings and etchings. Most of the prints were in poor condition, but their faded surface didn't detract from the violent, gory message they portrayed. Huge mammals spurting fountains of blood, boats being crushed in the pursuit and seamen facing death at the mercy of the angry sea and the more-than-angry animals they were trying to destroy.

Aline didn't care to spent too much time on this particular subject matter. She switched her attention to the large models of the whaling ships. These old beauties surely were Elcock's inspiration. Each ship was meticulously put together. The attention to detail, on a minute scale, was incredible to behold.

He stood apart from her and watched her moving around the displays. She felt his eyes following her every move. He was trying so hard to pull her into his soul. He could only share his utmost spirit with her if, and only if, she understood where his essence had had its beginnings, its birth.

23.

WEDNESDAY AFTERNOON. They briefly circled around the exhibition area for one last glance. Before leaving the gallery, Aline picked up some pamphlets and also purchased a small exhibition catalog which listed the artists' names and their dates.

Driving back, they both were pensive, mentally recalling the artwork and trying to relate to it. She was glad they were on their way home.

He wanted to know her reaction. "Did you enjoy the museum?"

"Yes. I'm glad you included it in our itinerary. I don't think the majority of Americans take the time to appreciate their history. But this exhibition isn't just history. Its essence, the heart and blood of all those sailors, is still in there. Their sacrifice and their raw courage were and are devastating to witness."

He didn't answer her and she knew his silence was a complete confirmation.

Elcock said, "Being from Maine is a very different identity. Not too many people want to take the time to comprehend what it entails."

Those were his last words for the time being. It started to rain very hard and his attention was on the road ahead, not his philosophy of life.

They reached Cape Warren after one-thirty. Because of potential flooding, they had decided to skip lunch.

The dirt road leading to his house was already awash and muddy. He parked next to her vehicle so she wouldn't get too wet.

When the ignition was turned off, he turned to her and pushed back against his seat. "Meeting you has been very rewarding for me, Aline. You have been instrumental in reviving my spirit to a greater extent thought possible for me to achieve at this point in my life."

His words were almost too overwhelming for her to comprehend at this moment. Evidently, this business arrangement meant more to him than she imagined. She was trying to remain composed and responded, "I can't remember feeling this fulfilled."

Elcock continued, "Well, we certainly have covered a lot of ground. I delight in your youth and friendship."

They parted on a compassionate note, Elcock waving good-bye. "Be careful and take it slow!"

It was really pouring now and sheets of water ran down her windshield with maximum intensity. The wipers could hardly keep up with the deluge. By the time she reached the main road, she wouldn't be able to see anything in front of her. It would be best to sit here for a while and wait for the rain to let up. Aline put the vehicle into park, listening to the rain pounding on the roof. While she waited, she retrieved a half empty bag of roasted peanuts from the glove compartment and began to eat them. The floor of her vehicle was covered with shells.

Once again, she contemplated returning to New York. It hovered like a black hole waiting to swallow her up, giving her nothing to look forward to. Her greatest fear was falling right back into her empty, depleting way of life as soon as she returned. She'd take drastic steps to prevent this from happening.

She had to get home and leave the safety of this driveway to venture out onto the wet pavement. Readjusting her seatbelt, she turned out onto the road, high beams on.

Finally, she arrived at Mitchell Street and parked in the back. Taking her house keys out of her purse, she ran for the porch, shaking off as much rainwater as she could. The front door was locked, meaning Cora wasn't home yet. It was almost two o'clock.

Inside the foyer, she took off her wet shoes, deciding to hang her coat in the shower upstairs. A hot bath would bring her back to life.

After bathing, Aline put on her robe and returned to her room, to review her date book. Studying it, she realized she promised to call Michael. He probably would want to see her over the weekend and she was starting to become intrigued about the prospect of seeing him again.

Taking some notepaper out from under the mound of newspapers and folders, she started jotting down her impressions and reactions of her observations at the museum. She needed to document everything she remembered when it was fresh in her mind, almost like the ships' logs. It would be impossible to try and recall everything if she didn't capture it now. After writing for a few hours, she was slowly becoming aware of the aroma of cooking. Aline put aside her paperwork, descending the front stairs on her way to the kitchen to greet Cora.

Her landlady heard her coming, but she didn't turn around. She was wearing a pink, flowered housedress and she stood at the sink, scrubbing vegetables. "Hi. Did you have a good day? I was worried about you, being out in the storm. Thought we'd eat a little early. Is that all right with you?"

"Yes. Sounds good to me."

"You can nibble on some cheese and crackers if you're too hungry."

"That's not necessary. I don't want to spoil my appetite. How can I help you, Cora?"

"You can set the table for me. The dishes are in the glass cabinet in the dining room. They were my mother's. I only use them on special occasions. The silverware is in the top drawer of the sideboard along with the linen napkins."

"Let me know if I can do anything else." Aline went into the dining room to set the table. She carefully took the antique plates out of the cabinet and placed them on the lace tablecloth that Cora had spread on the long mahogany table. This room was rarely used; it was similar to the quality of a room set up in a museum, displaying period furniture, old china, lace curtains, a bleached oriental rug and oil lamps mounted on the wall. The lamps were more decorative than useful. Aline flashed back to the whaling museum. The only difference was, this museum was lived in.

She returned to the kitchen after setting the table. Cora was in the process of poking at a small roast perched on the oven door.

She was concentrating on her cooking as she said, "I always like pot roast on rainy days."

Aline responded, "Your china is lovely. Having nice things is so special."

"I take good care of it. The plates were washed this morning, so everything is ready. I'll see you later. We'll eat around six."

Aline was being dismissed from duty. One thing about New Englanders—they didn't waste a lot of words. She went back upstairs and resumed the work she had been doing earlier.

At five forty-five Aline went downstairs to join her landlady for dinner. Cora was just taking off her apron when Aline entered the kitchen.

Cora announced, "Everything's ready."

They went into the dining room. The silverware and napkins were re-arranged to Cora's own liking. Serving dishes held green beans and mashed potatoes. A basket of soft rolls and a gravy boat, filled to the top, completed the offering. Thick slices of pot roast lay on the large dinner plates.

The women sat opposite each other on the short width of the table. They placed their napkins on their laps. The rain beat against the dining room windows. The chandelier was lit.

"Please help yourself, Aline. I don't drink, but I have a bottle of wine in the kitchen if you would care for some. One of the nurses at the clinic gave it to me for Christmas last year."

"Oh, no thank you. I have work to do tonight. Besides, I prefer water with my meal. Once in a while I'll have a glass of wine with my dinner if I'm out with my friends, but that's infrequent. Usually, I work late at the office and then go home and go straight to bed."

"Why don't you tell me a little bit about yourself. Your job sounds very demanding."

Aline told her about living in northern New Jersey with her mother before moving to New York to be closer to her career. Her father had passed away seven years ago, while she still was in school. Her younger sister, Cathy, was married to an electrical engineer and lived in southern California. They were not close.

"That's too bad. Family is important."

"Yes, I know. We still have some problems to work out." Aline was looking at her food instead of her hostess, indicating she preferred to end the discussion concerning her family. She took the lead. "How long have you lived in Cape Warren?"

"All my life. My parents and their parents were born here. I couldn't think of living anywhere else. I've lived in this old house since I was a child and my grandparents lived here before that. My father was a foreman in a paper mill and did quite well for himself. I have very fond memories of my parents. They gave me everything they could afford to give."

"Any sisters or brothers?"

"No. Wish I did. Sometimes you just want to talk to someone."

They were almost finished with their supper. Aline thought about her mother. The food tasted like her home- cooking. Her mother didn't want her daughter to live in New York and was very upset when Aline left for the city. Aline made a mental note to call her.

"Cora, do you have any children?" Aline also wanted to ask Cora about her husband, but felt it was best to avoid being too nosey. *Tread carefully.*

"No. Don't be too shy to take seconds."

"Don't worry. Everything is delicious and I'm starved."

She helped herself to more beans and potatoes, pouring gravy over both. The small talk came to a standstill. Silverware clicked against the plates. When Aline stopped eating to wipe her mouth, she noticed Cora studying her.

"So, tell me why you're here in Maine at this time of year?" Cora asked. She was closing in on the crux of the matter.

"I'm writing an article about a famous artist who lives here. He has a show on Madison Avenue this month and the magazine wants to feature him in the January issue. His name is Thomas J. Elcock."

Cora said, "We have quite a large art colony residing here in the summer months. Where 'bouts does he live?"

"He lives about twenty minutes from here, on the ocean."

"Really?"

"He paints landscapes and seascapes. His exhibition has been in all the New York papers. I'm sure he's been mentioned in your local paper. Have you heard of him?"

"Don't read the papers. I'll clear if you're finished." Cora stood up abruptly and started to take the empty dishes back to the kitchen.

Aline felt like she was standing on the edge of a precipice. Slowly, she stood up, not knowing her next move.

Cora ordered, "Stay in your seat. I'll bring in dessert and tea."

Aline obediently sat down, waiting for Cora to reappear. Somehow, her appetite was gone. Within minutes Cora returned carrying a tray holding a teapot with matching cups and a small cake covered with powdered sugar.

"I didn't bake this. Picked it up in town on the way home."

She poured the tea and cut the cake into two generous chunks, one of which she placed in front of Aline. Without looking at her guest, she asked, "What do you think of his work?"

The woman sitting across from Aline appeared stiff and unyielding and talking to her was becoming almost painful. Yet, Aline's good manners carried her. "His work is magnificent. I saw it firsthand at the exhibition. Most of it is very powerful and dramatic on a grand scale. I experienced the same impression at the Louvre in Paris when I was fortunate enough to view the paintings of the nineteenth-century French painters. Reproductions in art magazines can't possibly do any justice to the majesty and dimension of his talent."

They ate in silence. Occasionally, one of them would make a remark, but it passed unanswered. Pounding rain and tearing nature roared outside.

Aline felt she had said enough, perhaps too much. She didn't care to discuss Elcock's private life or share the confidentiality he granted her. It was her responsibility, as a reporter, to honor his trust. She found herself in an awkward position. Maintaining, but keeping discreet, two friendships in a small town was a tricky balancing act. To lose the rapport in either camp, could be detrimental to her purpose here.

Cora's questions continued: "Does he know where you're staying?"

"No. He hasn't asked. My personal life is of no real interest to him. All the interview time is spent discussing his art. He took me to a whaling museum today to see an early American collection of seascapes."

"The one near Camden?"

"Why, yes. Have you heard of it?"

"Everyone in Maine knows about it."

Cora's response made Aline feel ignorant. What a *stupid* question!

"Had enough to eat?" Cora's voice sounded tedious. She stood up, preparing to clear the table.

"Yes, thank you. Everything was wonderful."

Aline carried a full tray of dessert dishes back to the kitchen. Cora was already bent over the sink, scraping plates and getting ready to wash them.

"Why don't you let me do that?" Aline offered.

"Absolutely not. You're my guest tonight. Besides, you have work to do. I'll finish up here."

The chatting, the questions and the evening all came to an end. They both just stood there, with nothing more to say to each other, listening to the fury of the storm. Cora Prentis had no reason to continue on. She had already found out what she wanted to know.

Aline was back in her room, sitting on her bed and wondering why the evening ended the way it did-flat. It left her feeling hollow and empty. Probably she expected too much.

Maybe it was the age difference. Their backgrounds and upbringing were from two different worlds. Education wasn't a factor. Exchanging thoughts or expressing themselves didn't appear to be a problem.

No, it was something else, something went down very deep below the surface, below the façade. Cora simply shut Aline down, cut her off. The answer was somewhere in this town, in this assignment, in this house.

24.

THURSDAY MORNING. All night long, lying in the dark, she listened to the branches clawing at the side of the house. Finally, daylight arrived.

She went to a window to check out the aftermath of the northeaster. The sun's rays on her face felt reassuring.

Tree litter choked the street drains. Small branches and twigs covered the lawns and the roofs of parked cars. A look out the back window relieved her; the rental vehicle had been spared any mishap.

Before meeting with Elcock, she decided to pick up coffee on the way. She straightened up her room and went downstairs to get her coat.

Today Aline didn't care for Cora's coffee. She poured the whole pot down the drain. Last night's memory was too fresh. All she wanted was to get out of the house.

When she arrived at Elcock's, she cautiously started up the driveway, not knowing what to encounter. Not much damage here. The ponderous treetops must have acted as an umbrella to protect his property.

She pulled into the clearing. He was standing outside and he shouted to her to park beside his truck, as if he assumed they were going to be leaving right away. Instead, Aline went into his house and took off her coat.

He looked a bit perplexed. "I take it you have already made a plan for today." It was more of a query than a statement.

"I have an unusual request. You may not approve of it."

"I can't imagine what it might be."

"I would like very much to watch you paint."

He raised his eyebrows, his expression quizzical, at a loss for words. She didn't always give him enough time to counter-act her moves. He mused, "You certainly are full of surprises, I must say. Well, no one has ever watched me in action before, but I guess there's a first time for everything, as the saying goes."

"Is that a yes?"

Elcock just shook his head, indicating slight exasperation. Sometimes she was too much for him.

They took their coffee and headed for the back of the house. The air from last night's rain was raw and muggy, but she didn't care. She wrapped herself in one of his huge jackets and sat on a stool, watching him prepare himself for the execution of his art.

He lifted a large palette off a taboret and began squeezing oils, in generous blobs, all around the edge of it. Colors were arranged according to the spectrum, from titanium white to cadmium yellow, red, ochre, cobalt blue, ultramarine blue, burnt umber, and lamp black. After he finished arranging the paints, he poured clean linseed oil and turpentine into separate glass jars. All the necessary supplies were then placed into a large basket.

Before ascending the shaky staging, he stepped back as far as he could from the canvas and surveyed it, silently determining what section he was going to work on. He shuffled through some loose acrylic sketches rendered in color. When his mind was made up, he started to climb up into the supports. Aline couldn't help but think that he was climbing into the rigging of one of his ships. Once he reached his work level, he used the pulley system to raise the basket to his station.

She watched him for hours swinging his long arms in continuous sweeping movements as he applied the paint to the canvas. He was consumed by a driving energy possessing him beyond his own state of consciousness.

After three hours he put down his brushes. Turning his back to the wet paint, he leaned on the railing and hung his head down, totally exhausted.

Aline stood up, wondering if he needed assistance, but afraid to say or do anything. Gradually, he lifted his head and his eyes met her glance which was filled with concern.

"Aline, I'm all right. Don't look so worried."

She quietly sank back down on the stool. This passion was beyond her comprehension, quite apart from anything witnessed in her past research.

"Why don't you come down and take a break. I know I'd like something hot to drink."

As he placed the brushes in the jar of turpentine, she noticed his mobility was labored. He grabbed hold of the uprights with his big hands, carefully working his way down to her. When he reached ground level, her anxiety left her.

"I really feel my age after one of these sessions. Someday in the not too distant future, I won't have the endurance or the physical strength to do this."

Aline shook her head. "I can't believe that."

They went back inside the house and he promptly went over to a huge wooden bin stacked with logs. An ax with a bright red handle lay on top of the pile. After chopping some kindling and filling the wood-burning stove, he started a fire. Then he returned to his chair and fell into it. She didn't want him to move so she went into the kitchen and brought him back a mug of coffee.

Elcock thanked her. “Sometimes it’s very difficult to get the dampness out of the house and out of my bones. The stove will help.”

They sat listening to the crackle of the flames. Aline was still in a state of adulation after watching this explosion of human endurance and creativity.

She sat with him for a while and then stood up slowly to gather her coat and gloves. She went over to Elcock and gently kissed his forehead. “I’ll see you tomorrow morning.” She had tears in her eyes and didn’t look back.

25.

SLOWLY, SHE DROVE AWAY. Halfway down the road, she stopped the vehicle and put it in park, crossing her arms over the steering wheel and burying her face in the heavy fabric of her coat. She was thinking about tomorrow. It would be her last day with him and the finality of it was affecting her too much. She was becoming too attached to him, too sentimental.

In the past, she always remained detached from her subject matter. This was different; it felt like a sign of weakness. It was a new experience.

She wanted to call Martha. Martha would lift her spirits. They hadn't spoken to each other since she left New York and her friend was probably anxious to hear from her. When they reached out to each other for support, it always turned out to their own best advantage. They were close to each other and, more importantly, they needed each other. Aline thought to herself, *My friends and my mother have to become my top priority*.

Michael was expecting her to contact him. Sitting up, she was annoyed with herself for adding guilt to her situation.

Going back to Mitchell Street was out. Right now there were other things to attend to. She knew the Courthouse could assist her in finding a library. It would be the perfect place to think and work undisturbed. The car needed gas, a bath and a vacuum. Peanut shells covered the floor and the front seat. She spotted a gas station with a car wash connected to a convenience store and pulled in. After attending to the car's needs, she decided to call Michael.

The weekend lay ahead. Terri wanted to get together with her tomorrow night and Michael would try to see her at some point over Saturday or Sunday.

His business card was in her wallet and easily accessible. It was almost two-thirty. She was sure he'd be available. She dialed the bank's number.

"Shawmut Bank. How can I help you?"

"I would like to speak to Michael Williams, please."

"May I ask who's calling?"

"Aline Kranick."

He was on the line in seconds. "Hi! I was hoping you would call."

"I told you I would. How are you?"

"I'm doing great. How's your project coming along?"

"I'm very pleased with the progress. I wrap things up next week."

"I'd like to see you. Is it possible?"

"I think so."

"What are your plans for the weekend?" He sounded excited, almost breathless.

"I'm busy tomorrow night, but I have free time Saturday and Sunday."

"How would you like to spend some time in Augusta?"

"What's going on in Augusta?"

"I've been invited to a party and I'd like you to come with me. We can stay at my aunt's house. She adores company."

"Maybe it would do me good to get away for a few days. I have lots to tell you."

"I could pick you up at your house Saturday morning."

"Could you meet me somewhere else?"

"Is there a problem?"

"There could be. I'll explain later. You could pick me up at my girlfriend Terri's house. We're going to a movie tomorrow night and I'll probably stay over. Before we leave, I'll call you from her house to give you directions, around eight-thirty. Is that OK?"

"Sure. Sounds like your answer is yes?"

"Yes it is. I have to go now. I'll talk to you tomorrow night."

"You're going to have a good time."

She hung up, feeling satisfied she was meeting her commitment. And she was in control. *Was this going to be an end in itself—the control?* If so, she should be careful. Manipulating other people's feelings was a dangerous game.

26.

THURSDAY AFTERNOON. The library was a large brick building with a slate roof. It looked dated, but it represented a comfort zone for Aline. She found a parking space and walked around to the front so she could enter through the main entrance. As soon as she was beyond the glass doors, she was overcome with a sense of familiarity; spending many hours doing research culminated into a unique attitude toward libraries. To Aline, being in one was like exercising her membership in a private club.

She chose a secluded carrel where she could concentrate in peace. The circulation desk was very busy and all the sections were crowded with readers, even the stacks. All this was solace to her. She wanted to be a part of it, to feed off it.

Before she started to work, she took off her watch, resting it in the corner of the desk so she could keep track of the time. Martha always left exactly at five o'clock and went directly home to be at her mother's side. Whatever Aline was in the middle of, she would drop it and call her friend an hour later. She reminded herself to be careful not to become too engrossed in what she was doing. She didn't want to forget to call. The hours posted on the front door indicated that tonight the building would close at six. It was open until nine only on Mondays and Wednesdays. A warning bell would ring fifteen minutes before closing.

Aline plunged into her writing with fresh enthusiasm. She was totally absorbed in her work when the bell rang. It startled her. She quickly gathered up her paperwork, stuffing it into her briefcase. It would be more logical to call Martha from her car.

A line of cars was already leaving the library grounds and Aline decided to wait for a few minutes to avoid the traffic jam at the exit. While she waited for her turn to leave, she took out her cell phone. It was five fifty-three. She dialed Martha's number. After two rings, someone picked up.

"Hello?"

"Hi. It's Aline."

"Aline! It's about time! You've been gone two whole weeks. How are you?"

"I'm fine. I'm sorry I haven't been in touch earlier. You must be upset with me."

"No, just a little disappointed." Martha would be too timid to express herself fully.

"I miss you. How is work?" Aline asked.

"I miss you more. Work is the same. You know."

"Does Marty miss me? When I talked to him, he sounded like he could care less."

"When was that?"

"Last Friday. I can't believe I've already been in Maine for almost fifteen days."

"Neither can *I.* When are you coming home?"

"I plan to be here only one more week."

"The office just isn't the same without you."

"Thanks. I love it up here. This place was meant for you. It's so woodsy. If you ever came up here, Martha, you would never go back to New York. I mean it."

"I could never leave Mother. Maybe some day we could visit Maine together. You could show me around."

"The blind leading the blind! I only just found a library today. By the way, how is your mother doing?"

"About the same. She won't go back to the doctor. I'm at my wit's end with her."

"You have to be patient, Martha. I know it isn't easy. Taking on this much responsibility has been very hard on you. You deserve a lot of credit."

"Don't make me sound so noble, Aline. You know I don't have much choice."

"I understand."

Martha's mother was diabetic. The toes on her left foot were amputated last year. Frequent visits to her physician were mandatory, but she made it very difficult for her daughter when she refused to commit to this aspect of her condition. She was totally dependent on Martha.

"Anyway, I can't wait to see you. We'll have to do something special when you return to New York."

"Count on it. The readjustment to the city should be interesting. I'd love to redecorate my apartment completely—give it a country look."

"You're funny. When you see the city, you'll be glad to be back. You'll be home."

"I already feel like I am home."

"By the way, your plants are doing great."

"That's good. Hey, I have to run."

"*PLEASE* keep it touch, Aline. Write to me or call me collect."

"I promise. Give my love to your mother and tell the gang I'll see them soon."

"I will. Good-night."

"Good-night." Aline felt much better. She was a lot less guilty but she was still disgusted with herself. Martha was her only true friend and it was important to maintain her support. A notation to call and write to her had to be placed in the date book she carried around. If

Michael worked out, Aline decided to tell her about him when they got back together again.

Martha was avoiding the issue of Marty's status regarding Aline, probably because Martha really didn't know anything concerning how he felt. She simply didn't want to admit it. For his part, Marty was going to make it a point to guard against volunteering any information to anyone in the office concerning Aline. This was his policy toward all his employees. Marty was an expert manipulator. No one was clever enough to match wits with him.

27.

FRIDAY OF WEEK TWO. The last day. She had pushed her way into his life and now it was her moral obligation to push herself out of it. Only a few more encounters remained, but these would be completely social occasions and probably less consuming. Other people would be attending the town meeting and this she was thankful for. They would act like a cushion and make the final release more tolerable.

He didn't particularly like her observing him at his worst yesterday, being almost physically incapable of continuing any task. For him, it probably represented vulnerability, but for her, it symbolized the epitome of artistic strength and commitment.

She wanted to tell him this, but to say anything at all would be inappropriate and gratuitous. He was well aware of how she felt about him and his work, without her having to put it in words.

They spent the morning driving along the coastline. One stop was a lighthouse. From the top was a panoramic view of the territory. They relished the fresh air, sea birds and rugged beauty spreading out below them. It was breathtaking.

The last stop was a wildlife sanctuary. They parked in a designated area for public viewing overlooking the sea. A large island could be seen many miles offshore.

Elcock related to her the past history of its conservation experiment.

He was pensive. “There used to be deer out on the island, but hunters killed all of them. That’s why the state decided to make it a reserve. The animal rights groups brought a few pair out there five years ago to start a small herd, but you rarely see any. We don’t know whether the trial is going to be successful.”

Elcock’s reputation was to be very out-spoken at the town meetings, in support of preserving the environment. On the way home, he explained to Aline his involvement.

“It’s a side of me you are unaware of. I brought you out here for this very reason.”

She replied, “I’m not surprised. You are an incredible man, so connected to the earth and sea .”

“Not really, but I’m very concerned. There won’t be anything left of our planet to admire if we don’t do something. It’s already too late in some aspects.”

Aline nodded. “I’ve read Cousteau and Sagan. They were sounding the alarms decades ago, but no one was or is listening.”

“They will when we have nothing left.”

“While we’re on the subject, when is the next town meeting?”

“It’s usually the first Monday of each month. Why do you ask?”

“I wanted to have the experience of being part of one before I left, if I could fit it into my schedule.”

Elcock brightened. “You can come along with me if you like. The council members have had to move up the date to next Monday, the 20th, since the mayor will be out of town from October 27 through November 5. He wants to attend our meeting since it concerns new zoning laws. Will you still be in Cape Warren?”

"Yes, and I'd like very much to accompany you. I believe the meeting is at seven-thirty. What time do you want me to come to your house?"

"So, you've already read about it?" He turned to look at her, with a knowing expression on his face.

"I read about it in the paper and marked it down."

They made plans to go together. She was glad to have the chance to see him another time. He was glad to discover a measure of her presumptuous nature.

28.

SATURDAY MORNING. Michael arrived at Terri's house at exactly ten-thirty. Aline had called him to give him directions before she and Terri went out Friday night. Aline's instincts about him were right—she knew he would be on time.

The women heard his car crunching down the gravel driveway. He parked next to Aline's rental and was at the front door in seconds. Eager to meet him, Terri opened the door as soon as he knocked.

"Hello, I'm Michael Williams. I'm here to pick up Aline."

"Come on in. I'm her friend, Terri Shea. She's expecting you."

"Thanks, Terri."

As he entered the house, he noticed Aline sitting on a brown plaid sofa, waiting for him. He sat next to her, his face beaming.

"Good morning. Did you guys have fun last night?"

"We had a blast! Who would have guessed that a club was hidden back in the Maine woods? I bet you've spent some time at *Jason's.*"

"More time than I would care to admit. Everybody goes there. The choices are rather limited in these parts."

"How about some coffee, Michael?" Terri asked.

"Sounds good. Black, please."

She went into the kitchen. As soon as she returned, Michael asked, "How did you two meet?"

"I wait on tables at the diner downtown and Aline comes in there quite often for meals. She always chose my station when she came in, so we started to get to know each other."

Aline liked the way her date was dressed and realized for the first time since she had met him how handsome he was. He wore khaki trousers, cordovan loafers, a striped button-down shirt open at the neck, and a gray, heather crew neck sweater, very Ivy League. Aline thought, *My mother would adore this guy!* The women were sizing him up, asking questions. He wasn't used to so much attention.

He smiled a lot between answers and sips of coffee. "Enough of the third degree," he said, "I guess we better get going. My aunt expects us around noon."

Aline stood up. "I'm all ready."

There was a piece of soft nylon luggage sitting by the front door. He assumed it was hers. With a bit of humorous sarcasm in his voice, he asked, "Is this all you're taking?"

"That's it." She went to put on her jacket, checking the house quickly to make sure she didn't leave anything behind. Returning to the living room, she went over to Terri and kissed her on her cheek.

"Thanks for everything, Terri. I'll see you Sunday afternoon. I'll call you before I leave."

"Great. Have a wonderful time. It was very nice to meet you, Michael."

"The feeling is mutual. We'll see you Sunday."

Terri watched them get into his car and drive away. He tooted the horn as they disappeared from her sight. After meeting him, she felt pleased at the thought of her new friend spending the weekend in his company. What she was really thinking was, *Why couldn't I meet a man like that?* Maybe some day she'd get lucky.

29.

LATE SATURDAY AFTERNOON. All the roads in western Connecticut, as well as everywhere else, carried significant traffic at this time of the day. Most people had something to do or somewhere to go.

A slight figure started walking along the right shoulder of SR124. The hiker was dressed in gray double-knit slacks and canvas loafers. A bulky, hooded sheepskin coat obscured the hiker's face.

Hitchhikers were common on this road. Not everyone owns a car. In fact, their prevalence resulted in a police policy to stop handing out violations – too many reports to be filed and too much time spent in court.

The hiker's pace was slow, but deliberate. Perhaps the weight of the coat was causing the problem. There was no luggage to tote, just a shopping bag stuffed with newspapers.

A young couple from New Canaan was starting their night out on the town. They passed the hiker, stopped, backed up and asked the hiker if they could be of assistance.

"Excuse me, do you want a lift?"

The hiker replied, "That would be nice."

The husband got out of the car to assist the hiker to get settled in the back seat.

"How long have you been walking?" he asked.

"Not too long, maybe twenty minutes or so."

"What's your destination?"

"Station Place in Stamford" was the reply.

"Is that the Greyhound Station?" the couple queried.

"Yes. My bus leaves at six-twenty."

"Well, you're in luck because we're also going to Stamford. Where are you going?"

The hiker replied, "Boston."

"I guess we better hurry," the couple answered.

In half an hour, they arrived in front of Greyhound and helped the hiker by escorting their passenger into the bus station.

They said their good-byes and the hiker thanked them for their help.

The bus to Boston would arrive at South Station at approximately eleven-thirty, allowing plenty of time to read, nap and snack on the juice and cheese crackers resting at the bottom of the shopping bag.

The hiker took a seat, waiting for the departure call for the bus to Boston. An elderly gentleman, occupying the neighboring seat asked the hiker, "Is everything all right?"

The reply was, "Oh yes, thank you. Everything is going exactly as planned."

South Station was full of people at eleven-forty, coming and going on direct or connecting buses to all parts of the Northeast corridor. Most of the travelers were waiting for their departures or the arrival of friends and loved ones.

Small tables with seating filled the center of the concourse space, allowing passengers the opportunity to rest and revive themselves.

It was late, but the hiker wasn't concerned about the hour or the impending fatigue. The only concern now was the connecting bus to Maine from the Trailways terminal down the street. Unfortunately, it didn't leave until noon on Sundays. Twelve hours to wait. Waiting.

Always waiting for something. Waiting for life to continue, whether it be meaningful or meaningless.

The Trailways terminal was a ten-minute walk from South Station. The Concord Trailways line had added Rockland, Maine to its route and Rockland was less than thirty minutes from Cape Warren.

This was a smaller terminal with less security and much more dangerous to hang out in. At South Station, there were city police officers on patrol all night looking for pick-pockets or drunks who liked to pan-handle the travelers. It would be safer to wait in South Station.

The newspapers in the shopping bag were the hiker's traveling companions. They helped the hours slip away.

Hours later, the hiker started feeling drowsy, occasionally dosing off. During the night, the police kept trying to move the hiker from the station.

"I'm leaving early tomorrow morning. Please let me stay here. I'm very tired."

After much pleading and due to other considerations, they finally relinquished their demands.

Sunday morning dawned sunny but frigid. The hiker repacked the shopping bag, preparing to walk to the Trailways terminal. Once there, coffee and food were available. The day's papers left on the seats of departing patrons would replace the old ones. Anything was attainable, it was simply a matter of being resourceful.

Four days and three nights would achieve closure. It would consume more patience than most people were capable of finding within themselves. But, this was only a fraction of the total amount of patience, an eternity of it, that had been accumulating year after year after barren year.

30.

THE WEEKEND IN AUGUSTA was a grand success for both Aline and Michael. They needed the time to reestablish their relationship, to feel at ease with each other again. The long ride gave them this opportunity.

Michael was impressed with Terri and expressed his reaction to Aline.

"I like your friend Terri. I bet she likes a good time."

She replied, "Terri is one of the most honest people I've ever met. She is so compatible; we must have the same karma. She's also been very understanding about the landlady situation."

"Explain it to me. What's going on?"

Aline continued, "Well, in the beginning we were getting along just fine. I don't see much of her because we both are working. She was very considerate and friendly to me when we first met. She makes fresh coffee for me every morning before she leaves the house. But, it's changed."

"How do you mean?"

"I can't really put my finger on it. A shift in attitude, I guess. We actually were sharing a dinner together, finally, after staying in her house for almost two weeks—and at her invitation, mind you—when she kind of went frosty at the table."

"It does sounds strange."

"Yeah," said Aline, "I keep going over and over our dinner conversation, but I can't come up with anything insulting or offensive in my remarks."

"Maybe she just didn't feel well."

"No, it goes much deeper. It wasn't her health. She didn't cancel. After all, I'm a captive audience. I live there. I lie awake at night thinking about it. It doesn't matter how many times I review it, I always come up empty."

"You can't drive yourself nuts worrying about it, Aline. You have to go on with your life. It just isn't worth it."

"You're absolutely right, but it's easier said than done. Anyway, I haven't told her about meeting you, and I didn't want you to come to the front door and get an unfriendly reception. I asked you to meet me at Terri's house to avoid an awkward confrontation."

"I appreciate your concern for my feelings, but I'm sure it would have been all right."

"Maybe so. I just wanted the weekend to get off on an enjoyable note. I didn't want anything to spoil it."

"You probably made the right decision. Instinctive reactions are usually on target most of the time." He was trying to support her and more importantly, he was trying to change the subject, for both of their sakes.

The one topic he, personally, was most interested in, was the assignment and why she came to Maine in the first place. The minute he asked her to describe it to him, she was off and running. Now she alone was in the spotlight and he was fascinated. He wanted to know all about her, her dreams, her goals, her likes and dislikes, her tastes, her background and family, her plans for the future and her attitude toward the world around her. He couldn't get enough of her.

Michael's impression of Terri was matched by Aline's impression of his aunt, Marjorie Robertson. She presented herself as warm and loving to both of them. Aline kept a mental image of her in her mind: the soft smile, sparkling blue eyes, plump arms always ready with a hug, dressed in a lavender print silk dress and high heels—delightfully homey.

She and Michael became very close after the death of her sister, his mother, five years ago. He made a point of visiting her often and usually spent the holidays with her and his uncle.

Michael's father was a structural engineer who currently was working under contract in Europe and the two were rarely in touch. His father was devastated by the loss of his wife, Helen, and elected to work overseas to help bury his endless despair. Since Michael was an only child, his aunt and uncle were his only family. Marjorie and Charles Robertson had no children of their own and they considered Michael to be like a son.

They were both quite disappointed with Robert Williams. They considered him to be very selfish to choose Europe as his home instead of staying here to father his boy. In their eyes, he couldn't be forgiven. Marjorie was particularly bitter concerning the matter.

The house party and the rest of the weekend offered Aline the necessary diversion she was looking for, surrounded by people who cared about her and who were interested in her. Michael's friends were educated and stimulating.

She knew she wanted to continue her relationship with Michael; New York would not prove to be an obstacle.

When they returned to his aunt's house, he took her coat and stood watching her as she started up the stairs. Suddenly she turned on the first step to see him standing there watching her.

She beckoned softly, "Come here."

He didn't utter a word, just obeyed her. She wrapped her arms around his neck and pulled his mouth down onto hers in an open, full kiss. He held her firmly against his body, rigid with desire and longing.

Then she was gone, out of sight. He didn't move for a long time, still feeling the sensation of her kiss on his mouth.

And she was in the guest room, in the dark, standing with her back against the closed door, her eyes shut. She wanted him with every fiber in her young body.

31.

SUNDAY EVENING ALINE PICKED UP the SUV at Terri's house and spent a lot of time thanking both Terri and Michael for sharing a marvelous weekend with her. They wanted to spend as much time with her as they could before she returned to New York and their commitment to keep in touch with her after she returned was very reassuring to her.

Driving home, she relived the weekend in her mind. Michael was becoming more appealing and desirable every time she saw him. His sensitivity to her feelings impressed her considerably. She didn't want to lose him.

The moment she arrived at Mitchell Street, the urge to turn around and spend the night at Terri's was almost irresistible. Why? Intellectually, she felt she should be able to deal with this reaction on a more analytical level. It wasn't late, but the place looked closed down as always. By comparison, the familiarity of her room represented a harbor of solace to her. It seemed preposterous to Aline to picture this forbidding residence full of activity during the summer months, hosting a flow of tourists. Somehow the reality of this concept just didn't gel.

The work and wrapping up the details should help to make the remaining stay in Cape Warren go by smoothly. If she needed more time in the area, she could always stay at a motel or move closer to Michael. In any case, next Friday would be her last day here.

32.

MONDAY NIGHT, SEVEN-FIFTEEN. October was slipping away. This was the appropriate occasion to say goodbye. It was also the opportunity for her to voice her gratitude to Elcock for salvaging her career and reviving her depleted vitality. He was, in essence, responsible for resuscitating her purpose in life.

The thought of being in his company for the last time was a potentially overwhelming experience and she tried to block it out by rehearsing in her mind the conversation she was going to present to him when she saw him standing in his doorway, waiting for her. She wondered if he desired closure so he could get on with his work. Somehow, she doubted it. Bidding him farewell was the only aspect of the assignment she was dreading. But now, she couldn't postpone it for another day, another hour.

She would leave for New York toward the end of the week. The office was expecting her to report for work the following Monday. She made a mental note to call Martha and invite her to spend the first available weekend with her after she returned.

Entering Elcock's driveway, the darkness and the play of her high beams on the tree trunks gave the wooded approach to Elcock's house a final awful farewell. After today, this threat would be gone forever. The treetops were stirring in agitated, exaggerated waves.

Getting out of the vehicle, she pulled her coat tightly around her body and ran to the front door.

She stood there for a few seconds, but he evidently didn't hear her approach. He must be in another part of the house. For the first time, she was forced to knock. No response. Should she try to let herself in? She decided to hesitate a bit longer. She knocked again. Still no answer. Five more minutes later, she gently turned the doorknob.

The door swung open and she entered the house. A blast of air was right behind her, blustering into the front room, rustling everything it touched. Once inside, she slammed the door behind her, trying to make noise, and then stood frozen in her tracks. The room was in chaos. The old chest, holding his drawings, was tipped on its back and the sketches were strewn everywhere. How did this happen? All the windows were closed. Some sketches were face up, others face down and a few were ripped into crude pieces. This was the result of an onslaught, engulfing this space and creating a fury. The fury of it was still very much alive. She could feel it pressing against her.

But where was Elcock? She began to shout out his name. "Mr. Elcock!"

Silence. Only the wind could be heard outside nudging the house. She was afraid to move, afraid to touch anything.

"Mr. Elcock!"

He should have answered her by now if he was home.

"Hello, it's Aline!"

She had to find him. He must be in the studio. It was the only place left to look. Carefully she picked her way through the papers on the floor. Entering the kitchen, it looked in order, but the door leading to the back was ajar. A sharp draft was spilling out of the studio. *He never left this door open, so why was it unlatched ?*

Bursting into the studio, she was horrified at the sight before her. She let out a cry, dropping her handbag and covering her face with both hands.

Elcock lay on his stomach, arms stretched out in front of him. His head was floating in a large puddle of blood, facing her, wide-open eyes reflecting the horror of his last moments.

The scaffolding had been ripped apart by some force—the jagged, splintered wood resembling open wounds. He fell to his death from the top level, hitting his head on the cement floor. Powerful hands couldn't break the fall.

She became hysterical, staggering out to the deck, gasping for breath. The seagulls, shrieking overhead, echoing her agony. Their plaintive cries mimicking her pain. She held onto the railing with all of her remaining strength and sobbed uncontrollably.

What should she do? She must get a hold of herself. No one else knew he was dead. He was dead! She kept repeating it over and over again, trying to come to grips with the terrible reality of it. *Have to call the police!* In a numb trance she returned to the living room and located his phone. Her face was soaked with tears and her voice could barely be heard by the operator.

"Information."

Aline couldn't talk, her hesitation causing the operator to repeat herself.

"Information."

"Please get me the police."

"Excuse me, do you want 9-1-1?"

"I want the Cape Warren police department."

"I can't hear you, ma'am. Could you please speak a little louder."

"I want the Cape Warren police department."

"One moment, please."

The waiting was forever.

"Cape Warren police. Officer Brice. May I help you?"

"Mr. Elcock is dead."

"What was that, ma'am?"

"I'm at the home of Thomas J. Elcock. He's dead."

"May I please have your name, ma'am?"

"Aline Kranick."

"How do you spell your name, ma'am?"

While she spelled it out she felt a hot wave pass through her extremities.

"What's the address?"

"R.R.l, Route 17. There's a sign at the entrance to his road, pointing to his residence. Please send someone right away."

"How do you know he's dead?"

"Please send someone right away."

"One moment, please."

She felt faint and wanted desperately to sit down, to lie down. She started to cry again.

"Hello, ma'am? I'll be there as soon as I can. Just stay calm and don't touch anything. Is there a house number?"

And on and on it went, her despair building to an unbearable level, heightened by the detached attitude on the other end of the phone.

Why would they play with my emotions and sanity at a time like this? The tears poured out and she slumped to the floor, shivering in disbelief, to wait for the police. The nature surrounding her taunted her with its indifference.

33.

WHEN PATROL OFFICER JOHN BRICE and the rescue team arrived, she was still lying on the floor, curled up in a ball. Her face was swollen and her eyes were bloodshot from excessive periods of crying.

Brice let himself in when she didn't answer the door. He picked his way through the drawings and when he reached her, he bent down and put his right hand on her shoulder. He could see she was hardly breathing.

"Miss Kranick? Are you the lady that called?"

There was no answer from her parched lips. She couldn't move and didn't know what was going on around her, oblivious to Brice.

He pleaded with her in an exasperated tone. "Please get up, Aline. I'm here to help you. I'm Officer Brice."

Stiffly, she rose to her feet, her expression blank and distant. He pulled a wooden chair over to where she was standing and asked her to sit down. She dropped into it.

"Would you like a glass of water?"

She didn't respond.

"Could you please show us where Mr. Elcock is?"

She looked at him and started to sob.

"Please, Miss Kranick." Patience was beginning to run out.

Slowly, she raised her left arm, pointing in the direction of the kitchen.

"Don't move. We'll be right back."

Brice disappeared with the rescue team members in the direction she indicated. Within minutes, he returned alone. Aline was bent over, her forehead pushing against her knees.

"Brice here. I'm at the Elcock place. Is Sergeant Logan available?" He gave the desk sergeant the request to locate his supervisor.

"See if you can beep him. It's important."

He took a small pad out of one of his back pockets and scribbled down some notes. So much disorder was disturbing. After about ten minutes, Brice got the call.

"Hello, Tom? Yes, we were notified about half an hour ago. I'm here with Aline Kranick. Mr. Elcock is dead. Looks like he fell off a high platform and hit his head."

Tom Logan asked him questions. Officer Brice listened closely as his supervisor probed the situation.

"Well, I think there may be more to it. Yes, I think it calls for his attention." Logan knew the drill.

Brice ended the call, "O.K., I'll wait for him to arrive. I hope he's available."

The officer found another chair, placing it next to Aline. He wanted to return to the studio to get on with the investigation, but thought it would be a bad idea to leave her side. She was too distraught. He started taking more notes to fill the time until Detective Giles arrived. It was going on eight-thirty and even if Detective Giles could be located, it was developing into a long night ahead.

34.

DETECTIVE WALTER GILES arrived at eight forty-five. He was a man in his mid-forties, six feet tall, with sandy hair cut close to his head, military style. His body movements were quick, efficient. The lean muscles filling out his clothes proved he spent time in the weight room at the police department gym.

"Is this the young lady who made the 9-1-1?"

"Walter, this is Aline Kranick. She found the body."

Giles took one look at Aline and decided not to attempt any conversation. Turning to Brice, he said, "Where is he?"

Brice replied, "Follow me. We'll be back shortly, Aline. This is Detective Walter Giles." She didn't budge.

Giles didn't give her a second glance. He wanted to get on with it. The two men proceeded to the rear part of the house.

"Is she going to be all right?" Giles's voice sounded matter-of-fact.

"I don't know. When I got here, she was lying on the floor, all curled up. I had a hard time getting her to sit in the chair. She isn't talking. In trauma."

They entered the studio.

"Christ," commented Giles.

Brice watched the detective meticulously circle the body and survey the damage done to the supports. It didn't take Giles long to start adding things up. He muttered slowly, "The state police are sending over Detective Matt Lewis. He should be here soon."

"Good," Brice said, "he's the best they have."

Brice exited the studio to make some calls, and rejoin Aline. She was still in the same position, not relating to anything or anyone around her.

The flashing red lights ricocheting off the living room walls were followed by blinding light. Detective Matt Lewis of the state police slammed his car door shut and was in the house in seconds. Lewis was middle-aged, stocky, of average height and going bald. He was a fifteen year veteran of the police force, tough and uncompromising, a man of few words. His judgments were swift, to the point and almost always precisely correct.

Brice took Lewis over to where Aline was sitting. "Matt, this is Aline Kranick. She found Elcock."

Giles went over to greet Lewis. They enjoyed working together. Their collaboration over numerous cases went back over the years.

"Walter, good to see you. Where is the body?"

"Through the kitchen. He's in some kind of an art studio."

Aline was suddenly surrounded by voices and shuffling feet, but she didn't look up. She was in another world.

Lewis returned his attention to Aline. "Miss? My name is Detective Matt Lewis of the state police. We need your help."

Somehow, reversing the situation—where they needed her assistance more than she needed theirs—caused something to click. She lifted her head to look at Lewis and sat up, her arms limp in her lap.

"Can we get you anything? We just want to make sure that you are all right."

Brice was standing at the entrance to the kitchen, watching, taking mental notes on Lewis' technique and his success in bringing her around. He commented, "Maybe rescue should take a look at her before they leave."

Giles went over to Aline and held her forearms gently with his strong hands, trying to get her attention. "Officer Brice will stay with you while we work back there. Please don't be afraid to ask us for anything you might want."

Giles and Lewis retreated from the room. Giles couldn't hide his doubts regarding Aline. "We'll have to handle her with kid gloves. It won't be easy obtaining information from her."

With the departure of everyone except Officer Brice, a semblance of order settled around them. The policeman returned to his chair. Possibly, his company would bring her some companionship. She was not communicating and in a strange way, he was glad. He didn't want her to start crying again. He turned on more lights. The lack of a television set discouraged him. It would have offered some distraction. The only thing to look at was the chaos. It was unnerving.

In half an hour, everybody returned. The rescue unit departed after exchanging a few words with Giles and examining Aline. She was beginning to focus on the activity around her. Giles walked over and stood directly in front of her, demanding her attention. His body language was commanding.

"Aline, I know you are very upset, but I have to ask you some questions. Do you feel up to it?"

By looking at her, he realized the request couldn't be fulfilled. He dropped his chin and walked back toward the kitchen, indicating by a wave of his hand for Brice to join him. The men stood looking at her, filled with compassion and concern.

Giles continued, "She's in too much shock to be of much use to us at this time. I think the best move right now is to get her home and make arrangements for her to come down to the station for questioning tomorrow morning. Maybe, by then, she'll come around."

"I'll take her," Brice volunteered. "After I drop her off, do you want me to go back to Main Street?"

"No. Come back here. I want your input."

They returned to the studio. Giles called in the evidence technicians and notified Detective Peter Burton; his presence was requested. It was after ten o'clock by the time the Lincoln County's medical examiner's van arrived. Giles and Lewis went to greet the ME at the front entrance.

Giles grumbled, "Every time someone comes in here, these papers blow around the room. Securing this area isn't a simple task."

Joseph Devecchio showed up in a rumpled old trench coat and plaid cap. He looked tired and clearly wasn't pleased with the prospect of working this late.

"Walter, Matt, what have we got?"

"Follow us."

They left her alone again. She didn't care. Nothing mattered to her.

35.

WHEN DETECTIVE PETER BURTON entered the house, Giles and Lewis were standing where Aline was sitting. Lewis called her name, and to his surprise, she answered.

"Yes?"

"Miss Kranick, where do you live?"

She moved her head slightly, indicating to him she was ready to re-enter his world.

"Mitchell Street." Her words were barely audible.

"Very good. We're going to take you home now. You should attempt to get some rest. Officer Brice will be by in the morning to pick you up. When you come down to the police station, I would like to ask you some questions. Do you understand?"

"Yes."

"John, Officer Brice, will take you now. Your car will have to remain here tonight. It will be safe in our hands. You can pick it up tomorrow."

After they left, Giles turned to his associates. He looked relieved for the first time.

"She'll be all right, Peter. We'll get into it later. Right now, I want to take another look before the photographers arrive. I don't want any interruptions. Brice will be returning soon."

They were alone now and took the opportunity to go over the scene of death and concentrate on their work.

Soon the place would be crawling with photographers, video cameras, lighting technicians, fingerprint experts, and investigators searching the grounds for tire prints, shoe imprints, and any other clues. They didn't have much time. While Joe continued his examination, they stripped down to shirtsleeves and started the painstaking chore of scrutinizing the details.

Giles's eyes started roving over the pile of aged lumber near Elcock's body. All at once, he was riveted to one spot. "Hello, what do we have here?"

The others came over to where he was standing. He pointed.

"What is it, Walter?"

"It looks like an ax under all that wood."

"Holy shit!"

"Secure this section and don't move anything!"

Their gaze was fixed on the red handle of a wood ax which was mostly buried beneath the pieces of shattered supports. But, nobody noticed a tiny fuchsia thread that clung stubbornly to the end of a nearby exposed rusty nail.

36.

MONDAY NIGHT, TEN FORTY-FIVE. The cruiser came to a stop in front of Cora's house. Only a few of the large homes on the street displayed a light in a second-story window. Most of the residents were already in bed.

"Is anyone home, ma'am?"

"She never leaves any lights on after dark, except a few night lights in the parlor." This was the first full sentence she had uttered to him since they left Elcock's house.

"Who's that, ma'am?

"My landlady."

"Are you going to be O.K.?"

"I guess so. Thank you."

"Are you sure?"

"I'm sure."

"I'll be by in the morning to pick you up. I'll tell Detective Giles you'll be ready by ten. Is that a good time for you?"

"Yes." She let herself out of the police car and rushed toward the front door.

He waited until she vanished inside. The dismal old Victorian gave him an uneasy feeling.

Walter Giles was glad to see Brice when he walked through the studio door. "Everything go smoothly?"

"Yes, sir. She's talking a little."

"Where did she say she lived?"

"17 Mitchell Street."

"That's where Cora Prentis lives."

"The place is kinda spooky. No lights on."

"Interesting."

"How's that?"

"Oh, a long time ago, there were some rumors running around this town. I really don't want to talk about it right now."

"I'll remind you later."

Giles gave him a look indicating the subject was closed. There was too much to do and all of it demanded immediate attention.

This potential crime scene created special problems, one of which was the impending appearance of an army of personnel who were going to be disrupting the area while carrying out their duties. Staying out of each other's way was going to be a real challenge. With papers and artwork strewn all over the floor, it was going to be very hard to maneuver lights with tripods and equipment.

Giles would have to bring them in according to priority and a lot of time was going to be wasted while one group waited outside for access to the site while another group was working inside.

Politically, it was tricky. Everyone involved was important to the success of the investigation. And this was an investigation. Giles respected their expertise and they, in return, respected him and his reputation.

A few vans were ordered to report to the location to act in the capacity of a command center. Each was equipped with a short-wave radio and each offered a place to go to rest and at least get a cup of coffee.

Giles wanted the members of the task force to be very conscious of the magnitude of this case. They were all aware of Thomas Elcock. His fame in the art world brought a kind of legendary attention to the Cape Warren region, comparable to Norman Rockwell's creativity in Stockbridge, Massachusetts.

Cape Warren and Stockbridge were more than just small, colorful American towns. Their artists depicted them as representing heritage and history, time capsules of a maturing nation.

A dreary malaise hung over the studio as the various technicians began to arrive to commence the detailed work laying ahead of them.

Giles informed Burton, "Let me know when everyone gets here. I'll be in my car. I have some calls to make. Is Kranick's vehicle locked? Make sure it is."

The vans arrived with coffee and sandwiches. Most of the team went out to get something to eat while they waited for the next phase to begin. Burton asked them to park their vehicles in a row to the right of the clearing for the efficiency and convenience of those coming and going.

The press was a major concern for Giles to worry about. Eventually they were going to get wind of this. He must decide when he wanted to release Elcock's death to the papers. The medical examiner's office was in the county seat because Cape Warren was a small town and didn't have one. The body would be held there until the victim's identity and cause of death were determined. Then it would be placed in a funeral home. He would have to try to notify next of kin as soon as possible, while the body was at the medical examiner's office. That would be Tuesday. It would go to the funeral home on Wednesday.

He would probably fax the incident to the papers on Wednesday, business as usual. Cause of death would be listed as "accidental." It was too early in the investigation to start making public statements. He didn't want to bring extra attention to this death until all the reports were in. It was a small town and he wanted it handled as just another obituary.

After all, Giles thought, the man could have had a heart attack or a stroke and simply fallen off the scaffolding. Maybe Elcock left the ax at the bottom of the structure to remind himself to chop firewood when he finished painting for the day. These conclusions shouldn't be ruled out, not just yet. Anything was possible.

By most standards, Cape Warren was a quiet, peaceful town. There was no serious crime rate, no significant drug abuse, no domestic violence or arson. "The police blotter" was very mundane: a few speeding tickets, maybe an occasional drunk driver or someone disturbing the peace.

As far as Giles was concerned, this should be treated as a routine death. Nothing out of the ordinary. He wanted to maintain a low-key approach and didn't want to listen to a lot of personal opinions and speculations offered by the staff involved. After all the facts were in, the final report would reveal the direction he should follow.

He was, above all else, a man who always followed a pragmatic, rational course of action, simply follow standard police protocol.

37.

TUESDAY MORNING. A patrol car was idling in front of 17 Mitchell Street at precisely ten o'clock, the engine running. Officer John Brice lit a cigarette, patiently expecting the appearance of Aline.

Her night had been fitful, tossing and turning and crying. She woke up at six, lying on her back, staring at the ceiling, trying to put her thoughts into some meaningful order. Michael should be notified as soon as possible. It was a necessity to see him and ask him for his help. He would certainly give her the advice she so desperately needed. Marty Rosen was next on the list. What was to become of her article now? Elcock's death changed the entire picture. And now the police wanted answers. She had to be strong, for herself, her magazine, and all her friends and family who cared about her, especially her mother. Her mother would be terribly upset when she found out the predicament her daughter was involved in, but she would learn about it along with the others.

Aline got out of bed and went over to the oversized mirror on her dresser. She wasn't pleased with what she saw. Her face looked ravaged and drawn, devoid of color. Still was observing herself and thinking, w*ash your face, brush your teeth, comb your hair, put on some clothes and go down there and get this over with.* She knew the police car was already parked in front of the house.

Brice opened the passenger door of the cruiser and felt empathy for Aline Kranick. She looked so haggard.

"Good morning. How do you feel today?"

"Not very well, but I'm doing my best."

"I'm sorry we have to put you through this, ma'am."

"You don't have to apologize for doing your job."

He decided to stop talking and was grateful for the short ride to the station.

When they arrived, he walked around the front of the cruiser to open the passenger door for her, but she was already out of the car, on her way to the entrance.

Once inside, he caught up with her at the front desk. She was the picture of total wretchedness and he found it difficult to look at her. "Please follow me."

She quietly followed him. The interrogation room was at the end of a long hallway, where they found the glass door ajar. Brice pushed it open for her. She stood in the doorway.

Walter Giles and Matt Lewis were sitting on one side of an old wooden table which took up most of the available space. A ceiling fan was slowly turning, barely moving the stuffy air. Both men were dressed in casual clothes. Giles wore a brown tweed sports jacket, light blue button-down shirt, open at the neck, and khakis. Lewis was wearing gray slacks, a white shirt, and black wool jacket.

Giles stood up when he saw Aline standing in the doorway. Lewis was already pulling out a chair for her.

Giles said, "Good morning, please come in and sit down. Would you like some coffee?"

"Yes, please."

"Black? Cream and sugar?"

"Milk, no sugar." Aline recalled that Cora didn't make the usual pot of coffee for her this morning. *Was this now going to be eliminated from the daily program at Mitchell Street?*

"Do you mind Coffeemate?"

"That will be fine."

They all sat in silence until the coffee arrived. She quietly thanked the officer who brought it to her.

Giles folded his hands on the table and leaned forward slightly to begin the interrogation. "I don't want you to feel uncomfortable. This questioning is strictly routine. We're all trying to piece together this tragedy and come to some kind of a reasonable conclusion."

She hadn't really taken into account any of these officials last night—they were following the stipulations of their job responsibilities. The shock of what she witnessed blocked out everything. Now she was observing them as if they were total strangers.

Giles said, "Let's start from the beginning. What were you doing at the Elcock residence last night?"

"We were supposed to go to the town meeting together. He told me to meet him at his house a little before seven."

"How long have you known Thomas Elcock?"

"I've been his acquaintance since October 6th. I'm a reporter for *East Side/West Side Magazine* in New York. We're doing a feature article on Mr. Elcock for the January issue. I've been interviewing him all month. The town meeting was to be our last time together. I wanted to attend one before I left town and he kindly invited me to join him."

Giles put up his hand to stop her there, before she could continue. He said, "He's quite renowned around these parts, but I'm curious to know how you heard about him in New York."

"I read an article in the *Sunday Times* regarding his exhibition on Madison Avenue. I attended the show. It's been such a huge success. The gallery intended to hold it over for two more weeks."

Giles felt a little nonplused. Although his lack of interest in the arts and parochial attitude in general toward it made him unaware of the big picture, he wasn't going to be thrown off by a curve.

"What kind of a man was he?" he asked. "He seemed to be a man who didn't allow people to become too close to him. Evidently, you're the exception"

"He was generous and kind. Meeting with him every morning for two weeks was a special privilege I shall always cherish. He was very unselfish with his time and shared his private world and even his close acquaintances with me."

With the help of the coffee, Aline was feeling more refreshed . Her voice was calm as she recounted, "He took me down to the shipyard to meet his buddies and I witnessed with my own eyes the elements inspiring so much of his work. He also introduced me to his best friend, a sail maker, Mr. Hank Swenson, who made us lunch and spent most of an afternoon telling us old sea stories, entertaining us with his wit and marvelous experiences."

The detectives listened intently as Aline pulled them deeper into the detailed description of her relationship with Elcock. They were fascinated by her devotion and intensity. Neither Giles nor Lewis moved a muscle. For the first time since meeting Aline, they started to react to her as if they began to appreciate her and her purpose.

"Mr. Elcock also took me to the whaling museum and the wildlife sanctuary. I was even allowed to watch Mr. Elcock work on one of his huge canvases. It is hard for me to believe I was so easily accepted by him. The whole time spent with him has been more fulfilling than any experience in my lifetime."

The officers were captivated by her admiration but somewhat skeptical of the man she was depicting. Giles wanted to keep everything ground level. "Most folks considered him a recluse," he said evenly.

She replied, "I don't feel this is true, judging by the way he responded to me. I think a more realistic answer would be to consider him guarded about whom he spent his time with. He chose his true friends very carefully." Aline sat back, feeling more sure of herself.

Lewis took over the questioning. "Other than last night, when was the last time you saw him or spoke to him?"

"The last interview was Friday, October 17th. I always saw him in the mornings. The afternoons were left for him to paint, and after I left his house, I usually went to the library or worked on my project in my room on Mitchell Street."

"Did he ever seem depressed?"

"Hardly ever. He always welcomed me with a smile on his face. I never knocked. As soon as he heard me drive in, he appeared in his doorway."

"What day was it that you watched him paint?"

"It was Thursday, the 16th. At first he seemed reluctant, but he finally conceded. I was in a complete hypnotic state watching him work. No one can ever comprehend what it was like."

"Did the scaffolding seem unsteady to you?"

"Well, it groaned a little when he climbed up it, but it seemed strong enough to hold his weight. Don't forget, he was a big man and he was used to working on it. It didn't sway back and forth or look like it was about to collapse. I don't think it was unsafe. He knew his own limitations, believe me."

"Did he ever mention any enemies he had to you? You know, someone holding a grudge against him."

"How could a man of Thomas Elcock have any enemies?"

"I'm not inferring anything. To my limited knowledge concerning this man, you are the only one in this town who ever learned this much about him. The purpose here is to find out as much as we can about his personal life, his habits, his fears, and so on."

The questioning was beginning to make Aline uneasy. She became restless and moved around in her chair.

"Would you like to take a break?"

"No, it's all right."

"We can continue this tomorrow if you wish."

"I'd rather go on, please."

"Good . . . Did anyone ever call his house while you were there?"

"No."

"So, as far as you're concerned, everything was normal in regards to his daily schedule and disposition?"

"Yes."

The questioning continued. After another two hours, Giles stood up and walked over to the door. He turned around, putting his hands in his pockets. "Aline, you've been here for quite a while and I think this would be a good time to stop for today. I would like to talk to you further, so please don't leave town. Could you leave me your telephone number where you will be staying?"

At first she was hesitant, but finally jotted it down on the pad placed in front of her. She didn't want to draw attention to her unstable relationship with Cora. "When would you like to see me again?"

"Is tomorrow convenient with your schedule?"

"Yes. What time?"

"Ten is fine with us. We'll pick you up at the house."

"I'll be ready."

38.

TUESDAY AFTERNOON. It was twelve thirty-five when one of Giles's men drove Aline to Elcock's to pick up her vehicle. She was exhausted and having difficulty coping with common courtesy. She closed the door of the patrol car with a loud bang, neglecting to thank the driver. The officer didn't leave until she started her car.

After she returned to Mitchell Street, she went up to the telephone on the front hall table. She waited until today to make her calls, knowing she would be more in control of herself and would sound more sensible. While talking to Michael and Marty, in particular, she didn't want to be hysterical and in tears. If she expected their understanding, it was her responsibility to present herself as cohesive and accountable.

The first call would be to Michael. She was hoping he wasn't at lunch as she furiously dialed his number on the old phone. A receptionist rang his extension. Aline waited, almost holding her breath.

"Michael Williams. How may I help you?"

"Oh, Michael, thank God you're there."

"Aline? What's wrong!"

"Michael, Mr. Elcock is dead."

"What!"

"He's dead. We were supposed to go to a town meeting together last night, but when I got to his house, he didn't answer his door. I waited and waited and then finally let myself in. He was on the floor in his studio. The scaffolding gave way and he fell to his death. The weight of his body hitting the ground from such a high elevation killed him. I was the one who found him and called the police."

"I can't believe what I'm hearing. This is terrible!"

"You don't know. I'm a mess. The police are interrogating me. By the line of questioning, I interpret their initial impression is that of suspicion. They want to know all about our alliance."

"Do you mean to tell me that they might be considering you as a suspect?"

"Maybe I'm overreacting, but it looks like it."

"This is totally ridiculous! How are you holding up?"

"Not too well. I can't stop crying and I look like hell. Can you come over tonight? I have to hear your advice. Please help me."

"I'll leave work a little early. You know you can count on me to be there for you. Just try to hang on until I get there. Where do you want me to meet you? I can pick you up at your house."

"No, no. Meet me at the diner. I want to tell Terri what happened. Maybe we can have dinner there."

"Let's see, it's one thirty-five. I have a two o'clock meeting I can't get out of. It will probably run about an hour. The bank manager is expecting a proposal from me to be delivered to his office after the meeting. My secretary is working on it now. I should be at the diner between four and four-thirty."

Aline knew his responsibilities at the bank would preclude his being able to just drop everything and fly to her side. "I'll see you then, Michael. I can't wait to be with you." There—she said it and she meant it, every word.

"After dinner, we'll talk about how we can handle this situation. Have you called your boss?"

She felt him taking charge and at this moment she was depending on him to do just that.

"I haven't called Marty yet. I wanted to talk to you first. After I hang up, I'm going to call him. His reaction to this news is one I'm not looking forward to. He'll probably be more revolted than sorry."

"Don't worry about Marty. Concentrate on taking care of yourself. You're not alone. You have friends who care about you. Always keep it in mind. And don't forget to call your mother."

"Thank you, Michael. I already feel better just hearing your voice."

"I have to go. See you later."

After the click, she still held the receiver in her hand, as if she didn't want to let go of him.

The dial tone rang in her ears. Time to call New York. She felt a sick pull in her stomach as she dialed the number. She was so engrossed in her conversation with Michael that she didn't notice Cora framed in the kitchen doorway, standing motionless, her gaze penetrating Aline. She was drying her hands on a dish towel, but now her hands were still. She dropped the towel to the floor.

Slowly, Aline placed the heavy black receiver into its cradle. How long had Cora been standing there and how much did she hear?

Her landlady finally spoke. "I saw a police car pull up in front of the house. Is anything wrong?"

"I have been answering questions down at the station."

"Questions about what?" her voice demanded.

"Mr. Elcock is dead. I found him in his studio last night. He fell off the scaffolding while he was working on a painting."

Arms dangling at her side, Cora's eyes were riveted on Aline, but she did not speak.

"Uhh . . .I have to call my office. It looks like I'll be leaving town within a few days, as soon as the police are finished with me."

Time for Aline to break away—away from Cora, away from this street, away from this house. This atmosphere was choking her.

"Excuse me," Aline mumbled. As she started climbing the stairs, she looked back at Cora, who was still transfixed in the same location, as if under a spell. The dish towel was still lying in a crumpled heap in front of her.

Aline ran up the stairs. She was peeved with herself for using the house phone instead of her cell- *stupid, impulsive!* She didn't think Cora was home. The rest of her calls would have to be made outside the house, from her car. Maybe tonight she could stay with Terri. Packing would be a relief and would help fill the void until she could be with Michael.

After the bathroom was emptied of her toiletries, she returned to her room and started to gather together her clothes, office materials, manuscript and notes. Peanut shells and old newspapers were collected in an empty shopping bag. In twenty minutes she was ready. She started by taking the heavier items down first. Everything was lined up on the porch, then packed into her big, black SUV, which in itself felt like her home now.

On her first trip down the stairs, she noticed Cora was gone. The good-byes could wait.

39.

TUESDAY AFTERNOON. She was ready to leave, straightening her bedspread for the last time, knowing full well the bed would be immediately stripped as soon as Cora knew her tenant was gone.

Aline drove away from Mitchell Street. At the diner, she would tell Terri about Elcock.

Terri was working. Aline was relieved to see her on the other side of the diner. She wanted to be surrounded only by friends in this town. They would give her some consolation while she was going through this dreadful time in her life.

She tried to get Terri's attention by sitting at the counter because she passed this area often to pick up orders. Eventually she got it and waved her over.

Terri was glad to see Aline. "Hey, girl, where've you been? I almost called your house."

"I've been trying to finish up this assignment and I've been working late, but I have something very important to tell you."

"What's up?" Terri looked surprised.

"My wonderful Mr. Elcock is dead! I'm still in shock."

"God, Aline, that's horrible! How did it happen?"

"He fell off a platform while painting. I still can't believe it."

"When did this happen?"

"I don't know. We made had a date to go to the town meeting together last night. When I showed up, he didn't answer his door. I let myself in and found him dead. I was the one who called the police." She was trying to piece together the sentences in order of sequence.

Terri looked over her shoulder at the order window, "You'll have to give me the details later. I can't believe the story you're telling me. I go on break in half an hour. How about something to eat.?"

"Yes, I'll order here. I don't want a table. Michael is supposed to be here around four, four-thirty."

"Good. Listen, I'll be back."

Aline ordered a soda and a tuna salad sandwich. She wasn't hungry but she would try to eat something. Last night she went to bed without supper.

She kept looking at the clock. Marty always was in his office by two o'clock. She dreaded making this call. *What if Marty tries to force me to return to New York right away?*

She nibbled at her food. Finally, it was finally time to call Rosen. She ordered a piece of pie and a glass of milk and placed them on the counter in front of her seat, indicating she wasn't finished eating. The restaurant was so noisy she decided to call Marty from her car, using her cell phone.

The magazine's switchboard operator recognized Aline's voice immediately. "Aline! Hi, how are you? We all miss you so much."

"Thank you. I'm getting ready to come home. Is Marty in?"

"Yes. One minute."

"Aline?"

"Hi, Marty. I have very bad news to tell you."

"What is it? You sound morbid."

"Thomas Elcock is dead."

"You're kidding!"

"I wish I were."

"What happened?"

How many more times will I have to go over this? she thought, trying to remain calm. "He fell to his death from his work station which was over twenty feet high.

"God, that's incredible! Were you there? Did you see it happen?"

"No, no. We made arrangements to go to a town meeting and I was supposed to meet him at his house. When I got there, I discovered his body and notified the police."

"It's preposterous."

"I still can't accept it. The police want details concerning the last fifteen days of my life."

"Why are they wasting your time? It sounds like he simply lost his balance."

"Evidently, but they are not quite sure as to why he lost his balance."

"Ridiculous! It's cut and dry to me. Small-time officials love to make a big to-do out of anything out of the ordinary. It takes the monotony out of their jobs."

"I'm still in shock. A change of venue is in order. As soon as I get re-settled, I'll give you the number. Tonight I move out."

"I thought you liked it there."

Since Marty never bothered to keep in touch, he had no idea about the developing facts regarding Aline's connection with her landlady. He was completely out-of-date and out of touch. And what's more, he probably didn't care. She moved on to a subject he would care about. "I've finished the article. Can we still publish it?"

"Come back to New York and we'll discuss it. There's no point in prolonging your stay in Cape Warren. The project is over."

"I can't. The detectives told me not to leave town.."

"That's stupid. Do you want me to call the detective in charge of the case? I want you to come home *now*."

"Marty, you don't understand. Until the cause of death is determined, I have to stay here. Besides, I have to satisfy my own curiosity."

Marty's comeback was emphatic and demanding. "No, *you* don't seem to understand. This won't do. If you are not back in this office by Monday morning, I may be forced to fill your position with another reporter. I want to *end* this."

She expected as much. . . a lack of concern for her state of mind, a disregard for how she might be coping. His sensitivity level registered zero. She didn't even say good-bye. She hung up..

40.

TUESDAY AFTERNOON. Aline took her second cup of coffee and moved to a small table near the front of the diner where she could look out a window and watch for Michael's car. Terri sat with her during a short lull and Aline recalled to her the last seventeen hours. Aline was sick of talking about it, but she knew it was far from over. She would have to go over it again with Michael. Being close to him would make a difference for her state of mind. The clock over the pass-through window indicated only half an hour more until his approximate time of arrival.

Terri tried to encourage her. "He'll be here any minute. I'm sure he'll help you get through this."

"I need him so much," Aline agreed. "And I need you." With tears in her eyes, she reached for Terri's hand.

"Hey, take it easy. I'm here for you, too, you know." She squeezed Aline's hand firmly, filled with sympathy.

"Thanks." Aline was fighting back the deluge of tears. And then suddenly Michael was next to her, anxious and very concerned.

She stood up and fell into his arms, burying her wet face into his chest.

He held her close. "Don't cry, we'll get through this together."

Terri put her hand on his shoulder to let him know that she was also grateful he was here to give Aline his support. "Can I get you something, Michael?"

"No thanks, Terri." He sat next to Aline, putting his arm around her shoulders. "Would you rather go somewhere private?"

"Yes, I think so. I can't stop crying. Can we leave? I checked out of Mitchell Street this afternoon."

"That was the best move you could make now."

"Can you give me a few minutes? I'll go to the ladies' room to wash my face."

"Sure." He watched her move across the seating area toward the restrooms. He began reviewing in his mind how everything had so dramatically changed. Now she would have to lean on him to make most of the decisions regarding her strategy in this incident. He would have to take the role of leader, advisor and best friend, giving her the emotional foundation, the deciding factor to her survival. He could never let go of her.

Before they left the diner, they invited Terri for dinner at Michael's house the following night. She agreed to take some time off in order to accompany them and was flattered to be considered as more than a companion.

Michael didn't mention Elcock's death while still inside the restaurant. He wanted to be alone with Aline so she could relate the full story to him.

They walked out to where he was parked. "Why don't you follow me. I live fifteen minutes from here. If you're too tired, I'm sure that Terri could get permission for you to leave your car here for the night."

"I'm fine, really. Just don't drive too fast."

He winked at her and started his car. The street was not busy and she had no trouble backing out of her parking space and following him down main street. Out on the highway, he flashed his lights to indicate he was aware of her following behind him. The stress in her body started to gradually diminish as she realized that this man cared about her very much. She was very fortunate to know him.

They snaked their way through the dense, wooded landscape devoid of civilization or activity. The right blinker of Michael's car started flashing and he slowed down considerably. He turned down a narrow dirt road which led to an open field and a small, two-story framed house with a wrap-around porch.

After parking his car, he got out and motioned to her to move her car next to his.

He waited for her to open her door. "Where's your luggage? I'll carry it up for you."

"That would be great. My overnight case and a blue nylon bag are on the back seat."

It was obvious he wanted her to stay overnight. She liked the idea. To be alone in a motel room wouldn't work. She felt safe as long as they were together.

They climbed the staircase leading to the back entry, which opened into his kitchen. She followed him into the living room. The house was simple, uncluttered, clean, and looked casual. Original watercolors hung on the pine paneled walls. They depicted landscapes of a lake and Maine's snowy winter forests. A huge fireplace filled one end of the living room. The floors were polished and scattered with hand-made rag rugs. Wide-whale corduroy slipcovers gave the seating a plush, cozy appearance. Huge, textured terra cotta lamps with linen shades were crafted in tones of wheat and beige. The neutral color scheme was in deep contrast to the dark walls.

"I rent this house. It's in the sticks, as they say, but I like the peace and quiet. During the fall season, deer are always grazing on the lawn in the morning. There's a lake a quarter of a mile from the house. Maybe tomorrow, we can take a walk."

"I look forward to it. I could use the exercise."

"Do you like it?" he asked as he held her hand, leading her into a hallway.

"I love it. How many rooms do you have?"

"There are two small bedrooms upstairs with a bathroom in between. My bedroom is on the first floor next to the laundry room area which I use as an office. Come on, I'll give you a tour."

He said, "I rarely use the second floor, but I have a housekeeper once every ten days and she always cleans up there."

They returned to the living room. The entire home was cheerful and inviting, completely opposite of her Mitchell Street lodgings.

"I'll make a fire. Would you like a drink?"

"I could use one, but first, I'd like to take a shower and put on some fresh clothes."

"There's a linen closet down the hail, near the bathroom. Take all the towels you want."

"Can I leave my stuff in your room for now while I change?"

"Of course. But before you shower, let me get comfortable. I've been in this business suit for almost twelve hours." He left the room.

She called after him, "Why don't you let me get the drinks. What do you want?"

"I'll have a beer. There's some white wine in the refrigerator and scotch and rum under the sink if you want a mixed drink."

"Thanks. I'll help myself."

Michael re-appeared in jeans and a sweatshirt and had a fire going in just a couple of minutes. He replaced the heavy screen.

She handed him a beer.

"Thanks.Your turn. While you're freshening up, I'll put together some dinner. Are you hungry?"

"Famished. All the commotion took away my appetite. I haven't been able to think about meals."

"Spaghetti and salad O.K.?"

"My favorite. Perfect for tonight."

"Dinner will be ready in half an hour."

"I'm still in a state of denial."

"I can imagine. Well, actually, I can't imagine. Anyway, let me start dinner."

She went to his room and began to rummage through her suitcases, looking for something to wear. She couldn't wait to let the hot water run down her body to help rinse away some of the disbelief, still holding her in its grip.

41.

TUESDAY NIGHT. A dining table was set perpendicular against the wall leading into the kitchen. Michael set everything in place: a basket of bread in the center of the table and a large bowl of salad next to it. Tall candles were burning to add a sense of establishment. When she approached the table, he pulled out her chair and seated her, his movements deft and confident. He returned to the kitchen to serve the pasta.

"Why don't you serve the salad," he suggested from the kitchen.

"It's the least I can do. You've done all the work."

She placed two generous portions in each of their bowls. Salad dressings were placed on a dish in front of the salad bowl. He thought of everything.

He came to the table with two plates of pasta covered with marinara sauce and Parmesan cheese.

"Let me know if you want more cheese."

"Hmmm. If you gave me a choice of anything in the world to have for dinner, nine times out of ten, my numero uno choice would be pasta, any type of pasta."

"Enjoy your dinner. But first, a toast. Here's to your life getting better every day from this moment on." They clicked their glasses.

"You're welcome to stay here as long as you like, resting and removing yourself from anything reminding you of the trauma you've been through."

"I was going to check into a motel, a disastrous solution. The realistic answer is to be close to someone I can trust and confide in, sharing this experience with me so it doesn't eat me alive."

"After dinner, let's sit in front of the fire and you can tell me about it, starting from the beginning."

They finished their meal with relaxed conversation and mutual respect. The tranquility of the house and Michael's personality combined to form a protective shell around her. She was beginning to reach a level of composure. A few days ago this was beyond her grasp.

She helped him clear the table and load the dishwasher. After everything was put away, the two of them returned to the living room and sat on the sofa.

"Would you like another glass of wine?"

"No thank you. I'm very tired and more wine will make me too sleepy."

"How about a cup of coffee then?"

"I think not. I drank five cups at the diner."

"Tell me what happened. Don't skip any details."

Aline took a deep breath and began to tell the entire story, starting with the commitment she made with Elcock to attend the town meeting. Periodically, she would break down in tears and he would have to console her and wait for her to begin again. She was struggling to keep her composure and he kept telling her to let it go, it didn't matter. It was important for her to be able to release.

The emotion was draining her. Eventually she began to tire. She stopped talking. Her body sank deeper into the sofa.

He didn't expect her to continue beyond her saturation point, but he had to know only one thing before he let her stop. "Did you take a serious look at the condition of the scaffolding?"

She thought for a moment before answering. "No, I didn't. I was too upset. Unfortunately, I didn't notice anything beyond one fact. He was dead."

"If there was foul play, who would possibly want to hurt him? He was admired by the entire community."

"I know. It doesn't compute." She covered her eyes with her left hand.

"You, certainly, would be the last person to suspect."

"Right now they have no one else to interrogate. I was seeing him often and was closer to him than anyone else in this town. They're attracted to me because they have no other "person of interest" to consider. I'm a victim of circumstance."

"Maybe there is a side of Mr. Elcock that eluded you."

"I doubt it," She argued, tilting her head back and releasing a heavy sigh, agitated by his remark. "He brought me into his life to share his utmost intimate relationships and experiences, right down to the core of his inspiration. He trusted me."

Michael stood up and started pacing the living room. "Well, something isn't right about his death. He was a big man, had strong hands and built his support system to carry his body weight. He worked on it for years, without any problem, and certainly knew better than anyone if it became unsafe. He wouldn't take a chance with his own life if the structure wasn't secure. He was too intelligent." He stopped in his tracks and waited for her response.

"Your assumption makes perfect sense. I haven't stopped to put the facts together. My God, could this be homicide?" After uttering the word "homicide," Aline curled her legs under her and crossed her arms. "It can't be, it just can't! In my heart, I'll never begin to accept the idea."

He took her hands into his. "You may have to face the possibility that Mr. Elcock was murdered."

"No! No! Oh, Michael, please don't say that!"

He tried to calm her, annoyed with himself for upsetting her. "I think you have been through enough for one day. It's getting late, why don't you get some sleep. We can continue this at another time."

"Please, just hold me for a minute."

He pulled her into his lap and began to wipe the tears away. She was limp in his arms, weakened by the crying and the cruel reality of what he had just said. Softly, he ran his hand through her hair and buried his face into her neck. She wrapped her arms around his chest and melted into him.

"I need you," she whispered.

"Shhh."

He stood up and carried her to his bedroom. After gently laying her on top of the bed, he left to turn off the living room lights and knock down the dying fire.

When he returned to the bedroom, she was on her back, tearfully looking out through the blurred curtains. He lay down next to her, turning her face toward him and kissing her softly on the mouth and eyes. She put her arms around his neck, pulling him down to her. He didn't resist.

Effortlessly, they were out of their clothes. His hands traveled all over her smooth, firm body with tender eagerness. She guided his almost instant erection to the object of his desire—yearning for his penetration, his control, his dominance.

She hadn't had sex for a very long time. Her tightness made his desire for her even more intense, bordering on forcefulness. Their bodies writhed in sexual pleasure, both of them consumed with their individual lust for each other.

Finally, they fell apart, breathing heavily and soaked in sweat. She reached for his hand and when she found it, he rolled over and kissed her deeply. For a long while, they lay still. Words were unnecessary.

Then she turned onto her stomach and positioned herself on top of him, kissing him over and over. He had another erection. Sitting up, she mounted him and began slowly pumping her pelvis up and down on his penis. He was in ecstasy as she increased the rhythm of her buttocks, plunging herself deeper and deeper into his groin. The momentum kept building until her whole being shuddered and she collapsed onto his chest.

The fervor of their love-making sapped them of all their strength and they fell into a deep sleep in each other's arms.

42.

WEDNESDAY MORNING. At nine o'clock the alarm next to the bed shook Aline out of a deep sleep, giving her forty minutes to shower and dress. For a few minutes, she stretched lazily in the big bed, recalling their love-making during the night. Michael was strong and passionate, completely overpowering her in all respects.

Dreamily she got up and put on his shirt which was lying on the floor, the scent of his body still lingering in its folds. She walked down the hall to the kitchen and helped herself to a cup of coffee. On the counter, next to the coffeemaker, was a note.

Hope this morning goes well. Be tough. Call me later if you need to talk to me. I left you a key to the house on the kitchen table. See you tonight.

A *key* to the house. . . . It suddenly occurred to her she was still carrying the house key for Mitchell Street. She was in such a hurry to leave she forgot to return it to Cora. At some point during the day, she should drop it off.

Aline was ready in twenty minutes. She wore no makeup but she looked refreshed and rested. Before leaving, she put Michael's house key in her change purse. She would straighten up later before he came home from work. Maybe she would cook dinner for him and Terri tonight and surprise them. It was her turn. She filled her mind with pleasantries, attempting to put aside the gut-wrenching sensation seizing her during the police questioning. Today would be the last day of interrogation for a while.

When the police released her, she would try to touch base with Terri and leave her a map to Michael's house. She looked forward to sharing the intimacy of the evening with those who were concerned about her.

Michael's gift to her was a sense of femininity and sexuality. He gave her renewed energy and, for the first time in weeks, she was happy with herself. Walter Giles would spend the morning questioning a very different Aline Kranick.

Aline sat in her car directly in front of the police department. It was almost ten o'clock. She was never late for appointments and was grateful to have few minutes to prepare herself. Michael was right. Today would be better than yesterday.

Without further hesitation, she entered the building, passing the desk sergeant on her way to the interrogation room. As soon as she was seated, an officer poked his head around the door frame.

"No coffee today, thank you." she said, without turning around.

He hesitated for a second and then left.

After a few moments, Giles and Lewis presented themselves. Giles stood, his back to the door, with his hands in his pockets. Lewis sat at the table.

"How are you this morning?" Giles asked.

"I'm better, thank you."

"I'm glad. This won't take long. I just have a few more points to cover. I don't want you to become upset. As I mentioned before, this is a standard routine pertaining to this kind of investigation.. Do you understand?"

"Yes."

Giles continued his cross-examination. "We ended our conversation with you assuring me that you were convinced Thomas Elcock's life and situation were perfectly normal."

"That's correct. There was no change in disposition from day to day. It was always the same. He was always in a good mood. He became pensive on occasions, but never really depressed."

"At what time during your audience with him, did his mood change or become 'pensive,' as you describe it?"

"I recall a day when we went out to visit a point of land and an old house used as subject matter for a large body of his earlier work. We went to explore it and discovered it was in ruins. Seeing it in this condition made him a little sad."

"That's the old McLean house. It's been deserted for many years. The grandchildren didn't want to restore it. Most of them moved away, looking for work. To unload it, they sold the property to the town."

"I'm surprised you're familiar with the house," Aline commented.

He proceeded, "It was the only real estate in Cape Warren with a grand view of the whole harbor. Eventually the area became public domain and still is. In spite of the exceptional location, however, no one ever goes out there. It's too weedy and overgrown."

"Somehow, Mr. Elcock seemed very attached to it."

Lewis asked, "Did he ever have any company?"

"Not when I was there. If anyone ever came to visit, I was totally unaware of it. I only saw him for three hours in the mornings, unless he suggested a field trip. He used to visit Mr. Swenson at his place because the man never leaves his loft, except to shop for supplies. I don't know about Mr. Elcock's other acquaintances."

Giles moved to the table and sat down, facing her. He folded his hands together in his customary manner and nodded for Lewis to continue.

"Did Mr. Elcock ever mention his family to you?"

“He told me there were four brothers. His parents were dairy farmers. Two brothers died at a very young age of scarlet fever and the other two grew up to make their livings from the sea, one a fisherman, and the other a merchant seaman. They were not very close and communicated only occasionally, sometimes at Christmas.”

“Did Mr. Elcock ever mention his wife?”

“He talked about her a little when we first began the interviews. Evidently, she passed on a long time ago of Alzheimer’s disease. He always spoke well of her when he mentioned her name. Once they were very active together. They liked the outdoors. Then she became ill. I think he missed her very much.”

There was a moment of silence and Giles looked at his watch. The questioning by Lewis continued. Most of it concerned Aline’s family background and career history. Finally, Detective Giles pushed himself away from the table. “It’s almost eleven-thirty. I think we’ll end the session for today. I may ask you to come in again next week. Are you still staying at Mitchell Street?”

“No, right now I’m staying with some friends. I’ll give you some numbers where I can be reached.” She wrote down Michael and Terri’s home numbers and the number of the diner.

Giles asked her to inform him if she changed her location and again asked her to stay within the boundaries of Cape Warren. He walked her to the front entrance and opened the door for her. “I know that this whole experience has been terrible for you. But be assured we will find the answer as to how this man died. I won’t rest until we reach a plausible conclusion. That’s a guarantee. We appreciate your cooperation.”

Aline shook his hand to show him she understood his position. Respect for his dedication and intent was replacing her initial hostility.

He was still standing there, thinking about her, as she drove away.

43.

WEDNESDAY NIGHT. After locating the washer/dryer in the kitchen closet, Aline stripped the bed and washed all the linen, towels and clothes found scattered about the bedroom. While waiting for the laundry, she vacuumed the first floor. By the time Terri rang Michael's doorbell, the place looked immaculate.

Aline greeted her dinner guest, "Looks like you didn't have a problem finding us."

Terri replied, "Not at all. This is adorable. I'm impressed. By comparison, my place looks like a dump."

"Let me take your coat. I love it here. Mitchell Street seems like a bad dream compared to this."

"Exactly. Mitchell Street was like Cora, sinister and outdated."

"But I liked it there when I first moved in. It seemed to be a safe and satisfactory setting for my project. It started to change after the dinner we had together last Wednesday. There was a switch in attitude. I definitely touched a nerve."

"It's best you left when you did. You were handling too much all at once."

"I know. It's hard to explain the sense of foreboding which began to take hold of me."

"Let's change the subject. When do you expect Michael?"

"He should be here soon. I'll show you the rest of the house and then you can help me make dinner."

When they returned to the kitchen, Aline began pulling plastic bags of vegetables out of the refrigerator.

"Would you like a drink?" she asked.

"Not now. I'll wait for Michael to get home. What are you preparing?"

"Broiled chicken with onions and brown rice. It only takes forty minutes. I want to spend quality time with you two, not the oven."

"Sounds good. You'll have to show me where everything is. I feel awkward in another person's digs."

While they worked Aline gave Terri an update on the investigation. Her friend was struck silent with disbelief and dismay. Terri let her ramble on without responding in any way. She realized how vital her connection was to Aline's stability.

The food preparation was complete and they returned to the living room.

"Let's make a fire. This is the first thing he does when he comes home."

"How involved are you getting with this guy—or shouldn't I ask?"

"Right now, I feel very involved. To be perfectly truthful, I'm crazy about him. And I'm glad you asked me. It sounds exhilarating just putting it into words. Besides, I want you to know everything." They held each other for a moment.

"He came into your life at just the right time, Aline. I'm ecstatic for you."

"Your caring means a lot to me, Terri."

The fire began to catch and they sat in front of it, watching the flames licking and devouring the logs. Their closeness eliminated the need to talk.

They heard the sound of Michael's car. Aline rushed to greet him. As soon as he opened the kitchen door, her arms were around his neck and she was kissing him.

"Wow! Welcome home! Hey, Terri, hi. What a nice surprise, two women in my kitchen at the same time. Aline, how did it go this morning?"

"It went well. I'll tell you about it after dinner. Terri's been a big help preparing dinner."

He was impatient to hear about the result of her meeting with Giles, but he tried to disguise it with humor. "You're cooking? Surprise number two. Terri, do you think it's safe, or should we order takeout?" He had to duck in order to avoid the swat heading in his direction.

They were all talking at once, laughing and sparring. After making themselves drinks, they went to sit in front of the fire and exchange their thoughts of the day.

"Wow! Someone has been working very hard around here." Michael said, looking around. "I better get rid of my housekeeper and replace her with Aline. It'll save me a ton of money."

Terri watched the interaction between them and it filled her with a yearning for the same situation in her own life. "Let me go in and check the rice," she said.

As soon as she was out of the room, Aline and Michael were wrapped around each other.

When Terri returned, they were kissing. "Ahem," she said, announcing herself.

Aline pulled herself away. "I better start to put this meal together." In the kitchen she could hear her friends in the next room. Terri and Michael genuinely liked each other and this made her feel contentment.

During dinner, everyone skirted the subject of Thomas Elcock's death. Aline actually was cheerful. Neither Michael nor Terri wanted to spoil the mood.

"You realize, of course, that next Friday night is Halloween," Terri said.

"Good grief. What with all the commotion, I almost forgot about Halloween. Do you get a lot of kids out here, Michael?"

"I don't. Their parents don't let them come down this dark road in the woods. They stay in the well-lit housing developments, usually with an escort. Or they go to someone's church or home for a party."

"That makes sense," Terri said. "The world has changed. If I was a mother with young ones, the house party idea would get my vote."

Aline agreed, "In New York, parents accompany their children just within the confines of their apartment building. Even the parents don't want to go out into the city streets after dark. All sweets have to be sealed, no loose candy. It's just too risky in the Big Apple."

Michael replied, "Yeah, it's the same up here in the country. Speaking of sweets, what's for desert?"

"Terri picked up a pecan pie at the diner for us."

Michael looked pleased. "My first choice. How did you know?"

They joked with each other, enjoying the evening. Everybody chipped in to strip the table. In short order, the leftovers were put away, the countertops wiped, and the dishwasher was humming. Terri and Michael returned to the living room and made themselves comfortable. Aline joined them.

Then, she broke into the conversation that Terri and Michael wanted to avoid. "I'm curious as to how Cape Warren is going to handle Elcock's death." The words lay there like an open wound—nobody wanted to go near it.

Terri debated with herself as to whether she should let Michael handle it or come to his aid. Finally she answered, "It's unusual to have a murder here in Cape Warren, and even more unusual, to have it go so public. Thomas Elcock himself made us unique."

Michael gave Terri a look, questioning her motive for encouraging the discussion. "Civic matters usually dominate the headlines, not homicide," he commented in a clipped tone.

But Aline didn't pick up on his hint to change the subject. She, as usual, was too preoccupied with her own thoughts. "Michael has been looking through the Augusta and Portland papers for me, but he hasn't found anything," Aline said. "I assume that the police are trying to contact what's left of Elcock's family. It should be very interesting to see what they find out."

Michael and Terri were silent.

Aline continued, "I doubt if the police will release any information now. The investigation is still too fresh. Eventually, however, the papers will have to print an obituary." She looked at Michael, expecting a reply.

Michael agreed. "The editor-in chief of the Cape Warren *Chronicle* told me he contacts the police every week to publish the police blotter. Mention of his death is unavoidable."

Terri took her turn at attempting to end the discussion. "I guess we'll find out on Friday, when the paper comes out."

Michael asked Aline, "You were going to tell me about this morning. Do Giles and Lewis still want to question you?"

She uttered a tired sigh before she replied. "I don't know. All I do know is that they told me not to leave town."

Terri returned a knowing smile, "Maybe Michael had something to do with their decision. By the way, how is your boss taking all this?"

Aline gave her a look of disgust. "He's acting like a real jerk. He wants me back in New York immediately. If I'm not at my desk next Monday morning, he's threatened to replace me."

Michael cut in, "Is he real? How can you leave town when the police won't release you?"

"I know. Rosen hasn't cared about this project since its inception. All he really wanted out of it was for me to go on a pseudo-vacation to get some rest because I was burned out. Believe me, his needs have always come first. Now, all of a sudden, he wants to get involved. He even had the nerve to tell me he wanted to talk to the detective in charge of this so-called "case" so he could influence my return."

Michael scoffed, "He's flexing his muscles to no avail. The Cape Warren police don't care who he is or how he feels about your detention here. They won't allow him to become detrimental to their progress, no matter how much he rants and raves. Marty may be a big shot in New York, but here in Maine he's just another form of interference. He'll just end up making a fool out of himself if he gets too carried away."

"Aline, what are you going to do?" Terri asked.

"I'm not going to do anything. I'm going to stay right here until this awful predicament is resolved. I can't leave until it is, even if it means my job. I'm very determined about this."

Michael and Terri said nothing more concerning the subject. Aline finally shut the door on it for all of them.

Terri looked at her watch. "It's getting late. I better be running along. Thank you both for a wonderful evening."

Aline went to get her coat. The three of them walked to the back door, the two women hugging briefly before Terri exited into the cold night. Halfway down the staircase, she turned and called back to her friend.

"Follow your heart, Aline. You do have the courage of your convictions." She continued down the stairs. Michael and Aline didn't go inside until she had been swallowed up by the woods.

"You were more than lucky to find someone so loyal to you. I like her company."

"I'm very fond of her. She works so hard, never expecting too much out of life, just some simple pleasures, like a few laughs and the chance to spend her time off with people she enjoys. I hope some day she'll find the kind of happiness she deserves."

"I'm sure she will. She's very giving and genuinely good at heart."

They put out the fire, turned off the lights, and spent another night making love.

44.

FRIDAY. The couple enjoyed spending a few quiet days at home, preparing meals, renting movies and playing board games. Michael promised to teach her how to play chess. Their moments together were precious. When the work week started up again, the investigation would again take over her life. And even when it was closed, she would continue to be tortured mentally by its significance.

Uncertainty undermined her composure as well as her nerves. The attitude of the police and Detective Giles's subsequent implications were devastating. Then add Marty to this equation. His selfish reaction to her plight represented the final straw. Only Terri and Michael showed real compassion, probably because both of them loved her. They were the only ones who were really interested in her welfare. She would feel totally alone and desperate without them.

She chose to stay out of the public eye, but solitude wasn't the answer either. She needed time to recover her poise, and being with Michael would allow her to accomplish this. She couldn't continue if he wasn't in the picture.

Apprehension haunted her subconscious and more than once, she would drift off in the middle of their conversation without realizing it. He would bring her back and hold her in his arms. And it would be tangible again. Right now, he was her lifeline, the core of her existence.

Unfortunately, love didn't always lead to support. Following Michael's advice, Aline called her mother to explain her predicament. In return, she received a lecture on how out of control she was.

To counteract this response, she thought about telling her mother about meeting Michael. She knew this news would please her mother tremendously. Her daughter wasn't a lost cause after all. But Aline felt it wasn't the right time. She couldn't afford to be too impulsive, in case this new relationship didn't work out. Another failure to be criticized for.

Her mother's reaction hurt her more than she was willing to admit. She remembered her mother's words: "Why did you get so involved? This is much too dangerous. Why can't you find a job near home?"

Aline knew her mother resented her choosing a career over getting married and having children. A long time ago, Aline gave up trying to gain her mother's endorsement on anything she pursued.

Her father, however, never criticized her for her decision to go into journalism. His encouragement helped her make her career choice. He would forever be her champion. Her father's absence was a great loss to her..

Journalism, the paper. *Pick up the paper*. Michael would call her around ten-thirty—then she could go out. She went into the kitchen and made herself hot chocolate.

While she was sipping it, her thoughts went to Martha. By now, Aline was sure the whole office knew about Ecock's death. Martha probably was hurt to hear the news from Marty's lips instead of hearing it from Aline. She expected her friend would forgive her, but Aline was prepared to take the flak. Her alliances with her associates were shameful at best.

The phone rang. Aline picked up after one ring. "Michael?"

"Hi. You sound nervous. You all right?"

"Yes, I'm O.K. I just miss you."

"I miss you, too. You have to try to put this terrible event out of your mind. I know it'is difficult for you, but I can't sit by and watch it devour you. Please."

"I'm sorry. I'll try harder. I promise."

"Good. What are your plans for today? I know you don't want to go out." He sounded troubled.

"I'm going to get the papers. I think I'll call Martha later. There's plenty of things to do here."

"Do you think that calling her at work is a good idea?"

"What do you mean?"

"Calling the office will just make you more upset."

"She's my only ally in New York. If I don't keep in touch with her, I'll lose her."

"Aline, I'm not about to tell you what to do. I'm just trying to protect you. I hope you understand."

"I know you are. I guess I'm just lonely." She sounded unusually unsure of herself.

He didn't want to butt heads with her. He suggested, "Why don't you call her at her home tonight. Then you can avoid the office getting involved."

"You're right. Thanks. I keep heading for the brick wall. I'm sorry."

"You don't have to apologize. Listen, gotta run, late for a meeting. I'll be home early. Let's order some takeout. Would you like it if I picked up some videos?"

"Yes. I'll be counting the minutes."

"Take care."

She hung up. Somehow, he was always right. His perspective guided her around the path of self-destruction she insisted on following.

45.

FRIDAY NOON. The general store, where she usually shopped, was only about twenty minutes from Michael's house. She was certain the local paper would be available there.

As she drove down the country road, dry leaves pooled and spun behind her, stirred up by the speed of her SUV. She decided to slow down.

The colors of the autumn leaves appeared luminescent in contrast to the gray backdrop of leaden skies and leafless trees. Main Street had the usual activity level for this time of day. Most of the parking spaces hosted pickup trucks and vans. The Halloween decorations in storefront windows looked garish to her. They seemed to counteract her mood. Butterflies turned in her stomach as she looked for a place to park. After finding a spot behind a dump truck, she walked hastily in the direction of the store.

She came in for the paper, but would buy one item of clothing so it looked like she came in to shop. A sweatshirt would be the perfect item to purchase. Besides, she could always use an extra one with winter coming on.

As she entered the store she noted only two people. A woman was looking at rolls of fabric and a stock boy was pricing jars of fruit in large cardboard boxes surrounding him. Both were too busy to notice her.

A tall clerk dressed in khaki came up to her. “Can I help you find something?”

“Yes. I’m interested in a lady’s sweatshirt. The cold weather will be here before we know it.” She returned his smile.

“We just restocked our shelves. I’ll show you where they are.”

“Thank you.” As he spoke, Aline spotted a wire rack set down near the check-out counter. It was piled high with newspapers.

The clerk continued, “I remember you, but I haven’t seen you around here lately.”

“I’ve moved, but still come into town quite a lot to pick up supplies.” Aline followed him to the dry goods department.

“Here they are. Let me know if you need any help.” He patted the neatly stacked pile of folded shirts. Before he could say anything more, the woman in fabrics called for assistance.

Thankful to be alone, Aline began to search for a medium-sized sweatshirt. Since she didn’t care about the color, it didn’t take her long to settle on one. She carried it to the checkout counter and waited for the clerk, delicately lifting a copy of the Cape Warren *Chronicle* off the stack. She was handling it as if it would disintegrate in her hands. The headline was printed in large capital letters: “LOCAL ARTIST FOUND DEAD.”

“That will be twelve ninety-eight.” His words startled her.

“What?”

“Twelve ninety-eight. Do you want the paper?”

“Yes.”

“That’s thirteen dollars and thirteen cents. The paper’s fifteen cents.”

She handed him a twenty-dollar bill, her attention fastened on the headline’s message.

"It's a real tragedy, isn't it? A man with all that talent. What a shame." He was handing her the change.

She didn't answer him.

"Six eighty-seven back."

He was still standing there with it in his right hand. "Miss, your change. Did you know him?"

Aline looked up to answer him. "I know about his reputation as an artist."

"Feel sorry for the wife. Wonder if they'll tell her. Poor thing."

"What . . . his wife?"

"Yes, miss. He had a wife, you know."

"I was told she died a long time ago." Her grip on the paper began to tighten.

"Oh no, miss. She's still alive. Rumor has it she's in a private sanitarium somewhere near New York."

Aline took her change and tried to hide her dismay. "Who told you this?"

"It's common knowledge with the older townsfolk."

"What happened to her?"

"Seems like she had a mental breakdown caused by some personal shock. No one knows exactly what it was, but some people have an idea."

"How long ago was this?"

"Over twenty years ago, I'd say."

"Was she ill before this occurred?"

"She was always sickly. Stayed house-bound most of the time."

Nothing the clerk said matched the information described to her about Louise Elcock. She wondered if he was baiting her, playing some sort of a sick game with her because she was an out-of-towner. Maybe he was on some sort of power trip with his "insider information." *I have to be careful. I'm asking too many questions, playing into his hands.*

There was a glint in his eyes. She was a captive audience and he was relishing it. The clerk shook his head and said, "She was a sweet lady. Didn't deserve what she got."

Aline heard enough. She stuffed the change into the left pocket of her jacket, picked up the brown bag containing her purchases and left the store, slamming the door behind her. Anger and a sense of betrayal began to overwhelm her. She ran to her vehicle and once inside, pushed her tearful eyes deeply into the knuckles of both hands squeezing the top of the steering wheel. She let out a shriek and pounded the top of the wheel with closed fists. The smug, invasive attitude of the nosy clerk was impossible to erase. It pierced her heart and filled her with disgust.

If any of this was true, why did Elcock lie to her, especially when she was now part of the most private and personal aspects of his life? Her trust and adoration for him put him on a level where he stood alone. It must be nothing more than vicious gossip, a product of idle tongues.

What else could she think? Her skin was on fire, her heart racing. A cold sweat broke out all over her body. She had to get out of this town. She couldn't let the deception undermine her sanity. Everything around her was starting to fall apart.

46.

FRIDAY NIGHT. Almost seven o'clock. Michael came down the driveway leading to his house. Floodlights lit up the parking area. The windows in the kitchen were dark. At this time of day, Aline was usually getting dinner ready. She must be in another part of the house. He didn't bother locking his car, just ran up the stairs. The back door was unlocked.

"Aline?" Reflections of the fire, the only light, danced off the living room walls.

He found her lying on the couch, eyes closed. A blanket from the bed completely covered her. Empty peanut shells were scattered everywhere.

He sat next to her, searching for her hand. When he found it, it was ice cold. "Aline, what's wrong?"

She looked up to see his worried face looking down at her. "She's still alive."

"Who is?"

"Louise."

"Louise? Louise who?"

"Louise Elcock."

"What the hell are you talking about? *Help me, here!* I don't understand." Frustration distorted his voice.

"He told me she was dead. He lied to me."

"Aline, would it be all right if I put on some lights?"

"No. I'm tired. Only the fire." She sounded like a child, begging a parent's indulgence.

Michael stood up and went down the hall to his bedroom. He sat on the edge of the bed and put his head in his hands. What was he going to do with this girl? He couldn't penetrate her world. She was beginning to slip away from him. Finally, he removed his tie and started to undress. He hung up his suit, threw his shirt on the chair in the corner, and changed into a pair of jeans and a T-shirt.

He went into the bathroom and washed his face. For a few moments he stood looking at himself in the mirror. Was he going to take on the role of caretaker instead of lover? He should ask someone for guidance. Later, he would call his aunt. He felt certain that she would help him. When he went back into the living room, Aline was in the same position. He decided to take charge, even if it meant acting against her wishes.

"Aline, I want you to sit up. You should attempt to eat something."

He switched on all the lamps, then clicked on the TV. "I want to hear the news."

When he went into the kitchen, she stood up, pulling the blanket around her, dragging it toward the bedroom. Now he felt exasperated, but it was best to leave her alone. He placed a frozen entrée in the microwave and opened a beer. While his dinner was cooking, he remembered Wednesday night. The three of them were having an outstanding time together. He felt so much contentment. How could it have disintegrated to this level so fast? She was slowly sliding into an abyss and if he didn't act fast, she would be beyond reach.

The microwave bell interrupted his meditation. Mechanically, he removed the hot food from the microwave and placed it on the table. Then he walked away from it. He wasn't hungry. Instead, he took his cordless phone and sat on the edge of the couch to make his call. He knew Aline wouldn't hear his conversation.

He dialed Marjorie's number and played with the peanut shells on the coffee table. The newspaper lay folded in front of him, unread. He wondered why. He recalled how impatient she was to get her hands on it. Something was always happening to turn her world upside down.

"Hello?"

"Marjorie, it's Michael."

"Hi, darling, how are you? I was hoping you would call!" Her cheerful voice gave him a boost.

"I'm OK. How about you?"

"Just fine, dear. Putting on a little weight, but some things never change. How is Aline?"

"Not so good. That's why I'm calling you. I need some input from you as to what I should do. I'm at my wit's end."

"Oh, this sounds serious. Tell me about it."

Michael spent a few minutes explaining the situation to her. Recounting the events, he tried to simplify the details leading up to this moment. Too much narrative about Elcock's death, the police investigation and Louise's re-appearance into the drama, would only waste her time. The only thing he really cared about was saving his relationship with Aline.

He explained, "His death was such a blow to her. She spent so much time getting close to him and he confided in her and gave her insight into himself on a very personal level."

"It's terrible, dear. I feel so sorry for her. You know how fond I am of her."

"I want to marry her, Marge."

"Oh, darling, everything will work out. She just needs more time. You have to be even more patient and understanding than you already have been. Without you, she will not make it."

"I know, but I feel like I can't get through to her some of the time. She may need professional help, help I'm not able to provide for her."

"I think the only thing she needs is your love and your devotion. No doctor can give her those things."

His eyes started to well up as he listened to his aunt's encouraging words. His heart was aching. "I have to get her away from this town, this investigation."

"She can always come and stay with me."

"You're an angel. But I need her closer to Belfast because I want to touch base with her every day and the commute to Augusta would entail too much driving."

"I understand. Let me think. You could always use our summer cottage at the lake. It has electric heat."

"Well, she's comfortable here. Changing locations isn't the real issue. What I'm really talking about is making her divorce her mind from all this—somehow. Maybe if she had a new project to work on, she would become distracted from all this negative energy. Do you understand what I'm getting at?"

"Yes, but that may be more difficult than it sounds. She won't be able to concentrate on anything else until she can have some closure on his death."

He knew his aunt had hit the nail on the head. He was back to square one. But talking to her made him feel much better. "Thank you, Marge."

"It is going to be almost as difficult for you as it is going to be for her. But remember this: it will end. There is a light at the end of the tunnel. You have to be especially strong. Can you get some time off from work?"

"Yes. I could take part of my vacation. I get three weeks this year. What do you have in mind?"

"A cruise. You two would only be gone a week, ten days maximum. It would do her a world of good. Sun and fun would be a refreshing diversion for both of you."

"It's a great idea. The only hitch is, the police detectives don't want her to leave town."

"Well, what I would do in your shoes, is to go down to the police department, introduce yourself to the man in charge, explain how you are taking care of Aline, tell him she needs to pull herself together, give him the details on the trip and see what he has to say. You're not running away, you're just going out of town for a week. Everybody does it, what's the big deal?"

"You are fantastic. I love you." He heard her giggling on the other end of the phone. Then he started to laugh. It was the only solution. Convincing Giles wouldn't be a problem, but convincing Aline would be.

"Let me know how you make out."

They chatted on for a while and then said good-night. He told her again how much he loved her. After he hung up, he sat back, sipping his beer and wondering if this idea would work. It had to work.

He left the paper where it was. Reading it at this point was a total turnoff. It would just drag him down into the same abyss. Now he was hungry. He decided to eat, watch late TV, and sleep on the couch. Tomorrow was another day and this time, he was looking forward to the challenge.

47.

SATURDAY MORNING. Michael woke up with brilliant daylight washing his face. He looked at his watch. Nine twenty-five. Last night he dozed off while watching a forgettable late movie. The TV was still on. Aline must still be asleep. Rubbing his eyes, he went down the hall to the bedroom. The door was open, Aline was gone. He stood in the doorway, hands on his hips, looking at the bed. It was still made. She slept on top of the bedspread, covering herself with a blanket.

She planned to come back, since her clothes were still in the closet. He was filled with indignation, wavering toward defeat.

"Damn!" He slammed his fist against the wall. Where the hell did she go? Why didn't she wait and talk to him before she left?

He went back to the living room and sat on the couch, trying to imagine himself in her shoes. Louise Elcock was still alive and this triggered Aline's next action. Mr. Elcock told her his wife died. So he was a liar. The man she worshiped was guilty of deceiving her. So what was next? Maybe she went over to Terri's to confer with her. Sometimes women cling to each other in a crisis. It was early, but he decided to call Terri anyway.

The phone rang for a long time, but he was reluctant to hang up.

"Hello?" A drowsy voice answered the call.

"Hi, it's Michael. I'm sorry if I woke you."

"Hmm. What's up?"

Now he knew Aline wasn't there, but he followed through with his inclination. "Is Aline with you?"

"No, why? Is she missing?"

"Yes. When I woke up this morning, she was gone. Last night she was almost comatose. She wouldn't have any dinner. I slept on the couch."

"Shit, Michael! What is it this time?" Her sarcastic tone didn't cover up her disbelief.

"She got some bad news. Looks like Mr. Elcock's wife is still alive. The old man told her a tall tale about Louise Elcock passing away a long time ago. I wonder why he lied."

"I don't know and you don't know, but I *do* know that we are both fed up with this."

"Terri, have you had breakfast?"

"You bastard, you woke me up. I don't eat in my sleep."

"Good. Come on over and keep me company before I lose my mind. Maybe we can figure this thing out."

"I'll be right there as soon as I wake up. See you."

He decided to wash up and make coffee.

Terri arrived in half an hour. She looked well-rested and had a soft pink blush on her cheeks. Clinging to her coat was the fresh smell of autumn air, cool and woodsy.

"The aroma of your coffee is life-sustaining! I'd kill for it. Here's a little something to go with it." She handed him a small bag of sweet rolls.

"Oh, thanks. You're something else. How do you like your eggs?"

"Sunnyside up for me."

They sat at the table quietly eating breakfast, talking about their mutual foreboding relating to Aline's future.

"Did you read the paper?" Terri asked.

"No, it's still lying on the coffee table. When I got home from work last night, she was on the couch, curled up in a blanket, off in her little Elcock world. She was rambling on and on about Louise Elcock. I can't get through to her."

. "Michael, she's in too deep. She has to let go of it!"

"It isn't going to happen until they conclude their investigation. By the way, I called my aunt last night and she gave me some food for thought."

"Let's hear it."

"In essence, her conclusion was to get Aline out of town for a while. I mean, like a cruise. If I don't, it's over." He emphasized his words with high-flying arm gestures. "It's over for her, it's over for me, and it's over for *us*."

Terri was a bit intimidated by his aggressiveness. "Wow! You just said a mouthful. Unfortunately, you are absolutely right."

He calmed down. "Where in the name of God do you think she went?"

Terri leaned on the table and put her right hand under her chin. "I'd say, the first thing she is going to do is go somewhere offering her the information she wants. . .meaning the confirmation of whether Louise Elcock is dead or alive."

"Go on."

"My guess is she'll retrace her steps, returning to some of the locations they visited together. He let her get close to him, you know."

"Good point. Why didn't I think along those lines?"

"You're in love and you're too close to it. Under the circumstances, it's a wonder you can think at all!" She was trying to hide a smirk.

Terri continued thinking out loud. "Then there's the library. She might want to dig back into his past, looking for a clue as to the true story regarding his wife. He is a well-known character around here and is published often in the local papers. There's only one thing wrong with this idea. She'll want instant gratification at this point and I can't see her patiently spending time going through microfilm documentation."

Michael added, "And because it's Saturday, the Hall of Records in the town hall is closed."

"Right."

"What do you think I should do, Terri?"

"You can't do anything except sit tight. She'll be back. She'll want you to listen to the next chapter of the ongoing saga. She'll want to drag you in deeper. If I were you, Michael, I'd sound interested, but don't reveal your lack of encouragement. Hold her in your arms and let her play it out. You don't want her to turn on you, 'cause believe me, she will, if you try to stop her."

Michael listened, not liking everything he heard, but her insight could save him. If he lost Aline, life would be without purpose for him. His soul would remain blank. "God, what would I do without you. You see the facts so much clearer than I do."

"I'm a woman. I think like a woman. We have to keep in mind, Michael, the major factor here is Aline's fragile disposition. She's like a thin glass goblet teetering on the edge of a vibrating table. If we push too hard, she will end up in a thousand pieces."

"I get the picture. Patience has always been one of my strongest characteristics so I better start making it part of my profile."

"Listen, I'm going to leave. I don't want her to come home and find me here. We don't want to look like co-conspirators."

"You're right. Thanks for indulging me. I feel better, much better."

"You're not working through this by yourself, Michael. We're in it hand-in-hand."

She put on her coat and started for the door. Just before opening it, she turned to him. "You didn't miss anything by passing over the article about Elcock. No sensationalism. It's just a recollection of his art career, with a minor mention of his parents and family history. Very safe. No implications. The one thing I did find interesting, though, was the obit at the back—'Mr. Elcock is survived by two brothers.' No mention of the wife. Just the reference to the details of the funeral arrangements. Aline has definitely uncovered an issue which has been deliberately buried."

48.

FOR ALINE, FINDING HANK SWENSON'S SAIL loft was simple. The landmarks began to look familiar. She had paid close attention to the road and its surroundings when Elcock first brought her here, just in case she ever came back.

On the way, she went over the dialogue she would use to discuss the subject of Louise Elcock. Under the guise of consoling him concerning his friend's death, perhaps Swenson would reveal the status of Elcock's wife to her. He was either going to be very cooperative and open about it or be completely tight-lipped, honoring the memory of his old friend. She didn't have high expectations, but she was certain he knew the truth and he was the only one who did.

No thought on her part was being given to Michael or his possible concern about her absence. She was on a mission, blocking out everything. Her compulsive-obsessive drive to find out the answers gave her tunnel vision. This was her only opportunity.

The excitement began to build as she got closer and closer to confronting Hank. And then, there it was, silhouetted against the sky, just as she remembered it. Soon she was on the approach road, expecting Hank to be surprised and delighted to see her.

She parked by the front door. There was no sign of his truck. Burlap covered the bottom half of the windows on the first floor. It was obvious he wasn't home. She got out of the SUV and walked around the building. Newspapers covered the picture window overlooking the marshland.

Confusion and finality took hold of her. Why wasn't he here? He was always home. Returning to the front of the house, she examined the front door. No message was tacked to it. She started pounding on it, calling out his name. No response.

Her exasperation intensified. She had been too sure of herself. Knowing his personality, why didn't she conclude he would desire to avoid confronting anyone? . Maybe he thought the police would question him, trying to draw out of him the confidential facts he kept secret all these years. In any case, he fled. No trace to follow. He was not about to sabotage his only close alliance.

She sat in her vehicle. It was Saturday and all the public buildings were closed, so finding out any conclusion today was out of the question. The health department might have a record of Louise's death certificate *if* she was deceased, but she didn't know any officials in City Hall, either, so it was a dead end.

Driving back to Michael's house put her in a mood of deep depression. He would ask her how she spent her morning. She didn't feel like justifying her actions. She was tired and just wanted to go back to sleep.

49.

MICHAEL WAS WATCHING TV when Aline returned to the house. He heard her help herself to some coffee. When she came into the living room, she was still wearing her coat. She didn't say anything, just stood looking at him, holding her coffee mug with both hands.

"Where have you been?" he asked, not turning his head.

"Oh, I was just driving around, trying to think."

He knew she was lying. "Want some breakfast?"

"No, thank you. I want to lie down for a while."

"Suit yourself." His voice was tense.

"Please wake me up later."

As she exited the room, he called after her. "I'm going grocery shopping. Feel like anything special for dinner?"

She didn't answer.

He walked down the hall to the bedroom, still trying to intrude into her detachment. She was undressing, her back to him. Standing in the doorway, he asked, "Would you like to go to the mall later?"

"I don't know, Michael. I'll let you know."

She was taking charge again and he could sense the barricades going up around her. He walked away and the bedroom door closed after him. He wanted to shake her until she cried out for him to stop.

Get out of the house. Now it was his turn. He slammed the back door, and loped down the stairs to his car, trying to get control of himself. She was closing him out when she needed him the most. Couldn't she see it made him feel inadequate and useless? She didn't have the right to treat him this way. He was her lover, her partner, not some obedient fool waiting in the wings to respond to her demands.

Grocery shopping would give him something constructive to do. On the way to the store, he thought about the rest of the day. He decided to call Terri from the market to let her know Aline was home. Her companionship was the only reassurance he had.

He bumped into some neighbors at the market and exchanged small talk. Before he started filling up his cart, he pulled out his cell phone and called Terri. The phone only rang once.

"Hi, she's home."

"Oh? What's the mood?"

"Detached, distant. All she wants to do is sleep. It's going to be a hell of a weekend."

"Hang in there, Michael."

"I'm trying, believe me."

"Listen, I'm working tonight. If you want to get out of the house for a while, come down for a cup of java."

"I may take you up on the invitation. Who knows what's in store for me this evening?"

"Try to ignore her and just go about your business. You can't let her do a number on you. You're too intelligent."

"Right now, you're my biggest fan."

"I'm counting on you."

"I'll call you if I get a chance."

"Later."

He hung up and resumed his shopping. He felt like he was back on track.

Even though it was almost November, the sun was bright and warm. People were out, dressed in flannel shirts, raking their lawns and bagging piles of leaves. Their children were running around, jumping into the piles, squealing with pure joy. The sight of it made him think of childhood memories, happier times. Someday he would be absorbed in the very same activity with a family of his own.

It was going on one o'clock when he returned home from the market. After unloading the groceries, he made himself some soup and sat enjoying his lunch recalling the beautiful fall day.

"Mmm. Is there enough for me?" She was standing next to him in her bathrobe. Creases in the sheets showed up as impression marks on her face. To Michael, she represented a lost little girl, looking for comfort and approval. He never knew what to expect from her anymore.

"Sure. Have a seat. I'll get some for you." He returned to the kitchen and came back with a large bowl of soup which he placed in front of her, exploring her face for a trace of how she felt.

She was calm, in a state of surrender.

"Would you like anything to go with your soup? I bought soda crackers."

"Could I have some spring water?"

He put her crackers and water on the table, and sat down to continue eating his lunch.

"This tastes wonderful. Thank you."

"It's a beautiful day. We should get out and do something. Everyone is out working on their lawns or washing their cars."

"After I take a shower we can go to the mall. Let's go shopping. What's for dinner?" She was trying very hard to get back to where he was.

"I'm going to grill a steak outside. It's still warm enough."

She was ravenous and quickly finished the soup. After wiping her mouth, she took their dishes into the kitchen to wash them.

He turned in his chair, watching her move gracefully through her task.

Soon she was back, holding his head against her chest and burying her face in his hair. “I’m sorry if I was snappy. I’m not myself.”

“I know.” He put his arms around her waist and held her close to him, all the while thinking, *take it slow, boy*.”

Softly, she kissed his lips and then released him. “I’ll get ready.”

He sat at the table with his back to the wall, in a state of suspension. It was going to be a roller coaster ride, the likes of which he had never experienced before. He prayed to God to give him the strength to endure it.

50.

SATURDAY AFTERNOON. With the holiday season close at hand, the mall was packed. Halloween was always the catalyst for putting people in the mood to shop. The spirit of Christmas was everywhere and many of the stores were in the process of decorating their display windows with extra lights, bright colors, and tinsel. People appeared to be in high spirits, laughing and talking in an exaggerated manner. The bumping and jostling of bodies made it difficult to walk, but in a way, it added to the excitement.

Michael and Aline enjoyed being part of the energy around them. They were caught up in something outside of themselves, something that would take their attention away from the current forces eating at them.

Michael stopped in front of a ladies' dress shop display. "What should I buy my aunt for Christmas."

"How about a halo?"

"There you go! I don't think they come extra-large, the only size appropriate enough to fit Marge. "

"My mother is the hardest person in the world to shop for. She never likes the gifts I buy her and I always have to return them. She relishes rejecting me."

"Ouch! That bad?"

"I'm afraid so. We aren't close at all."

"Excuse my frankness, but I wondered why you seldom mentioned her."

"Don't worry. Most of my friends notice the same thing. I rarely call her and vice versa. Every time we do talk, I get another lecture on how I'm wasting my life."

"It is a mother's second nature to do a lot of lecturing. My father and I are not close at all. He never recovered from mother's death. Chose to live and work in Europe. I never hear from him. My mere existence is a reminder of his loss. He does call Marge once in a while."

"Incredible. I don't mean to sound bitter, but I bet if either one of us became famous, the two of them wouldn't leave us alone."

"Maybe your mother would haunt you, but I'm not so sure about my dad."

"Your aunt is wonderful. I wish my mother was more like her."

"You should see her house at Christmas time. It's like a trip into a world of fantasy."

"I can imagine. It must be spectacular."

"I'd like you to spend Christmas eve with me there."

Aline hesitated. "My mother will expect me to spend Christmas with her, but I promise to find the time to share the holidays with you."

They strolled along, holding hands, making frequent stops to get a closer look at some object in a window. Eventually, they became weary and Aline suggested they sit down and have some cocoa at one of the cafés.

The coffee house was full of patrons and the hostess told them there would be a table available in ten minutes. As long as they were close and spending the day together, they didn't mind waiting for a table.

A couple with two small children stood in line in front of them. Michael and Aline started interacting with the kids, tickling them and gently tugging at their clothes. The little ones would giggle and break into spurts of high-pitched squeals. Their parents enjoyed the play and the teasing.

The turnover was quick and three tables opened up at the same time. Michael chose the most private one, out of the traffic flow. They ordered and sat watching all the movement around them. In a few minutes, the waitress brought them the hot, aromatic brew.

"Yum. This is going to taste fantastic." Aline bent down to inhale the sweet, chocolate steam rising from her cup.

They savored their treat. As expected, it was delicious and its warmth soothed them. When it was time to leave, neither of them wanted to get up.

"Do you have any singles for the tip."

"I think so." She opened her purse, searching for her wallet. "All I have is a five, but I know I have a lot of quarters." She started hunting through the coins in the change pocket.

"Oh, darn it."

"What's wrong?"

"I still haven't returned this damn key!"

"What key?"

"The key to Mitchell Street. Cora gave it to me when I rented the room. I still haven't returned it. I was in a big hurry to get out of there, remember?"

"We can drop it off on the way home."

"If she isn't there, I'll put it in an envelope and slip it through the mail slot."

They retraced their steps to the other end of the mall, where Michael's car was parked. Dusk was beginning to set it by the time they left the mall.

Michael inhaled deeply, and said, "I like the cold air. It was getting stuffy in there."

"I hate crowds, too, but today was a ball," replied Aline, "It put me in the spirit of what's to come. I love Christmas."

"We'll be home in an hour. I'm starved."

"Me too. Do you like to cook?"

"Yes. I grill outside all winter. Even in the snow. The floodlights provide more than enough light."

"You've got a lot of style, Michael Williams." She was smiling at him and he was relishing it.

51.

SATURDAY NIGHT. It was just before six o'clock when they pulled up in front of 17 Mitchell Street, and Aline looked for an envelope in her purse.

"No lights on, as usual," Aline noted.

"She probably isn't home."

"I didn't see her car. Maybe it's in the garage. On the weekends, she sometimes puts it there and locks it up."

"Find one? I may have some bank stationery in my briefcase. It's still on the back seat."

Aline pulled a crumpled envelope out of her purse. "This will do. It's part of an old bill I've already paid. Some day I'll clean out all this useless stuff."

"Are you going to write a note?"

"I should. I never really said good-bye. Not very mature on my part."

"You have plenty of time to do that. You two weren't exactly bosom buddies."

"I didn't understand her. Maybe I read too much into her reactions. She's alone most of the time. I don't think she socializes. Entertaining doesn't appeal to her."

Aline scribbled a brief sentence on the outside of the envelope and slipped the key inside. "I'll be right back."

Michael watched her move up the walk, up the steps, and onto the front porch. She knocked on the huge door, but it didn't open. He was right, Cora wasn't home.

To Michael's dismay, Aline was letting herself in. Maybe she elected to say good-bye after all. Then, the door swung open and Aline disappeared into the foyer.

He got out of the car and walked to the house, stopping in front of the porch steps. An uneasy sensation gripping him. He felt a chill race through his body. Why did she go inside and not turn on any lights? She must know where the switches are. He planted himself to the spot, waiting for something to give. The front door remained ajar.

And then he heard it—a long, tortuous scream. It jolted him to the core of his very being, sounding like the unearthly howl of a dying beast before it trailed off. The howl belonged to Aline.

Clearing the steps in two leaps, he burst into the house, desperately looking for the source of the cry.

"Aline!" No answer. He could barely make out the layout of the first floor through the dim light filtering in from the street. It took a few seconds before his eyes could readjust to where he was. To the right of the front staircase was a long hallway. At the end of it, a faint light was coming up from a basement area.

Running down the hall, he passed closed doors on the right and left. They were probably closets or bedrooms. He reached a staircase leading to the cellar. Taking hold of the old railing, he cautiously, but quickly, started down the stairs.

He found a switch and turned it on. A bare bulb, hanging on a frayed electrical cord, threw light to the back of the cellar. Still further in the distance, he could see a brightly illuminated room. It must be for storage.

"Aline!"

She was standing, with her back to him, covering her face with both hands. He ran up behind her and looked up. Hanging from a thick, cast-iron pipe was the body of Cora Prentis. Her eyes were rolled back and her arms hung at her side like a rag doll. The sash of her bathrobe was used to hang herself. A step ladder lay on its side next to the crumpled heap of her robe.

Michael turned Aline around so she could not witness the grisly scene anymore. She collapsed against him. Stepping backwards, he edged her out of the room. It was of utmost importance to get her out of there as fast as possible. Taking her by the hand, he led her upstairs to his car.

After easing her into the passenger seat, he leaned over her, holding her and kissing her hair. "I'll call the police." His cell phone was in the glove box. He reached for it and dialed the operator.

"Operator. How may I help you?"

"Get me the police."

"Cape Warren, sir?"

"Yes." He waited.

"Cape Warren police department. Officer Miller."

"You better send a cruiser to 17 Mitchell Street."

"What's the problem?"

"Cora Prentis hung herself."

52.

SATURDAY NIGHT. Michael and Aline sat in the car in the dark. The police would arrive at any moment. A steady rain began to fall. Aline laid her head on Michael's lap, facing him. She didn't move. He kept stroking her hair, but he knew she didn't feel anything. Droplets of water began trickling down the windshield, one by one. Occasionally a car would go by and make a swishing sound on the wet pavement. The rain water would catch the light of the blue-white streetlamps or scarlet taillights of a passing car and briefly become ignited before it ran down the glass, scurrying away into obscurity, as if being chased by some voracious predator.

There was no sense of time anymore. Just a vacuum of space in which they both seemed to be drifting. Occasionally an oversized drop of water, falling from a high branch of an overhanging tree, would ping on the roof. The sound would interrupt Michael's thoughts.

Flashing blue lights appeared from nowhere. The cruiser parked directly in front of Michael. A door slammed shut with a dull thud and a flashlight was turned on. Brice walked up to the driver's side and tapped on the glass with his light. Michael lowered the window.

"Officer John Brice. Who are you?"

"Michael Williams. I'm Aline's boyfriend."

“Is that her? He was looking at the limp figure lying on Michael’s lap.”

“Yes.”

“What are you two doing here?”

“We stopped by to return Miss Prentis’ house key. Aline forgot to leave it with her when she moved out.”

“When was that?”

“Tuesday.”

“Stay here. I’m going inside.”

“I want to take her home.”

“Home?”

“My place.”

“Wait until I come back out. By the way, where is Miss Prentis located?”

“There’s a closet in the back of the basement. You’ll find her there.”

Brice walked toward the house at a brisk pace. The flashlight bobbing up and down as he hurried out of sight. As soon as he entered the property, all the lights on the first floor began to be turned on, one after another. Within a couple minutes, the place was lit up like a beacon in the rainy night. It was the only time it ever would be again.

53.

BRICE CAME DOWN THE FRONT PATH and went directly to his cruiser. He turned on the map light and began the process of reporting in to receive his instructions. The light went out and he walked to Michael's car.

"I have to wait here for some people to arrive. I'm sorry to detain you."

"When can we leave?"

"After Detective Giles gets here, I'll let you know. He should be here shortly." Brice returned to his vehicle to write down some notes.

He didn't have to wait long. A pair of headlights belonging to Detective Giles' cruiser parked behind Michael and before the ignition was turned off, Brice was standing next to it. Michael watched the two of them in his rear view mirror as they walked up to talk to him.

"Detective Giles, this is Michael Williams, a friend of Aline Kranick."

"Hello, Michael. Is that Aline with you?"

"Yes, sir."

"Please stay here until we return." They left him and entered Cora's house.

Michael let out a loud sigh of futility. *All I want is to take Aline home. How much longer is this night going to drag on?*

When the officers finally exited the house, they went promptly to confront Michael.

Giles grabbed the wet sill of Michael's window and leaned against it with outstretched arms. "Michael, I've contacted Detective Lewis. He will be here in five minutes. He wants you to wait for him."

Michael was too angry to acknowledge Giles' commentary.

"Did you hear me, Michael?"

"Yes, yes."

"I regret this as much as you do." He and Brice returned to the police car and sat in the front seat, talking and making phone calls on Giles' cell phone.

Within ten minutes, the rescue unit arrived and parked across the street, heading in the opposite direction of the other vehicles.

Lewis arrived around seven- thirty and the street was bathed with intense light. Some of the neighbors began peering out of their second-story windows behind drawn curtains. They had never seen so much activity on their street before.

As soon as Lewis's car was parked, Brice and Giles joined him. They waited while Lewis introduced himself to Michael. Then the three of them went inside the house again.

Michael rested his head on the back of the car seat and shut his eyes. He would have to sweat it out. He would also have to act as a spokesperson for Aline. He assumed she was asleep because she refused to answer him when he spoke to her. He was getting zero backup.

He knew he loved this woman, but he didn't feel as though he could help her. She was almost beyond assistance at this point. Even Marjorie couldn't pull him through this one, but Terri was turning into his life line. He needed her more than ever. He wanted to talk to her, but didn't want to wake up Aline. He would call her when he was home, after he put Aline to bed.

He could feel the stamina draining out of his body. Thank God he didn't have to work tomorrow. He sat listening to the rain, wishing the two of them could float away on one of the leaves that passed by on the streams of rainwater sweeping down the flooded street.

54.

"CAREFUL OF THESE STAIRS! There isn't much light down here," Brice warned, leading Lewis and Giles down the narrow staircase into the basement. As they reached the bottom step, the musty odor of damp earth and dried-out wood penetrated their nostrils. "She's all the way in the rear of the building."

Lewis and Brice stepped aside to let Giles approach the area ahead of them. They expected the rescue unit to go down first. Giles stood watching the technicians close up their cases. They finished their work and were preparing to leave. One by one, they stood up, turning to face Giles. Their expressions were dispirited.

"Strangulation—asphyxiation by the bathrobe belt," one of them stated. "Devecchio can approximate how long she's been dead. I'll leave my report on your desk tonight before I go home."

"I'd appreciate that."

After they left, Giles remained at the entrance of the room, surveying its dimensions. Approximately eight by ten feet and lined with shelving on the two sides adjacent to the doorway. Canned vegetables, glass mason jars filled with fruit and tomatoes, Christmas tins, and laundry detergent were neatly organized.

The room was constructed of scrap lumber. None of the boards matched in length or color. A roughly-hewn door with a padlock was clumsily hinged at the entrance.

It was open at an angle, hardly the product of a handyman. In the far left corner of the room stood a small, two-drawer file cabinet covered with scratches and dust. On the right-hand wall was an undersized desk with one drawer and an oil lamp, its chimney coated with soot. A chrome tubular chair with red plastic upholstery accompanied the desk. The corners of the seat were split, revealing the foam rubber stuffing.

The step ladder helped her to raise herself up high enough to reach the heavy cast-iron pipes running across the ceiling. She wore an old colorless dress and no shoes.

The sight of Cora Prentis hanging from the ceiling was demoralizing for everyone. Giles busied himself with putting on a pair of latex gloves in order to momentarily divert his attention away from her.

He said, "John, can you get me more light in here? See if you can find a one-hundred-watt bulb to replace this sixty hanging from the ceiling. Let me have your flashlight."

Giles approached the back wall, carefully avoiding the dangling feet. Brice handed him a large flashlight and he began to train it over rows of faded snapshots neatly tacked onto the wall in some kind of sequence. The first shots were very light, almost bleached out with age. As they progressed from left to right, they were easier to make out. Most of them portrayed the figure of a large man, but his facial features were hard to distinguish. Many of the photographs were composed of a couple, standing together with their arms wrapped around each others' waists.

Giles bent over to look at the pictures in the bottom row. These seemed to be more recent—they were much more clear. There was no mistake, the woman in the photographs was Cora Prentis. But who was the man? And who took the pictures of them together?

There were dozens of pictures here to examine and the more he looked, the more he was surprised. One photo in particular caught his attention. Cora and her male companion were posing in front of an old house. Giles recognized it as the McLean house. As his light ran along the rows of pictures, he noticed the same house in many of the shots. Giles observed, "They must have spent a considerable amount of their time together out there on the point. It probably gave them the privacy that their relationship demanded."

Lewis and Brice stood quietly in the background watching Giles pore over the photos. Brice decided not to make any comments in the presence of the older, more experienced men. Then Lewis moved up, next to Giles.

Lewis remarked, "My, my! This new development is rather intriguing."

Giles didn't appreciate the remark. And his expression indicated he was not in the mood to make light of the situation.

Giles ordered, "Let's get Devecchio and our technical people in here right away. I need to have this body taken care of as soon as they finish. Brice, get on with it."

Brice responded by immediately exiting the room. Lewis didn't move, a bit perturbed that Giles wasn't ready to speculate with him about the situation. Before they left, Giles went over to the small desk. He slowly pulled the drawer handle toward him. Inside was a maroon-colored scrapbook, its edges worn with handling. He deftly lifted it out of the drawer and placed it on top of the desk. Lewis stepped up to peer over his shoulder at the contents.

"Do you have another flashlight?" Giles asked without looking up.

"I do in my car."

"Get it."

Lewis disappeared into the cellar. While he was gone, Giles used a credit card to turn a few of the brittle pages of the scrapbook. "Holy shit."

The pages of the scrapbook were filled with articles about Thomas J. Elcock, his showings, his Maine upbringing, his art and his career. Most of the articles were over twenty years old. They had been published in local papers only. The condition of the newsprint was very fragile, but the newspaper dates were easily distinguishable. Giles gently closed the cover and stood there, staring down at the book. The reappearance of Lewis redirected his thought.

Lewis stuck out his hand. "Here's the beam."

"This scrapbook is full of articles about Tom Elcock. Unless I miss my guess, he must be the mystery man in the photos."

Lewis showed no reaction. "We'll have to bag all this stuff. You and I can go over it later. We better look at the file cabinet."

Lewis also put on a pair of latex gloves. He gingerly opened the file cabinet drawer. It was rusty and hard to open, but he finally got a hold of it. Inside, there was an array of yellowed manila folders. Most of them held receipts for appliances and stubs from paid bills. The last folder in the back of the drawer held packets of letters, wrapped in tissue paper. Lewis didn't unwrap them. He didn't have to because he could read the handwriting on the envelopes through the transparent paper. There were no return addresses.

"I'll bet these have some connection," Lewis said. "Should make for some interesting reading."

"Anything else in there?" Giles's arms were folded across his chest.

"Other than the letters, most of this paper looks like household business. Let me check the bottom drawer." Lewis closed the top drawer and opened the lower one. Inside was a large folder. It was taped shut. "I don't want to tamper with anything until it is photographed. The contents of this will have to wait."

"Let's get out of here," Giles replied. " Michael and Aline are still up there waiting for us. We've been down here for forty minutes."

As they ascended the stairs, the evidence experts were just arriving. Giles went upstairs and out to their van. "I want everything bagged and brought downtown as soon as you finish here. I'll be in my office until very late."

Lewis left for the police station, but Brice remained at the house with the evidence team.

Giles walked up to Michael's car. The window was still down. "I know it's getting late, but I want to talk to you both before you go home. I'll try to keep it as brief as possible. Why don't you follow me."

He drove away at a slow pace. Michael turned on his headlights, following him, not making any effort to move Aline.

55.

AROUND EIGHT-THIRTY, all the vehicles pulled up in front of the police station simultaneously. Lewis was the first to go inside, ahead of everybody else. Giles remained outside, holding the front door open for Aline. He noticed how detached and vacant she appeared. Her hair was mussed and she looked wasted. The young woman was aging before his eyes.

After entering the building, Giles turned to Michael. "Michael, I'll talk to you first. After this meeting, I think you better take her home. Is she relating to you at all?"

"No. I had a hell of a time getting her out of the car. She won't answer me."

"Bring her into my office. One of the officers will bring her something to drink and keep an eye on her."

Giles joined Lewis in the interrogation room. When Michael entered and sat down, Giles gave him a minute to catch his breath.

"Black coffee?"

"No thank you." It remained there untouched.

"You look like all of this is taking its toll on you as well."

"It's wearing me out."

"You told Officer Brice you're Aline's boyfriend."

"You might call me that," Michael answered sarcastically.

"How long have you known Aline?"

"I met her the second Saturday in October at *Harborview.*"

"Is she living with you now?"

"Yes."

"Why did she leave Mitchell Street?"

"She told me that she didn't feel welcome there any more."

"Why?"

"She and Mrs. Prentis more or less had a falling out. Aline noticed a strong change of attitude toward her."

"Can you explain what you mean?"

"I think Aline can explain it better than I can."

"What were you two doing at the Prentis house tonight?"

"Aline wanted to say good-bye and drop off her house key."

"Didn't she say good-bye when she left?"

"Not really. She left in a hurry."

"Do you think Aline said anything to upset Cora Prentis?"

"No way. Aline respected her."

"I mean unintentionally."

"I don't know."

"Old people get rattled very easily. Maybe Aline did something to disturb the old lady."

"That's ridiculous."

"Well, when I question her, maybe she can be more specific."

"Why don't you get off her back." Michael snarled, not quite under his breath.

"Take it easy, Michael, I'm just doing my job."

"I'm sorry. I love her and I don't want to see her get hurt anymore. Since her arrival here, she's already had enough emotional pain to last her a lifetime!"

"I can appreciate your feelings, Michael, believe me. I want to resolve this just as much as you do."

"You know she's innocent."

"I'm assuming that. But, we're dealing with two deaths within a week in Cape Warren and every time I arrive at the death scene, I find your girlfriend. She is a first-hand witness to what I have to investigate. Put yourself in my position for a moment. There really is no one else to question at this point, is there? Do you understand?"

Michael sat scowling at the top of the table. He knew Giles was going by the book. He just didn't want to condone it.

He answered, "You have to make her believe you don't suspect her, because she thinks you do, and it is torturing her. Do *you* understand?"

Giles admired Michael's fire. The young man was Aline's lover as well as her fierce guardian. He thought to himself, *I wouldn't want you to react to me in any other way.*

56.

ON THE WAY HOME, Michael and Aline exchanged looks only once. It was still raining and the rhythmic sound of the windshield wipers was almost therapeutic, breaking the tension inside the car.

After questioning Michael, Giles agreed to the completion of the questioning on Monday morning. He and Michael both realized Aline would probably be more receptive then, anyway.

She sat with her head leaning against the window, eyes closed, her face turned away from him. Her hands lay lifeless in her lap. He wanted to get her home as quickly as possible, hoping she would snap out of it.

At last, they were at the entrance to his driveway. He parked the car close to the house and went over to the passenger's side to open the door. When he opened it she almost fell out. He caught her in his arms and lifted her to her feet.

"We're home, Aline and I'm too tired to argue with you."

She leaned on him heavily as he guided her up the stairs and into the kitchen. Instantly, she headed into his bedroom and he followed. He wanted to remove her jacket and shoes before she got into bed. Without resisting, she let him assist her and then fell onto the bed, burying her face in the pillows. He covered her with a blanket and bent down to kiss her. Gently closing the door behind him, he left her to her grief. There was nothing he could do. He had to see Terri.

Terri usually worked Saturday nights, so he called the diner first. The manager answered and informed Michael that he would have Terri call him during her break. They were extremely busy at the moment and she couldn't come to the phone.

"When does she go on break?"

"Ten. What's your number?"

"Please tell her it is important."

He gave the man his number and hung up. He went into the kitchen to get himself a glass of water. If Terri could meet him, he could lock up the house and leave Aline alone, to sleep. When she was upset, that's all she wanted to do. Besides, trying to communicate with her now was out of the question. Past experience made this very clear. In any case, she would be safe here if he left for a short period of time.

He put the cordless phone on the coffee table in front of him, dimmed the lights, and stretched out on the couch, waiting for Terri to call back. It was nine forty-five. Even though he was concentrating on the phone, it still startled him when it rang.

"Michael?"

"Hi! Am I glad to hear your voice!"

"Is anything wrong?"

"Everything is wrong. Cora Prentis is dead. She hung herself. Aline and I found her over four hours ago. I just put Aline to bed."

"Oh, my God! This is horrible!" Terri exclaimed.

"I have to see you, Terri."

"I punch out at eleven. If it gets slow later, I'll try to leave early. Do you want to come down here?"

"No, I have to have some quiet in order to think. Why don't you meet me for a drink after you leave the diner."

"Where?"

"Your call."

"There's a bar and grill outside of town. I've only been in there once or twice, but it's never crowded. The place always looks empty, even on Saturday nights. A few locals hang out there, but I don't think Cape Warren would consider it a first choice."

"Give me directions. I'll find it."

"I'll call you to let you know when I'm leaving."

"O.K."

"I'm afraid to ask about Aline."

"Here we go again. She's already asleep. Not talking."

"The poor girl needs help, the kind of help we can't give her."

"I'm getting fed up with her, to tell you the truth. I don't think I've ever been this burned out."

"I have to go."

He hung up and lay back down on the couch. Maybe he should try to get some sleep himself. He thought about calling his aunt but he didn't want to frighten her. Because of his involvement, she might take this latest development as threatening to his welfare. He would meet with Terri first and then decide how to tell Marjorie.

He turned on the TV and lowered the sound. After skipping around the channels, he found an old Joan Crawford movie. The big hair and broad shoulder pads fascinated him. He was impressed by Joan's sense of style and aggressiveness. She had great eyebrows.

In half an hour, the phone rang again.

It was Terri. "Michael, I'm leaving now. I'll give you directions."

He went down the hall to wash his face. He looked at himself in the bathroom mirror. A stranger looked back at him. Lack of sleep left the predictable black circles under eyes. His muscles felt stiff and his whole body seemed to be depleted of its endurance.

Before leaving, he checked in on Aline. She was in the same position. For a few minutes he stood there watching her sleep. How was he going to bridge the gap? His heart was breaking.

Returning to the living room, he turned up the lights. From outside it would look as if he were home. The floods were on timers, as well as the house lights, so if he returned late, the lights would shut off at the usual programmed hours, status quo.

As silently as possible, he locked the back door and slipped down the back stairs to his car. It wouldn't be necessary to put on his headlights until he was halfway down the road. The illuminated grounds provided more than enough light to aid him in the exit.

He didn't want to leave, but he had to talk to someone. Terri was a pragmatist. He knew he could depend on her.

Totally preoccupied, he barely saw the car fly by the end of his driveway. He slammed on his brakes. *I have to be more careful. My personal problems are starting to take possession of my mind.*

57.

WHEN MICHAEL ENTERED the *Coast Bar & Grill*, he found Terri sitting at the bar facing the front door. Just as she predicted, it was void of patrons and very secluded. Two other customers sat in back near the jukebox. They were talking to the bartender, who was drying glasses.

The wooden paneling was plastered with neon beer promotions. Large TVs, hanging from the ceiling on both sides of the bar, were tuned into a cable sports network, but no one was watching. The atmosphere reeked of lager beer and stale cigarette smoke.

Michael went up to Terri and planted a kiss on her right cheek.

"Does this place meet with your approval?" she asked.

He'd seen much worse in the city. "Sure, it'll do," he assured her.

"Do you want to sit in a booth?"

"No, let's just sit at the far end of the room. We'll have some privacy there."

The bartender approached them to take their order. As soon as he left, Michael and Terri made their move. They deposited their coats on the empty stools next to them and chose a seat.

"Michael, what the hell is going on?" Terri's expression was pleading with him for an answer.

He waited before responding to her question. "I don't know and I don't think I want to know. Aline has stumbled into the middle of something and she can't handle it."

"What do *you* think, Michael—was Elcock's death accidental?"

He was pensive. "I want to believe it was. There has to be a simple solution to all these incidents. Unfortunately, Aline now thinks he was murdered. At least that's what the police are leading her to believe."

"What do you really think happened out there? I'm very impatient to learn the truth."

"I'm having difficulty buying the concept of foul play. Terri, you know Cape Warren doesn't offer the backdrop for such a cruel act."

"The paper was ho-hum. Nothing out of the ordinary." She sounded dumbfounded.

"Well, we didn't see the police report. It may be shrouding some facts indicating a different story."

"I think the police are withholding information from you, Michael."

"No. They have to finish their investigation before they can make a clear statement. Without sufficient evidence, anything they say is purely conjecture. Giles and Lewis are not going to put themselves on the spot. They're too experienced."

"I thought you liked those two cops."

"I do," Michael replied. "They impressed me with their professionalism. The investigation is in good hands." He sounded very sure of himself.

Terri persisted. "And what about Cora Prentis? How does she fit into this tragedy?"

"I can't answer your question. I haven't been involved until recently. I never even met the woman. Aline didn't want me to confront her. Nosy lady."

"You're right, Michael, she and Aline seemed to be getting along well at first. Then something happened and she started to close Aline out."

While he listened to her, he started peeling the label off his beer bottle. "That's what Aline said. Can you pinpoint when this occurred?"

Terri continued, "Two weeks ago, when they shared dinner together. Aline told me Cora turned cold and unresponsive by the time the meal was over. It's too bad. They both were looking forward to spending some time together. Aline couldn't figure out why the evening went sour."

"Terri, she told me the same story on the way to Augusta. I assumed she said something offensive to Cora. Aline can be very outspoken."

"Outspoken and headstrong! I bet it gets her in trouble more than occasionally."

"Any idea about the content of their dinner conversation?"

Terri thought for a moment, "They told each other about their backgrounds and Aline described her assignment to Cora. I guess her landlady was curious as to the reason why Aline arrived in Maine."

He couldn't believe his ears. "Are you telling me that Cora Prentis didn't find out about the Elcock interviews until the second week of living with Aline?"

"That's right."

He shook his head. "I find it hard to believe, almost sounds like they were consciously avoiding each other from the beginning."

Terri gathered the shredded label, rolling it into a ball. "Doesn't it, though? The two of them were the proverbial ships passing in the night. Cora was rarely ever home or simply not around when Aline was in the house. I do know the woman did volunteer work and had a part-time job, but this still doesn't explain the constant no-show."

Michael surmised, “A woman rents out part of her house to a perfect stranger and then never shows her face. If she was such a private person, why did she let anyone into her house at all? It’s unnatural.”

“Well, I’ll take it one step further. I think it’s just plain weird.”

He was still sitting sideways on his barstool, looking directly at her. “Did you know anything about this woman? I’ve never even heard anyone in this town mention her name.”

“Neither have I,” Terri said. “The older residents may know about her, but most of the people who recently settled here are from out-of-town. Her name wouldn’t be a household word.”

Michael didn’t try to hide the bitterness in his voice. “Around here, everybody pretends like they know nothin’ about nothin’. They put on a good act.”

“Maybe the woman was in a deep depression for a long time and her death is just a coincidence.”

“There has to be a simple explanation,” Michael said, trying to convince himself.

“But there’s one thing that I can’t erase from the back of my mind.”

“What’s that Terri?” he asked as he turned back to the bar.

“Aline told Cora about Elcock’s death on Tuesday. The paper printed the article about him on Friday. And Cora was found dead the next day.”

“God. Do you think there’s a connection?” Now suspicion was replacing his bitterness.

“I’m afraid to think anything, Michael. All I do know is I’m just as concerned about Aline’s mental attitude as you are. What can we do?”

“We have to convince her to drop her involvement with Elcock and Prentis. As soon as the police are convinced of her innocence and release her, I have to convince her to leave Cape Warren for a while.”

Terri already knew the answer to her next question but she asked it anyway. "Will she go back to New York?"

"I doubt it. I don't think the magazine will hold her position open after Monday. She was given an ultimatum to return by then. It just isn't going to happen."

Just as she thought, he was on the same page. "And then what? If she doesn't go back to New York, what's going to become of her?"

"She has to drop this and move on. I can't tolerate much more of it, myself."

"Michael, you know that you can't make her do anything. She's too determined and independent."

With the bottom of the bottle he beat his words out on the table with soft thuds for emphasis and finality. "If she is going to stay with me, she will have to follow my lead."

"Or?" Terri asked, also knowing the answer to this question.

"Or, we split up. I can't stand by and watch her gradually destroy herself. I won't do it. She means too much to me."

"Do you know what you're saying? You're her lover—she needs you."

"I know, Terri, but if I can't help her, she has to find someone who can. Someone professional."

She started to play with her cocktail napkin. She felt troubled dealing with the truth. He was at a dead end.

The two of them fell into silence, avoiding each other's eyes. Meanwhile, the bartender came over to them and was leaning on the edge of the bar, trying to drum up more business.

"Another round?"

"I should go, Michael."

"Please don't." He gave the bartender a sign for more drinks.

She didn't reply, just looked at her watch. Aline could take care of herself, but Terri wanted to sound concerned. "Aren't you worried about leaving her alone?"

"No, she'll be all right. Sleep is the best thing for her. I guarantee she won't move until morning."

"You seem very nonchalant about this." She wanted him to know she disapproved of his presumptuousness. .

"I know what I'm doing."

The bartender set two cold beers in front of them and re-joined his friends on the other side of the bar.

Terri stood up and put her coat on. She leaned against the bar, turning to look at Michael. "So what happens next?"

"Aline and I are expected to show up at the station Monday morning for questioning. The bank owes me some time off. I've been putting in a lot of Saturdays."

"I could never take off more than one day at the diner. What do you think Aline's going to do now? You're living with her. You must have a clue."

"Sorry, Terri. Coexistence doesn't give me the edge. I think that as soon as she can recover enough to get back on track, she'll start hunting down the facts. She's looking for Hank Swenson. Evidently, he's left town."

"Why does she want to find him?"

"He's Elcock's best friend and he probably can shed some light onto Elcock's private history, especially in regard to Louise Elcock."

"It sounds like he's ducking any confrontation regarding Elcock."

"I know. It's so obvious. Aline told me he never leaves his loft—ever. And now, as soon as Elcock dies, he splits. No note on the front door. All the windows covered. Naturally, he is the one person who knows the most about Elcock. And he also knows the police will want to question him."

"But why would he leave town? The newspaper article didn't hint of anything out of the ordinary. It was treated as a routine death. And how do we know if he even saw the paper? He's a bit of a recluse himself, isn't he?"

"Yes, but he gets his mail and he probably gets the paper delivered. My guess is he saw the headline, took a drive over to Elcock's place and saw the yellow tape."

"Why would he go to Elcock's house?"

"Maybe he wanted to see if the house was secure. He and Elcock looked out for each other."

"And the minute he saw the police tape he knew there was an investigation under way."

"You got it. Terri, can you think of anyone else in the cast of characters surrounding Elcock, who might be considered a suspect besides Aline?"

"No. How many friends did Elcock have, anyway?"

"He had a few acquaintances, but he had only one friend. . . Hank Swenson."

58.

FOR MICHAEL, Sunday and Monday were going to be difficult days to get through. He didn't dread the questioning by the police as much as he did filling the space spent with Aline. She was silent and withdrawn and spent most of the time in his bedroom with the door closed.

He should probably treat Sunday like any other Sunday, reading the paper, preparing breakfast and watching TV. He would be sure to knock on the bedroom door to remind Aline to partake of the food prepared for them, but he didn't push it. He was, however, starting to be concerned for his own welfare, just as much as hers. He liked his job and wasn't about to jeopardize it by surrendering himself to her one-track fixation.

He could wait for her to return to him on some level, but he had maxed out on his sympathy level and dedication to her struggle. He knew she would have to face the facts, sooner or later. If she wasn't willing to let go of her involvement when he requested it, then there was no point in continuing on with her.

He felt relieved making a clear decision as to his position. For him there was no ambiguity or uncertainty. He could move out of it as easily as he had moved in. He would not let himself become another victim of circumstance.

After brunch, he gathered the papers together and put them in a neat pile on the coffee table in case Aline wanted to read them later. He washed his dishes, cleaned up the kitchen, and sat in the living room, thinking it out. Television didn't interest him. He had too much to mull over and couldn't really concentrate on the programming. The options were to go to the mall and look for a new fall raincoat, call one of his buddies to take in a movie, or wash his car. He could get in touch with Terri, but decided to leave her in peace.

He decided on the mall. After shopping, he could still go to a movie and later stop to eat. Before leaving, he wrote a long note to Aline, explaining his itinerary. He listed the stores and the name of his favorite café. He suggested she join him there later. He left a plate of food for her in the refrigerator, wrapped in plastic wrap, ready to put into the microwave. He also told her he was going to the seven o'clock show and told her where he'd be sitting. The note was anchored onto the dining table by a salt shaker.

He then went down the hall to his bedroom and opened the door without making a sound. As quietly as he could he took some changes of underwear, shirts, ties, a few suits, and a few sweaters from the room. If he was to be sleeping on the sofa, he needed a change of clothes, especially for the upcoming week. She never knew he was in the room. After collecting all the necessary items, he returned to the living room. The front hall closet would have to do for his clothes. He left the coffee pot turned on, knowing she would look for coffee when she woke up.

He had been as considerate as he felt he should be and he felt good about how he was handling himself. He was giving her all the space she wanted and going on with his own life.

Driving to the mall, he knew in his heart she would not come to join him there. In a way, he didn't want her to come. He needed his space too. He intended to ground himself against the events that were determined to derail him. He was doing exactly what he should be doing. He was living his life in spite of it.

59.

MONDAY MORNING, THE LAST WEEK OF OCTOBER. At exactly ten o'clock, Aline and Michael entered the Cape Warren police headquarters. The officer at the front desk escorted them to the interrogation room.

Giles and Lewis were waiting for them. On the desk, in front of Giles, was a yellow legal pad covered with his outlined study. Lewis was pushed back in his seat, arms folded on his chest. Neither of the detectives stood up as the couple entered their domain.

"Good morning," Giles said. "I'd like to talk to you first, Michael. Aline, would you mind waiting outside for a few minutes?"

Without saying a word, she left the room. An officer standing outside in the hall led her to a bench near the front door.

Giles clasped his hands together on top of the desk, as he addressed Michael. "She looks terrible."

"I know. I'm at my wit's end."

"Has she opened up to you at all?"

"No. She isn't talking to me. I spent yesterday by myself in the mall. I cook for her, but she doesn't eat. All she wants to do is sleep. Pure escape. I'm living on my sofa."

Giles let out a deep sigh. "This is going to be like pulling teeth. You must be going through hell. I don't envy you." They were talking man to man.

"Is this ever going to end? At some point, for me, personally, it has to."

"We have a long way to go," Giles replied.

"I'll stay with you as long as I can, Detective Giles, but I'm getting pretty sick of the whole business."

"I can appreciate how you feel, Michael. You have become an unwilling bystander."

"Not for much longer."

"What are your plans?"

"I'll stay with her until you release her from being a suspect. And then, if she doesn't move on, she'll have to find another place to live. It's real simple."

"I'm sorry you had to get involved. I don't have a lot of questions for you. This investigation primarily concerns Aline."

"Let's get on with it. I took this morning off from work. The bank will be understanding to a point."

Detective Giles fired back the first question. "Did you know Cora Prentis on a social level?"

"No. Aline never introduced her to me."

"So Saturday night, when you found her body, was it the first time you actually came into contact with her?"

"Yes, we went over there to drop off the house key. Aline forgot to leave it with Cora when she checked out. When Aline left Cora's house, she was very distraught and wanted to see me as soon as possible. Returning the key was the last thing on her mind."

"Did Aline ever mention to you anything regarding Cora's reaction to her assignment?"

"Yes. She felt a sudden reversal in her landlady's demeanor toward her. I guess this occurred during the evening they had dinner together. Aline was describing her interviews with Mr. Elcock and Cora turned to ice right before her eyes."

"And when did this occur?"

"Around two weeks ago. I think it was a Wednesday night."

"Do you have anything else to add to the information you've already told me?"

"No."

"Now I want to talk to Aline and after I question her, I would like you to join us. Detective Lewis and I want you both to hear our conclusion after examining the evidence. I may need you, Michael, to give her as much emotional support as possible. She may refuse to accept our decision."

"Is she a suspect?"

"We will discuss this with you both, shortly."

"Can't you tell me now?"

Giles rose from his chair. "I'll see you in a few minutes. When you go out, will you please send in Aline?"

Michael left disgruntled. He felt as if he was being played with. All the melodrama. *Can't Giles be frank with me?* He had had enough. He dropped down hard on the bench next to Aline and snapped, "It's your turn."

60.

As Aline walked past Michael on her way to the interrogation room, her movements were rigid and mechanical. Giles left the door open for her, anticipating her. She strolled into the room and sank heavily into the chair designated for her.

Giles returned to his seat and briefly scanned his notes. Then he tried to make eye contact with her. She was staring straight through him without blinking.

"Aline?"

She did not react.

"Aline, we need to get on with this. As soon as you begin to cooperate, you can go home."

"All right." She said deliberately.

"I need your help."

"May I have a glass of water?"

"Of course. We have coffee and soda if you would prefer either of those."

"Just water, please."

He left the room. While he was gone, she took off her coat and hung it on the back of her chair. Lewis watched her intently, not uttering a word. Giles returned to the room and closed the door. He placed a large glass of water in front of her.

"Thank you."

"I will try to make this as concise as possible, knowing you are under a considerable amount of pressure."

She took a sip of water, mentally preparing herself for the questioning.

"Aline, please try to remember as many details as possible. It's vital to the success of closing this case."

"I understand."

"Were you aware of any intimacy between Thomas Elcock and Cora Prentis?"

"No."

"How can you be sure?"

"They never mentioned each other's names to me."

"Did Mr. Elcock know you were living in Cora Prentis' house?"

"No. He never asked me where I was staying. All he was concerned about was his work and discussing his career with me."

"Did you ever ask him about his personal life?"

"No, his personal life was none of my business. My article was about his art, not some form of sensationalism about his private affairs."

"Did he ever talk about his wife?"

"Yes. He told me she had been very sick with Alzheimer's disease. She died about twenty years ago."

"Did you know she was still alive?"

"Yes, I found out by accident."

"By accident?"

"I went to buy the newspaper at the general store last Friday and the clerk insisted in commenting on Mr. Elcock's death. Obviously, he saw the headline in Friday's paper. He made remarks concerning Louise Elcock."

"What kind of remarks?"

"He said he felt sorry for her and it was rumored she was in a private sanitarium in Connecticut. I didn't like his intonation—or his comments."

"Why?"

"He was a sinister, self-righteous creep. He made me frantic."

“Every town has one. He’s not the most popular man in Cape Warren.”

“I wanted to slap his face.”

“What else did Mr. Elcock discuss with you concerning his wife?”

“He told me when her health was good, they used to spend a substantial amount of time together hiking, sailing, and traveling. Evidently, they were quite close.”

Giles started writing on the legal pad and Aline was challenged by the effort of deciphering the upside-down scribbling. It was a while before he continued the questioning.

“Did Cora Prentis ever show you the back of the house or her basement area?”

“No, the doors leading to those quarters were always closed. I was a boarder, renting a room upstairs. It never even occurred to me to go beyond the confines of my room and the kitchen. I’m not a snoop.”

“I didn’t mean to infer any such thing. This is an investigation, Aline, and it’s my responsibility to find out as much information as I possibly can.”

“Cora didn’t broadcast to me every move she was going to take” Her voice was laced with resentment. “I don’t know what the hell she was up to most of the time.”

“Did you develop a friendship with her?”

“Hardly. We rarely saw each other. She worked two jobs and I was either interviewing Mr. Elcock, writing in my room, or working in the library.”

“How did she behave towards you?”

“Indifferent. At first, she was pleasant enough, but she changed.”

“What do you think caused the change?”

“It seemed to happen as soon as I started to describe to her the details of my project. When I began to talk about Mr. Elcock, she abruptly ended the meal we were sharing.”

Giles was scribbling again. This time he took copious notes, almost filling an entire page before he stopped. He looked up. “I think Michael should join us now. What Detective Lewis and I want to say should be addressed to both of you.” He left the room to find Michael.

Aline closed her eyes and tipped back her head. She was thinking about Louise Elcock. She must find her.

61.

ALINE SAT UP when Michael and Giles entered the room, trying to appear attentive.

As soon as everyone was settled, Giles turned the legal pad face down on the table. He crossed his legs and locked his entwined fingers into a tight ball in his lap. The expression on his face hadn't changed. It was grave but not stern. The empathy he was experiencing for these two young people was reflected in his eyes.

"To begin with, I want to make one thing clear. This department does not consider either of you under the category of prime suspects. We are concentrating on Aline in order to gain some further insight into the cause of these unfortunate circumstances. Since she alone was the sole contact for Thomas Elcock and Cora Prentis, she is our most valuable source of information."

A hint of a smile could be detected on Michael's face. It was a display of contempt, not relief.

"It would appear, from the evidence already collected, that Mr. Elcock and Cora Prentis had been lovers in the past. Their deaths are related in some manner. However, at this point in the investigation, this is still merely an assumption. We still have extensive work to complete before we can make a definitive statement representing our findings."

Michael leaned forward to the edge of the table. "How did Elcock die?"

“I’m not in a position to release any part of the investigative work until the case is finalized.”

Michael lurched back into his chair with enough force to show his displeasure at being denied an answer.

Aline, on the other hand, was tongue-tied, in mild shock caused by the revelation of Giles’s words. She was hearing facts she couldn’t accept.

“As far as you two are concerned, you are free to go. However, please stay in town until further notice. I may want to talk to you at a later date. I want to thank both of you for your cooperation. Stay in touch.”

Giles went over to open the door for them. After they left, he sat down at the table and turned the pad face up.

Suddenly, Michael was standing in front of the desk, frowning at him. “Is this a homicide?”

Giles didn’t answer his question. He already had.

62.

MONDAY. ELEVEN FORTY-FIVE. Michael opened the door on the passenger side of his car for Aline. After he was seated behind the wheel, he turned to her, his hand resting on her headrest. “Do you want to have some lunch?”

“Sure.”

“Any place special?”

“No, it doesn’t matter.”

He drove out of town. There was a luncheonette near his house. He didn’t feel like driving too far. Within fifteen minutes they were there.

The hostess knew him on a first-name basis since he usually ate here on Saturdays.

“Hi, Michael. Booth or counter?”

“That booth near the window will be fine, Ellie.”

They followed the waitress to the booth and took off their coats. Ellie put menus on their placemats and took their order for coffee. Michael didn’t want to start a conversation with Aline until after it was served.

Ellie returned with a coffee pot and a saucer full of small creamers. She filled their cups and stepped back from the table. “I’ll be back in a minute.”

Michael settled himself in the booth, nestling into the corner where the seat met the wall. He put his left arm on the windowsill and his right arm on top of the thick cushion covering the back of the seat. “So, can you tell me about your plans now, Aline?" His voice was flat and devoid of feeling.

"My work isn't finished yet."

"I was afraid you were going to say those words. Can you give me some details?"

"I shouldn't have to explain it to you. I'm sure you know what my next move is going to be."

"You're going to track down Louise Elcock and Hank Swenson."

"I don't need to find both of them. One will suffice."

"Is this simply to confirm her existence?"

"That's part of it."

"Part of it? You mean to tell me there's more!" The edginess was creeping back into his voice.

Ellie interrupted them by suddenly appearing at the table with her pen and pad. "And what would we like for lunch today?" Her pleasant smile was almost clown-like in comparison to the mood hanging in the air over the table.

"I'll have tuna salad on wheat toast, Ellie. No chips."

"Make that two."

"Would you like coleslaw?"

"Yes, thank you."

"And you, dear?" she asked Aline.

"None for me."

After Ellie left, Michael sat staring out the window. He was stalling, not anxious to tell her how he saw things. The promise he made to himself must be met. It could wait another half hour. They ate the meal without speaking. Everything they shared together was breaking down, including the intrigue. He was an innocent victim himself, a simple bystander, being pulled unwillingly into a churning whirlpool. He was drowning.

When they finished eating, Ellie came to clear the dishes off the table. "Can I get you anything else?"

"I'd like another cup of coffee, Ellie."

"And you, dear?"

"No thank you," Aline replied.

The waitress returned, filled Michael's cup and departed, leaving the bill upside down on the edge of the table.

He stirred his coffee, waiting for his opening.

"You're awfully quiet, Michael. I'd love to know what you're thinking right now. You must have drawn some conclusions regarding this 'case.' Can't you share them with me?"

She gave him his cue. This time she was on her own. He wouldn't be able to pull her through this one.

"Look, Aline, it's like this. I'm in closure. It's finished for me, but just beginning for you. The next chapter of this journey, on which you are about to embark, will have to be explored without me. I can not be there to help you resolve it."

"Are you telling me it is over between us?"

"It is over only if you refuse to let go of this mess. Let the police solve it. They do it for a living."

"Don't patronize me."

"Aline, I love you! I want you. But I can't watch this case tear you to shreds. You are too vulnerable at this point. You have been through too much suffering. You owe it to yourself to focus on your health and mental stability. You are no longer a suspect."

"Are you making insinuations concerning my lack of stability?"

"Of course not. The death of this great man has shaken you to your roots. You still haven't recovered. Get away from it for a while or it will consume you."

"I guess you have no idea what I'm going through. If you really loved me, you would understand."

"We're on different pages, Aline. The trouble with me is I care about you too much. And now it's hurting me, too."

"I just can't back away from all of it, Michael. It's part of me now."

He didn't say anything for a long time. "Are you going back to New York? You had a deadline today, remember?"

"I remember. You know damn well I can't go back. Not yet."

"Are you going to call Marty?"

"No."

"Don't you think you owe it to him?"

"I owe nothing to that condescending bastard."

"Aline, what's happening to you?"

"Whatever is happening to me is of little interest to you, it would seem. As soon as I find a motel room, I'll be out of your house."

"I don't want it to end like this."

"There's no point to it anymore. Let's go, I have things to do."

He felt sick to his stomach. Terri was right on target. He repeated her words in his mind: *You know you can't make her do anything. She's too determined and independent.*

Aline's voice interrupted his musing "I'd like some space this afternoon, if you don't mind. I have to pack and find a place to live."

"I'll drop you off and spend the afternoon at the bank. Can we have dinner together later?"

"I'll see."

He parked the car in his backyard, but didn't turn off the ignition. As he turned to face her, she jumped out and ran up the back stairs. No wave, no looking back, no nothing.

63.

MONDAY AFTERNOON. Detective Lewis sat in his office reading reports. Walter Giles was on his way. They planned to meet right after lunch, to compare ideas and study the available evidence. He was impatient to move ahead in the investigation. As always, he was in a hurry to wrap up the case.

A few taps on his open door confirmed the presence of Giles, expecting to be invited in.

"Walter, come in. Please close the door."

Giles planted himself in the large wooden chair placed in front of Lewis's desk. "God, Matt, I hate this chair!"

"Sorry, Walter, why don't you sit in the leather armchair in the corner."

Giles went over to the plush maroon wingback and pulled it closer to Lewis's desk. "This is more like it."

Lewis didn't waste any time. "Kranick hasn't been much help, has she?"

"No, Matt, she hasn't. But at least she's talking. Unfortunately, she doesn't know anything. A real babe in the woods."

"I wasn't expecting anything else. Let's start off with some of the hard facts surrounding this investigation." Lewis always cut to the chase.

"O.K. Elcock died due to a forceful action beyond his control. The blow to the head, when he impacted the floor, crushed part of his skull. His heart was fine and he didn't have a stroke. The coroner's report confirms this. In other words, he was in good health for his age."

"What about the estimated time of death?"

Giles continued. "It was only sixty four degrees in the room where we examined him, so that particular variable is important to take into consideration. However, the coroner's report indicates that Elcock's corneas were slightly milky and he was still in rigor. It looks like he had been dead at least twenty four hours when she found him. He probably died Sunday evening."

"Any trace of liquor consumption or medication in his blood?"

"None. His blood was clean. There were no pills in the medicine cabinet or in the sleeping area."

Lewis looked skeptical. "Not even aspirin?"

"No. Just shaving gear, shampoo, a hairbrush, and deodorant."

Lewis smiled. "He must have been a tough old bird."

"Not tough enough," Giles stated, tapping his pen on the stack of papers on his lap. "The point of contact, where he hit the ground, is on the right side of his head, not the back. He fell forward."

Lewis was absorbing Giles's every word. His eyes turned into two slits, as he began to put his thoughts into words. "It looks to me like someone gained access to the studio, without Elcock's knowledge, while he was working. That individual started to smash apart the supports with the blunt end of the ax head found at the scene. Elcock must have turned around to confront his assailant and clung desperately to the structure with all his might while it was being destroyed. His back was to the painting. He was looking down at his attacker when he fell."

Giles had stopped the tapping and turned quiet and sympathetic. "The poor soul. There was nothing he could do to save himself."

Lewis charged ahead. "Also, the splinters embedded in the palms of his hands, indicated he was holding onto the railing in front of him for dear life."

Giles was visualizing the scene as Lewis spoke. "Would it take a lot of strength to smash apart that wood?" he asked.

"I don't think so. It was heavy, but it was very dry. Brittle. The ax head was heavy. A full swing, building up the momentum of the blow, would have been enough to do the damage."

"Could a woman be capable of such an act?" Giles believed the force of the blow would not be affected by whether the perpetrator was male or female, but he wanted his associate's opinion.

"Yes, I think so. Remember Lizzie Borden? Why, are you looking at Aline as a possible suspect?"

Giles rested his chin between his left thumb and fore-finger. His left elbow rested on the arm of his chair. "No, I don't think so, especially when you observe her behavior. She worshipped the man. His death devastated her. However, we have to look at all the possibilities."

"Maybe so. You certainly know her better than I do. I trust your gut reactions. . . . You're usually right. The problem is, I don't think she's a very good actress." Be-ing compassionate wasn't part of Lewis's makeup.

Giles disagreed. "I think I'm right on this one. Be-sides, I have her prints on a coffee cup she left in the interrogation room. It's in the lab as we speak. I'll know very shortly if those prints are a match to those found on the ax handle."

"Good work, Giles. Who's left to consider?"

"There's Hank Swenson. He left town immediately after he found out Elcock was dead. Not very smart of him. We'll catch up to him eventually. Anyway, I count him out. He and Elcock were best friends, like blood brothers. They protected each other's interests with a vengeance."

"Speaking of vengeance, what have we got for a motive?" Lewis wasn't as familiar with all the players as Giles was. He depended on Giles to fill him in.

Giles answered without hesitation. "I don't think it was robbery. He was in the back, engrossed in his painting. Anyone breaking and entering could have cleaned out the front of the house. If the perpetrator used caution, the old man probably wouldn't have heard his place being ransacked."

Lewis was still evaluating the players. "Did he know a lot of people in this town?"

"He had a few close friends, but his acquaintances did not add up to much of a list. He stayed mostly to himself. Aline's ability to become confidential with him really surprises me."

Lewis slouched down in his seat. "Walter, I think you and I are going to draw the same conclusion." His posture was one of resignation.

Giles didn't hesitate. "I keep going back to one person. The only one I can think of who was deeply involved with him and who was closer to him than anyone else we've already mentioned . . . Cora Prentis."

Lewis suddenly moved forward. "I was wondering when you were going to mention her!"

Giles was on a roll. "She could have gone to his house in a rage and attacked him while he worked. Something could have triggered her anger."

"Do you think they were still seeing each other?"

Lewis's question evoked a chuckle from Giles. He shook his head in an exaggerated negative gesture. "No way . . . it was old. They were pretty cagey about their affair, but the town gossip eventually drove them apart."

"A lot of people have affairs. And if theirs was ancient history, why would Cora suddenly turn into a murderer?" Lewis liked to add doubt into a conjecture, covering all the angles.

"Aline started talking about Elcock the night she and Cora dined together. Maybe she re-kindled the fire from the ashes."

Lewis added, "If Cora was upset that he never married her, she may have wanted to punish him when he became a celebrity without her being by his side."

"I see your point. It could have been resentment," Giles agreed. "He was becoming very well known, what with his New York show and being featured in a major cosmopolitan magazine. Could be she felt left out, cast aside."

"So," Lewis concluded, "she took his life and then, out of pure remorse, she took her own, unable to go on without him."

Giles interlaced his hands on top of his head and looked directly at Lewis. "It's only one theory. And right now, it's the best one we have."

"Walter, what about the old newspaper articles in the envelope we uncovered? The reports about the disappearance of her husband."

"The articles we found in the bottom drawer of the file cabinet?"

"Yes. According to the dates on the papers, the disappearance of Oscar Prentis was in close proximity to the time Elcock and Cora were having their affair."

Giles started leafing through one of his folders. "Incredible. Oscar was never found."

"Do you think he left town when he discovered his wife was involved with Elcock?"

Giles closed the file. "That's unlikely. From the comments in those love letters we examined, Oscar was totally unaware. The two of them were laughing at her husband behind his back. He was a joke."

Lewis looked disgusted. "And what about the rumor about Louise Elcock being alive and well and living out her days in a private hospital in Connecticut?"

Giles grimaced "If this is true, she was far more clever than Oscar Prentis. It's possible she found out about the affair and its glaring reality resulted in a mental breakdown. Elcock must have had her committed. Because of the private location of his house, he and his wife were never in the public eye. No one would ever miss her."

"So both spouses were technically out of the picture."

"Yes. Aline mentioned something which still puzzles me. Elcock described to her, in considerable detail, the physical activities shared by himself and his wife: hiking, sailing, traveling, etcetera. But, Louise Elcock was an invalid, always sick and usually hospitalized with pneumonia, or some other form of illness. It's inconceivable to think she could partake of all these physical activities. He was actually talking about Cora. Cora was robust, healthy, an outdoor person. When you drove by her house, she was always raking leaves or up on a ladder cleaning gutters."

"Aline is so naive." Lewis's statement was without feeling.

"Matt, Elcock completely captivated her. She was putty in his hands. He simply used her to promote himself and his art."

"What are you going to do now?"

"I'm going to act on another one of my gut reactions, as you call it."

"Oh, and what might that be?"

Walter Giles stood up and walked up to Lewis's desk. "Hand me your phone."

64.

MONDAY AFTERNOON. Good bye, Cape Warren. It was over. The assignment, the vacation, the lives of two people, the love affair with Michael, and her future with *East Side/West Side* in New York City. However, for Aline, one aspect of this whole endeavor still remained unfinished. The solution. The final answer to the one haunting question in her mind and the many smaller, but pertinent questions still unanswered. For her, the research was just beginning.

She needed a new base from which to operate. A city large enough to have a library system with an extensive reference department. A city where she would not have to encounter anyone who knew her or who knew of her. All her ties with the individuals comprising her social life had to be broken. Her energy would be devoted to the work awaiting her. Nothing and no one could interfere.

Before she launched herself into this extension of her existing project, there remained one more thing to do. Reconnect with those close to her in New York. Her mother was at the top of the list and Martha Wilson was a close second. Her goal was to re-establish her business contacts, touching base with her associates who worked for other magazines and the New York newspapers. All of these friends had been sadly neglected by her. Hopefully, some of them would forgive her. Eventually she would end up back in New York. In a way, she regretted leaving there in the first place.

Her job was lost and she wanted desperately to defend her position against the release, which in her eyes, had been unfair and without just cause. If her associates became aware of all the facts, she was certain they would side with her. Their support was suddenly very important to her durability and her future.

Portland offered her what she was looking for. Much of the urban areas were now refurbished, fashioned after Boston's Faneuil Hall Marketplace and waterfront. There was an upbeat atmosphere in the downtown area and at night it was full of activity. It would be perfect for her needs.

All she had left to do was find a place to live. This had to be carefully thought out. A motel was out of the question. If she stayed in a motel or a hotel, she would be too easy to trace. Michael and Terri would be looking for her.

Also, the magazine wasn't going to pick up the tab for a hotel. All expenses from this point on were going to be coming out of her own pocket. As much as she didn't want to admit it, she knew another rooming house was the best solution. The thought of it chilled her, but it was the only answer—it was cheap and it didn't leave a paper trail. She could draw money on her credit cards and pay for everything with cash.

She would be eating all her meals out and would probably be doing some traveling. The total time spent in any one place would be short-term, anyway, so she could tolerate any place that didn't exactly meet with her approval. For now, she simply needed a room on the outskirts of town for a few days. She thought about changing her name, but decided against it. She would never be in one place long enough for it to make a difference. And she would never leave a forwarding address.

She would find a room outside of Cape Warren for the night. Tomorrow, once in Portland, she would get settled, and spend the rest of the day in the library. Once she found out the information she was looking for, she would be heading for Connecticut. Trying to find Hank Swenson was a lost cause. He could be squirreled up almost anywhere. And wherever he was, she was certain she would never find him.

But Louise Elcock was another story. Most likely, she was incarcerated in some quiet, out-of-the-way facility. Aline thought, *I simply find her and see her with my own eyes.* And she also needed to find out how and why Louise ended up in such a cruel situation, the solution to her husband's predicament.

When and if Aline could pull together the facts, she might or might not relate her findings to Walter Giles or Matt Lewis. She would consider it more thoroughly when the time came to make that decision.

And then there was Cora Prentis, Elcock's lover. God—the realization of it still tore at Aline's guts. She was so damn blind, a fool! She would never forgive herself for this lack of consciousness.

Knowing her own tenacity and drive, she had no doubt she would eventually find the answers. The thing bothering her the most, however, was a terrible realization. She didn't know the whole awful story, and more than likely it would be more than she could handle.

65.

MONDAY NIGHT. Michael left work just before six o'clock. He hadn't called the house during the work day, avoiding any conflict between himself and Aline. Once he was home and in her presence, he was certain there would be a reconciliation. He planned to ask her to join him for dinner at *Harborview*, the restaurant where they first met. If she would agree to spending the evening there, he thought the surroundings might renew the intimacy in their relationship and smooth out the rough edges.

Night was upon him and the back roads were deserted. He increased his speed slightly and hoped a change in her mood would be receptive to his proposal. In spite of it all, he felt Aline truly cared for him.

His headlights penetrated the woods and granite boulders lining the entrance to his house. Pulling up to the back stairs, he noticed her car was not there.

The back door was locked and he let himself in and immediately went to his bedroom. The bed was made and the room straightened up. He opened the closet. It was empty. All her luggage was gone. He went into the bathroom. Her toothbrush, shampoo, and personal items were no longer there. He rushed back into the kitchen, looking for a note. There was none. He started to search the living room for any message. Again he found nothing. She even cleaned up the peanut shells and threw away all the old newspapers before she left.

Exasperated, he felt empty and nauseous. He should contact Terri. Maybe she knew something.

The telephone only rang once at the diner and the owner answered it, sounding out of breath.

"Hello, this is Michael Williams. Is Terri there? I would like to speak to her for a second. It's urgent."

"She's here, in the back. Please make it short, it's hectic right now."

"Sure." He massaged the back of his neck with his left hand while he waited for Terri to come to the phone.

"Michael?"

"Hi. Listen, have you heard from Aline?"

"No, why?"

"She's gone."

"What?"

"She split. All her stuff is out of my house. She didn't even leave a note."

"You're kidding. What's the problem now?"

"We had words. About her dropping the case. She was pissed at me. Said I didn't understand."

"I warned you."

"I know. Don't remind me. This is just hard to accept. "

"After she cools off, she'll be back. She loves you."

"That's questionable. She's on to the next phase and she knows I don't want to be a part of it."

"I don't know what to say, Michael. I haven't heard a word from her. I guess I'm excluded, too."

"I'll let you get back to work. When you get home tonight, please call me."

"I will. If I hear from her in the meanwhile, I'll let you know."

"I'll be here later even if I go out."

“I’ll be in touch.” She hung up and when she did, that final click dashed his hopes. He was certain Aline would contact Terri, even if she didn’t want to speak to him.

Just sitting there, staring at the living room walls, was driving him mad. He had to do something. He locked up the house, leaving all the lights on, and sprinted down the back stairs. Only one other person might know where she was. Walter Giles.

The parking lot in front of the Cape Warren Police Department looked deserted, so he parked in a reserved space to save time. Within seconds, he was standing in front of the sergeant sitting at the night desk.

“Can I be of assistance?”

“Is Detective Giles here?”

“No, he’s not in the building.”

“Could you tell me where I might be able to find him?”

“He’s down at Mitchell Street.”

“Mitchell Street?”

“Yes, he’s working in the field. Why do you have to see him?”

“My name is Michael Williams. I need to tell him something.”

“Well, why don’t you come back in the morning. Maybe you could leave him a message. I’d be glad to give it to him.”

“No, I have to see him myself.”

“He doesn’t want to be disturbed.”

“He’ll be very interested in what I have to tell him.”

“When he’s working on an investigation he can’t be interrupted.”

“*I am* part of the investigation.”

Before the officer could respond, Michael was running out the door. He could be on Mitchell Street in ten minutes. If Aline left town, Giles would be annoyed. He had clearly requested that she not do so. Maybe she gave

Giles a forwarding address before she left. It was Michael's last chance..

Approaching his destination, Michael noticed a bright glow in the sky. Turning into the street, he could see several vehicles and vans blocking the area around Cora's house. Police cruisers were in the driveway and parked haphazardly on the front lawn. There was nowhere else to park. He left his car at the end of the street and walked down to the house. The whole property was being lit up by huge spotlights mounted on flatbed trucks.

Police personnel were walking back and forth, some dressed in yellow plastic slickers and rubber boots. Before he could reach the back yard, an officer stopped him with an outstretched arm. "Excuse me, this area is closed off to the publc. You will have to leave the premises."

"Please tell Walter Giles that Michael Williams is here to see him. I only need his attention for a second."

"Does he know you?"

"Yes, I'm involved in what he's doing." That always seemed to put them in motion.

"Don't move." The officer left to find Giles. Meanwhile, Michael was moving into a mild state of disbelief and wondering, *What the hell is happening here?*

Giles walked toward him with a fast step and wild eyes. "What are you doing here?"

"I need to ask you a question."

"What's that? I'm busy here. You'll have to exit this property."

"Aline is gone. She moved out, lock, stock and barrel. No note."

"When did this happen?"

"This afternoon. Can you help me?"

"Damn! She didn't notify me."

"We're nowhere. You were my last hope."

"If you find out her whereabouts, let me know as soon as possible."

"Believe me, if I do find out, you'll be the first to know."

"You better go now. I have work to do."

He turned and was out of sight, leaving Michael standing there with tears welling in the corners of his eyes. Instead of leaving, Michael walked toward the back of the yard adjoining 17 Mitchell Street. He ducked down behind a grove of tall, overgrown lilacs to avoid contact with the policemen next door. The opaque line of trees ran parallel to Cora's driveway. When he was abreast of Cora's house, the noise began. It was deafening. To his dismay, he was witnessing a frightening sight.

Working under the intense light was an immense orange backhoe, in the process of digging up Cora Prentis's back yard.

66.

TUESDAY MORNING. Portland, at one time the capital, was the largest city in Maine. It was built on a peninsula, projecting out into Casco Bay. The current capital Augusta, by comparison, was about one-third the size of this port.

Aline was eager to get settled here. She wanted to be back in an urban environment with the noise, traffic, movement of people and hustle-bustle associated with it. She wanted a complete change of venue and Portland would give it to her.

She spent the night in a motel about an hour south of Cape Warren and parked behind the row of rooms so her vehicle could not be seen from the road. The night passed quickly and she checked out early, the morning light filtering through the woods which acted like a backdrop for the motel. Finding another rooming house was the goal for this day.

The drive south to the city shouldn't take more than two hours. She had plenty of time to stop for breakfast along the way. Eating in diners, along with the truckers was a sure bet. They always knew where the good food was and her friends wouldn't be looking for her car hidden behind the huge semi's.

Maybe later, she would contact Terri and Michael. At this time, they weren't part of the schedule. Besides, they would attempt to thwart her efforts. She just didn't have time for them. They would have to wait.

She did intend to contact her mother, however. Her mother expected Aline to return to New York and would take more drastic action to locate her if she didn't show up. Aline's mother and Martha would be her only contacts. She trusted Martha. Martha would understand and would do what was asked of her. Aline could manipulate Martha.

Being back in control again felt reassuring. No matter what happened, she knew in her heart she would always return to this point. She was much stronger than any of them could have imagined. Her personal faith in herself always gave her courage in times of pressure and it wasn't going to fail her now. Uncovering the truth was near, gaving her additional strength. Soon it would all be finished and she could go on living.

67.

NOON. IT WAS ALREADY the last week of October, Halloween week, and the temperature was dropping significantly. The sunny, yellow days characterizing early autumn were long gone. The light reflected a bluegray cast and most of the trees were missing their gaudy mantle of leaves. Winter tones of dull lavenders, browns, taupes and charcoals gave the landscape a somber expression which matched her own. Black, stripped branches, like scrawny fingers, scratched at the subdued horizon. The stage and the scenery were set for the last act.

Compared to the heart of the city itself, the outskirts of Portland appeared drab and outdated. Aline decided to search the side streets as the best location to find a rooming house offering off-street parking. Locating an acceptable set-up was going to take time, but the entire day was open for her to hunt.

Private homes began to be replaced by apartment buildings as the downtown district drew closer. Most of them were narrow, three-story structures built close to the street. Alleyways ran between them, leading to small back yards. Aline drove around the streets for hours, trying not to become frustrated or impatient. She knew she should choose carefully. At last, she spotted a handwritten sign leaning against the pane of a bay window on the first floor of one of these buildings. It read: "WEEKLY RATES."

She parked across the street and sat for a few minutes, examining the rooming house. It was covered with gray aluminum siding and had dark brown trim, giving it a neat but rather dismal façade.

Slowly, she got out of the SUV, and without further hesitation, ran up the front steps to ring the door bell. No one answered, so she rang it again. There was a peep-hole facing her and she heard movement behind it. She knew she was being observed. The unmistakable sound of locks being unlatched briefly amused her. Fort Knox. A brass chain kept the door from opening completely, allowing the face behind it to examine solicitors.

"Yes?"

"I'm looking for a room. Do you rent?"

"What's your name?"

Aline hated it when someone couldn't answer a simple question flat out. "Aline Kranick. I'm working on a project in the Portland area and I'm looking for a place to stay."

"How long would you need a room?"

"Probably for a week, maybe a little longer."

The chain was released, indicating the possibility of entering this establishment. Standing in the threshold was a tiny elderly lady dressed entirely in clothing devoid of any color. She wore bifocals and a frayed apron covered her housedress. Her wispy gray hair was piled up on top of her head in a large knot and covered with a hairnet.

"It's a hundred and ten dollars a week, paid in advance. No smoking, no cooking, no guests, no pets."

The black and white cat staring down into the street from a second-story window obviously belonged to this lady.

"May I see the room?"

The woman allowed Aline to enter the house, stating, "My name is Miss Avery."

"Nice to meet you." Aline extended her hand, but Miss Avery declined to respond to it. Instead, she swept her hand back through her hair to avoid the physical contact.

"Any luggage?"

"Yes. It's in the car."

"Follow me."

They started climbing up the steep, creaky staircase to the second floor. Miss Avery struggled ahead of Aline, clinging to the heavy balustrade with her bony hands as she slowly and painstakingly pulled herself up the stairs. Once she reached the second-story landing, she stopped to catch her breath.

"It's down at the far end."

The corridor was poorly lit and musty. There were rooms on both sides. All the doorways were painted dark gray and there was no carpeting on the flooring. The echo of their footsteps sounded loud and obtrusive. The whole house gave the impression of being worn-out and overlooked, like a dusty, crushed dress locked in the bottom of an old truck in the attic. It was neglected and forgotten, like Miss Avery.

They stopped in front of a door at the end of the hall and the landlady unlocked it.

Pushing open the door, she waited for Aline to pass in front of her. "Take a look."

Aline entered the nondescript room. Like the rest of the house, it was monotonous and stuffy from lack of use, lack of life, and lack of air. Tattered scatter rugs dotted the bare floor which was scratched and abused from wear and tear. Furniture dragging over it, left gouges in its finish. A single bed and an antique dresser and night table comprised the furniture. Their condition matched the look of the floor. A tan Bates bedspread with white and black stripes coordinated with the limp curtains on the only window in the nine by twelve room. The window and the curtains were dirty.

Two framed ovals displaying a lady's and a gentleman's black silhouetted profiles on a white background were the only examples of hanging art. They were placed over the bed. The view from the window looked out on the back yards and electrical wires of the buildings in the next block. Weeds and untrimmed bushes filled the small spaces.

Aline's heart sank. She thought of her old room on Mitchell Street, clean and bright. It's success was its simple honesty, uncluttered and unpretentious.

"Do you want it?" Miss Avery's voice snapped.

"It's O.K."

"You have to share the shower at the other end of the hall. I'll bring you some towels."

As the old woman started to walk away, Aline called after her. "Where can I park?"

Miss Avery answered her without turning around. "There's a grocery store on the corner. If you pay the owner ten dollars a week, he'll let you park in the back behind the dumpster."

"Thank you. I have to go out, so you can leave the towels on the first floor landing. I can pick them up when I return."

"Suit yourself. I'll leave them in a paper shopping bag so they won't get soiled."

Aline couldn't stand the thought of this woman struggling up the front stairs again, just to place a few towels in her room.

They returned to the first floor and Aline paid her a week's rent. She told Miss Avery she would let her know by Friday if she needed the room for an additional week. Miss Avery gave her a receipt and keys to the front door and her room. Before she departed, she went over the house rules again.

When Aline left the building, it was early afternoon and she was hungry. She would find a place to have some lunch and then go in search of the library. At the grocery store, she showed the proprietor her rent receipt. Walking her out the delivery door at the back of the store, he showed her an area where she could park. He wrote down her license plate number, stuffing the ten dollars into his shirt pocket.

She sat in her vehicle, going over in her mind her situation. Her room was awful by comparison to Cape Warren, but it was time to make sacrifices and this location provided a perfect cover for her. No one would be looking for her here. It was an unassuming neighborhood and she could feel free to operate out of it.

Besides, she would not be spending much time here. She would doing research or traveling. This was simply a crash pad. Also, it was becoming dark early and slipping into her room at the end of the day would probably go unnoticed. The setup would work.

68.

TUESDAY AFTERNOON. The reference librarian at the main Portland Library was very helpful to Aline, taking her back into the stacks to locate specific publications which would offer the information necessary to start the search.

The government phone book for the state of Connecticut listed all the state and government telephone numbers for departments pertaining to public health. Aline expressed her appreciation to the busy librarian for taking the time to assist her, then copied down the necessary information. The next step was purchasing a new cell phone in a local store, using phone cards. As far as New York was concerned, the assignment was finished. If additional charges were continuing to come in, she was sure an effort would be made to bring usage of her phone to a dead halt. Also, she didn't want to risk her calls being traced on her old cell phone. She would be using her personal credit cards. Charges on them would be billed to her New York address.

She didn't want anyone finding out she was in Portland. Everyone, including the state police, would be searching for her here if they found out where she was.

The strip malls would have Radio Shacks and telephone stores where she could buy a phone. Finding a quiet place to work and make calls was all she needed to do to start her in the right direction.

Her room wouldn't provide the appropriate place to work. She didn't want Miss Avery snooping around or eavesdropping. She couldn't make personal calls from the library, but she could order some food in a fast-food restaurant, making her calls at her table. The clientele would be moving in and out quickly and no one would be hanging around there long enough to care about her activity.

Tonight she would call her mother, telling her she was coming home the beginning of November to share Thanksgiving with her. Her mother would be thrilled.

Before leaving Maine, she should return to Cape Warren to say good-bye to Michael and Terri. She believed they would forgive her for remaining incognito for so long. She wanted to leave them on good terms and was planning to continue her friendship with both of them after returning home.

Once in New York, a new apartment, a new job and a fresh start would be her priorities. This would include improving on the time spent with her mother. A true communication with her mother hadn't been addressed in a long time. A new life was beginning.

69.

THURSDAY MORNING. Aline worked in the Portland library for two days, researching the hospitals in Connecticut. She considered giving Miss Avery another week's rent, even though the thought of extending her stay was almost unbearable. But, this consideration had no relevance because the assignment was almost over.

Sometimes she would lie in bed in the early morning hours, wondering how this seemingly creative and pleasing project was still evolving into such a horrendous monster, completely illogical and unforgiving. The culmination of her research was overdue to be buried.

This glaring fact was tearing her to shreds, emotionally. She couldn't let the outsiders destroy it, outsiders who showed no real interest in it from the beginning. She must follow it through, no matter what the cost. Even if she lost her job, she could try to sell it to another magazine. Free-lancing was always an option. Many of her associates made a good living as free-lance writers and they would be able to give her the leads she needed. She wouldn't give it up. In spite of everything, Thomas Elcock deserved his curtain call and she promised herself she would honor his memory by finalizing her goal and getting this tribute to him in print.

Aline covered a lot of ground in a week. Everyone she contacted at the state agencies was efficient and thorough in assisting her to find the appropriate agencies she was looking for.

The Administrative Services Department of Mental Health and Addiction for the state of Connecticut informed her of the sanitariums run by the state. They strongly recommended she contact the Connecticut Department of Public Health for a list of private psychiatric hospitals, since this was the other alternative. Aline decided to start with them first.

Much to her surprise, there was a current listing of only six of these facilities for the state of Connecticut. This would facilitate the hunt. Public Health also offered to fax the information to her if she could provide them with a fax number. Any Mail Boxes, Etc. or office supply store would have a fax machine for her to use.

She was intent on ending the deception of this plot. Finding Louise Elcock was necessary to satisfy her own ego. Except for this fact, nothing was preventing her from going home. She supposed most of her acquaintances would consider her unreasonable, stubborn and selfish, but she didn't look at it that way. Too much emotion had been exchanged between herself and Thomas Elcock. Getting to the root of the charade was urgent.

Was she really such a fool, blocking out the truth with her hero worship and devotion? Did he simply play her to advance himself and his craft? What were the true circumstances under which he was forced to have Louise committed? Facing the last cruel answers to these questions was going to be painful.

Michael and Terri would always be there for her. And so would Martha. They would help her get through this final development.

She found a fax machine and called back the Department of Public Health. Within twenty minutes, her request came through. If she was fortunate enough to locate the facility in which Louise resided, she could drive to Connecticut tomorrow.

She copied many maps of the state in the library and marked the location of the six hospitals with a highlighter. Calculating the miles and driving hours would be the last step. Where should she make the calls? It was too cold to sit in the park and too public to work in a Laundromat. She decided to wait until around three-thirty to go look for a restaurant.

70.

THURSDAY AFTERNOON. Aline sat near a large plate glass window in Burger King, looking over her list. A few patrons were scattered about the dining area. Because of the lull in business, the employees were out of sight. After contacting five of the hospitals, Aline came up empty. None ever heard of Louise Elcock. There was only one more to call, the one in the New Canaan area.

At first she hesitated. If this one turned out to be a dead end, it meant starting to work on the sanitariums run by the state. This would extend her stay in New England for yet another week, maybe more. It also meant she would have to find another rooming house. She had to keep moving around to avoid detection. The only problem was she didn't know if her energy level was sufficient to continue the search.

She must finish this last step To quit now would betray all the work already achieved. She dialed the phone number and waited.

"May I help you? Hello, may I help you?"

Aline hesitated to answer, afraid of failure. "Yes, I'm sorry. My name is Aline Kranick and I am looking for a Louise Elcock. I was wondering if she might be one of your residents."

"Are you a member of the immediate family?"

"No, but I am a personal friend of her husband, Thomas J. Elcock."

"Only family members are allowed visitation privileges."

Her spirit soared and her thoughts flashed, *She is there! She is alive and she is there.*

"I'm going to be passing through the New Canaan area and wanted to stop in to pay my respects."

"I'm sorry, Ms. Kranick, but I can't allow it. Hospital rules."

"Can't you make an exception in my case? I just want to look in on her."

"I will have to discuss this matter with my supervisor and she isn't here today. Why don't you call back tomorrow morning. Ask for Mrs. Payne."

"Mr. Elcock and I were very close," she pleaded, "and I know in my heart he would have wanted me to stop and see her on my way home."

"Please call back tomorrow," was the monotone answer.

It was evident that they already knew of Elcock's death by their lack of response to her past tense reference. Aline's verbal maneuvering was not going to change this nurse's mind.

"I'll call back tomorrow morning. Thank you for your help."

Aline ended the call and said out loud, "Thank you for nothing." The patrons ignored her. Not all of it was negative, however. Even if she was being denied access to the visitation, at least she knew where Louise was located.

The rest of the day was going to drag on. Dinner and a movie would help kill some time. Tomorrow, if the answer was still going to be a flat "no," then she would have to think of another way to get in. She refused to be turned away, not now.

New Canaan was close to the New York border. After seeing Louise, she could go straight home. Or should she see Michael first? Maybe she should contact him before driving to Connecticut. No, he might try to stop her. It would be better to call him before going home.

If she received a favorable response from him, she would make an effort to see him once more before leaving Maine. If not, she would simply depart. Their future would be his decision.

71.

THURSDAY NIGHT. Aline left Monday. Michael spent most of his evenings lying on the couch, waiting for Terri to get in touch with him when she took her break. The TV was on but he wasn't watching it or even listening to it. It became background noise, a form of companionship to help fill his hours of loneliness.

Losing Aline was easier to accept than the hard fact of his life returning into the same empty void it was before he met her. Listening to the reassuring tones of Terri's voice, as she tried in vain to nurse him through his grief, was his only salvation.

If she didn't get out of work too late, they would meet for a nightcap and console each other. She felt the same as he did, but to a lesser degree. They both shared the feelings of being deserted, used and taken advantage of. Aline's lack of communication with them just caused these feelings to be blown way out of proportion. The whole situation was beyond reason, inhumane, as far as they were concerned. They both felt they did everything in their power to be supportive, understanding and loving, each sacrificing their time, effort and emotions to fulfill Aline's desperation.

And she, in return, was totally indifferent, unconscious to their personal involvement in her cause. Her goals had become their goals. Her happiness and well-being were their quest. They felt she rewarded their loyalty by casting them aside when she was finished with them.

All the lights but one were turned off in Michael's living room. His eyes were closed, his hands folded on his chest. He was still in his work clothes, including his shoes, the suit jacket hanging over the back of a chair. Without her presence, he couldn't sleep in his bed.

The cordless phone rang on the coffee table. He knew it was Terri, but in a way he didn't want to answer it. The conversation would be the same and he was tired of going over the subject of Aline again and again.

Terri would nag him about skipping meals, not getting enough sleep, drowning himself in self-pity. It was starting to annoy him. Finally, he picked up.

"Michael? Were you in the other room?"

"Yes, I was washing my face and hands."

"Did you have dinner?"

"No, I'm not hungry."

"Michael, snap out of this. I'm disappointed in you."

"*PLEASE*, don't lecture me tonight. I don't want to hear it."

She took the impact of his anger. For a moment, she didn't say anything. She ventured, "I'm worried about you."

"Don't waste your time. I'll survive." His sentences were biting.

"Thanks a lot. I do care about you, you know."

She was hurt and he could hear it in her voice. He felt badly about answering her in such a rude manner. "I'm sorry. I'm not myself tonight."

"You haven't heard a word from her since she left town. I don't think she's coming back."

"I know she isn't."

"You should try to get out of the house more. Stop dwelling on your loss."

"I know. I'm just not fit company for anyone I care about, especially you."

"Why don't we do something this weekend. Maybe get out of town."

"What do you suggest?"

"Let's drive to Boston and take in a show. What do you think?"

"It won't help."

"And anchoring yourself to your house every night will?"

"I'll let you know tomorrow."

"Would you like me to come over?" She kept trying.

"I don't think so. I just want to watch some sports on the tube."

"I'll be here if you change your mind."

"Thanks." His lackluster tone let her know it really didn't matter to him if she showed up or not.

"I'll probably do something with one of my girlfriends. Anyway, take it easy Michael."

"Yeah. Talk to you soon."

He hung up and rolled over on his side to go to sleep. He still wore his shoes.

72.

FRIDAY. HALLOWEEN. Aline was up early. She decided to call the hospital back around ten o'clock. It would give the staff time to go through their early morning routines.

She stopped at the usual luncheonette down the street for breakfast. It was hot and noisy and she liked it because it reminded her of the diner in Cape Warren. The service was fast. After breakfast there was an hour and a-half to wait before she could call.

Some window-shopping would make the time pass quickly. It only took fifteen minutes to reach the downtown district of Portland. Most of the shops would still be closed, but it didn't matter. The fresh air and exercise would do her good.

As she drove downtown, she was imagining the response of the supervisor to her call and thinking of a counter-response. It wasn't going to be easy, writing a script in her mind and playing both roles. If she appealed to Mrs. Payne in sympathetic terms and avoided obstinacy, she felt her request would be honored.

She parked in a public lot and began walking along the streets, looking often at her watch. Still forty-five minutes to go. The city's extensive program of upgrading its commercial area was a grand success. Faneuil Hall Marketplace in Boston represented a strong influence here. The quality of the shops was very upscale, giving the city a needed contemporary veneer.

Almost ten o'clock. She decided to return to her SUV to make the call. After she climbed inside, she turned on the ignition and the heat. Next to her was a pad of paper and a pen to take down directions. She entered the number on her cell phone and waited.

"Good morning, may I help you?"

"I would like to speak to Mrs. Payne. Is she available?"

"May I ask who is calling?"

"Aline Kranick. I spoke to the head nurse yesterday and she advised me to call Mrs. Payne this morning."

"Would that be Mrs. Austin?"

"Yes."

"One moment, please." Aline was holding and her impatience was not being appeased by the recorded message assuring her that "your call is important to us."

"Miss Kranick? This is Mrs. Payne. How may I help you?"

"Mrs. Payne, I am a close friend of the Elcock family and I was wondering if I could stop in to see Mrs. Elcock on my way back to New York."

"Close friend in what capacity?"

"I was very close to Mr. Thomas J. Elcock. My magazine was writing an article about him before his death. I did all the research on that project."

"Miss Kranick, I don't think it would be very productive for you to see Mrs. Elcock. She lives in more or less of a dream state. Attempting to carry on a conversation with her would be a waste of your time."

"Well, I just wanted to look in on her."

"I must say, I find you overly persistent. I don't quite understand why it is so important for you to see Mrs. Elcock. Besides, I'm sure you were told about the visitation rights given only to the immediate family. I hesitate to interrupt her routine. She needs her rest, especially now."

Especially now? No visitors. It was a hard fact to swallow. Aline didn't want to ask the next question, but she knew she had to. "Did her husband ever come to see her?"

"Really, Ms. Kranick. I'm not in a position to disclose personal family information of this nature to you."

Aline took Mrs. Payne's answer as a confirmation of Elcock's desire to have his wife out of the way. She was inconvenient for him. For him and Cora. Although this actuality numbed Aline's senses, she tried again: "If you let me just let me look at her, I promise I'll leave. I won't make any attempt to speak with her. She won't even know I'm there. You can accompany me to guarantee it. I'll never bother you or your staff again. I'm returning to New York to continue my career."

"Why are you so insistent, Miss Kranick?"

"When I was interviewing her husband, he spoke of his wife in such loving terms. I guess I would like to think of them as a couple. I feel as though I know her after hearing so much about her. His memory will always live on with me and I want her to be part of that memory. This may be very hard for you to understand, Mrs. Payne, but it would mean a great deal to me if I could take back to New York a visual picture of this dear old lady."

Aline was really overstating her case, but it was her last endeavor to find closure.

There was a moment of silence from Mrs. Payne. "Visiting hours are on the weekends, from two to five. I don't work on the weekends, but if you come by this evening, before five o'clock, I will accompany you to her room for only a few seconds. This is highly irregular."

"I'll be there. Thank you so much for your cooperation."

Aline scribbled the directions to the hospital. It was described as being located in a wooded area and she would have to travel down some secondary roads to find it. Sheer determination and New York drive would get her there.

It was ten-fifteen. She would have to hurry. The trip would take at least seven hours, maybe more, depending on traffic. She drove back to the rooming house as fast as she could and quickly packed. Before rushing out the building, she slipped her house keys under the office door in a plain envelope. The trip would be tiring, and she didn't want to waste time stopping to eat. The corner store would provide her with bottled water and snacks. She could get gas on the way to the turnpike.

It didn't take long to gather the items she needed in the store. On her way out, she was occupied with putting her money back into her wallet and didn't notice the stack of morning papers piled nearby. One of the headlines on the front page read: SKELETAL REMAINS OF MISSING CAPE WARREN MAN FOUND IN WIDOW'S BACK YARD.

73.

STAFFORD GARDENS WAS A PRIVATE HOSPITAL located in southwestern Connecticut on an old estate framed by a scenic woodland, just off a well-traveled secondary road. Occupancy was limited to approximately thirty residents. Staffing was highly selective and the nurses in this hospital were very experienced, professional, and committed to the care of the individuals assigned to them. The nursing shifts were 24/7 and a resident physician occupied an adjoining house connected to the main building. The architecture of the complex was Victorian and most of the buildings had recently been restored. The hospital portrayed stately composure and total tranquility.

Activity increased as the employees started to prepare for the supper hour which came early here. Night staff gathered around the nurses' station, checking charts, looking at their watches and busying themselves with their duties. Chatter was limited. The time to talk would come later, when things quieted down and the residents were asleep.

The head nurse left specific instructions for the nurses to give special attention to the monitors. One of the patients walked out of the facility recently and wandered off. This was always a problem in small nursing homes and private institutions where security wasn't as tight as a state hospital. With limited personnel who were constantly occupied, it was a major concern. Someone had to be accountable for walk-outs.

In the case of this last occurrence, Mary Rabino took the blame. She was an excellent nurse, with impeccable credentials, and she took this slip-up very hard. Now, she was fighting off severe depression and low self-esteem because of her error. She was severely reprimanded and was doing extra duty to compensate for her mistake. It was her way of satisfying her own sense of atonement.

Eventually, the state police returned the resident to the hospital in perfect condition. Everyone was relieved. The resident had been missing for four days. A dispatcher in the Stamford bus station noticed an elderly passenger wandering around looking disoriented and called the facility to check on the walk-outs. It was a first-time incident for the station.

Staff on duty was trying to be more alert. Mary was very popular with the other nurses and the head nurse, in particular. Her failing would be short-lived as far as her associates were concerned.

In spite of this, she was very jittery today. "I hope we don't get those snow flurries," she said, trying to get her mind off the matter. She spoke to another nurse who was busy placing medications into small paper cups, concentrating on the task at hand.

"It shouldn't be too intense, Mary. The weatherman said we might get an inch. But it might be slippery just the same. I bet you're glad to get your new coat back! Just in time."

Mary answered, not looking up from her work. She was suffering from a case of double-embarrassment, the walk-out plus the missing coat.

"Maybe it will turn to rain. I need new tires and I have to find the time to buy them. My husband already gave me the money for them. He'll be upset with me if I don't get it done soon. Somehow, I never remember to put it at the top of my to-do list."

"Mary, you better take care of that right away. Winter is here, girl, and you don't want to get caught."

"I know. I'm planning to take care of it on my next day off." She looked at her watch again.

The other nurse stopped what she was doing to get her friend's attention. "When was the last time you checked on her?"

"Twenty minutes ago. Should I go again? I was going to wait until I brought her the dinner tray."

The other nurse just kept looking at Mary.

"O.K., O.K. I'll go right now. We don't want to lose her again, do we?" She hurried down the hall.

"Don't forget to collect those old *New York Times*. She's turning into a clutter bug."

74.

FRIDAY AFTERNOON. At last, Aline was on her way. It was over, all of it. Maybe she should call Giles, to let him know about finding Louise Elcock. But after thinking about it carefully, she knew it was not a smart idea. He'd want to drag her back to Cape Warren for additional questioning.

She must continue, alone in her quest. A sense of detachment came over her spirit, in spite of one fact. She was finally closing the door on all of it. Yet there was no feeling of accomplishment. Now returning to New York was the only important event in her future.

The light was failing quickly because of a heavy overcast and the air smelled like snow. In New England it wasn't unusual for the weather to turn nasty early in the season. Dusk was settling in and the sky was losing its sparse color. As she drew closer to her destination, the woodsy areas became more prevalent. Acres of dense, barren trees made up the miles of horizon stretching before her. Soon it would be dark. She had to keep her eyes on the road ahead.

The car in front of her slowed down to pick up a hitchhiker. She saw a few of them earlier in the afternoon. Most of the traffic consisted of pick-up trucks, small commercial vans, numerous SUVs and passenger cars. Another hour and twenty minutes or so should meet with the deadline given to her by the head nurse.

The only other decision to make was what to do after seeing Louise. She debated in her mind as to whether she should continue on to New York. In a way, she yearned to be back in the city, to touch base with her friends there, to see her mother.

On the other hand, maybe she should return to Maine to see Terri and Michael. She didn't know how he was going to react to her when she contacted them. She left him angry and stubborn, but knew she wanted to continue seeing him and would ask him to forgive her. If she didn't do this before returning to New York, he would be lost to her forever.

She was certain her instincts would help her make the right decision. When she turned on the ignition in the hospital parking lot-her search complete-she would know what to do.

It was beginning to snow.

75.

FRIDAY NIGHT. Terri finally convinced Michael to join her for dinner. She wanted him to channel his mindset into a more productive direction. Maybe her efforts were fruitless, but she would try.

He had told her he would pick her up at seven-thirty and he would be wearing a suit and tie. If they were going to dine out, he wanted them to choose a restaurant with some atmosphere and an above-average cuisine.

She was looking forward to seeing him and wanted to look especially nice. She was wearing her roommate's best dress and was helped with her hair and make-up. Terri usually didn't put the time or enthusiasm into her personal appearance, but today was different. When she was finished getting ready, she looked at herself in the mirror. Her roommate did an excellent job. They were pleased with what they saw and felt Michael would also approve.

He was on time, as usual, and after he rang the bell, she took a deep breath, slowly walking to greet him. The door was swung open wide and he entered the room without looking at her. When he turned to her, a slight look of surprise spread over his face. "You look fabulous."

"Thank you." She blushed deep red.

"You should wear a dress more often."

"I'll get my coat." She said nervously.

He said good night to her roommate, helped Terri on with her coat and escorted her out of the house.

The air was cool to the skin and braced her. "A little nippy today, but I like the cold weather better than those sweltering summer months," she said.

"I agree. Somehow, you have more energy in the winter months. When it's humid, I'm in slow motion."

He opened the door on the passenger's side of the car and softly closed it after she was seated.

Once inside himself, he turned to her, putting his right arm across the back of her seat. "Where would you like to go? It will have to be somewhere special because you look so nice."

"You know we don't have too many choices around here. We could always go north to the coast and do some exploring. It would be more fun if we found someplace new."

"That sounds good to me. Let's go."

He seemed to be coming around and she felt content. Everything was perfect. Today would be a day for her to remember for a long time.

They drove for an hour and a-half, headed east. The conversation skirted the subject of Aline, but Terri knew in her heart that sooner or later he would begin to discuss his lost love. She hoped it would be later.

The sunlight was failing and small pinpoints of yellow lights began to appear from the surrounding residential areas. Michael was looking for a restaurant. "I don't know about you, but I'm very hungry.."

"I didn't eat any lunch," she replied. "I was saving my appetite for tonight."

"Let's take this coast road. I see some lights up ahead."

"Where are we?"

"I think we're outside of Rockland, but I'm not exactly sure. I don't drive up here very often," he admitted.

Eventually they found a restaurant they both agreed on. They parked and went inside.

A hostess met them at the door. After stopping by the coat room to check their coats, she directed them to the nonsmoking area. They were lucky enough to get a table at the back of the main dining room, in a corner. It was out of the main stream of traffic and busboys and it overlooked the water.

"This is exactly what I had in mind," Michael told the hostess.

"I love it," Terri added.

A waiter came over to their table and poured ice water into their glasses. "Your server will be right with you." He handed them the menus.

While Terri studied her menu, Michael studied her face. He was always too absorbed with Aline to pay much attention to her friend. Compared to Aline, Terri's complexion was healthy and robust. Her auburn hair was shiny, her skin clear. Her eyes were the color of honey, bright and full of expression. There were no lines of stress or anxiety to spoil her appearance. He never took the time to notice how attractive she was and this new revelation fascinated him.

They ordered their food and a bottle of wine. The hustle-bustle of the dining room was only a minor distraction. It was actually soothing, considering both of them led virtually solitary lives. The restaurant was busy and almost all the tables were occupied. The waiter arrived at their table with a bottle of red burgundy. He poured a small amount into Michael's glass and waited for him to taste it.

"This is excellent."

The waiter served them wine and departed.

"Terri, let's have a toast. Here's to a fresh start and a better life."

"And happier times for both of us."

They clicked their glasses gently and drank to their hopes. Michael leaned back in his chair and looked at Terri. For a few moments he said nothing, but she knew he was pulling together his thoughts and he was about to launch into a conversation. She held her breath. She didn't want a full night of discussing Aline to ruin her evening. Tonight was her night.

Michael smiled at her and said, "I'm glad you coaxed me out. I can't go on like this any more. You're right, it's taking too much out of me."

"Don't beat yourself up. We've both been through a terrible ordeal. We have to move on."

"I know. I don't think I want to renew my relationship with Aline even if she returns to Cape Warren. She revealed a side of her personality I'm not compatible with. She's a hard lady to come to terms with when you're standing in her way or disagreeing with her. I've had enough of it."

"I'm sorry she hurt you."

"She hurt both of us, just threw us away like one of her old newspapers. I'm pretty upset about it."

"So am I, but I can't let it ruin my life. I just have to be more careful in the future to select my friends with more caution. Don't forget, she used me, too."

Terri's voice was bitter and she wanted him to know it, but she didn't want to sound stupid by acting totally devastated by Aline's pseudo-friendship.

Michael continued, "I think we both need a big break from Aline."

She liked the sound of the words, but she wondered if he really meant it. "Michael, you and I have to start taking advantage of being young and single. There is so much to see and do out there. We owe it to ourselves to take part in it before other commitments prevent us from doing so."

"Now you're talking. I spend too many nights alone, watching that damn TV. I can do that later when I'm an old man. "

"We live close to Portland and even Boston. We should start going to the theatre, to the ballet, the Pops concerts. Why don't we go to New York some weekend? There's a lot of life to live. Let's start living it."

"That's a great idea. I'd love to take in New York."

The evening was turning into something special. He was shedding his skin. Their conversation took on an enthusiastic note. Aline's name was dropped from it entirely. They were sharing in each other's companionship, loyalty and mutual pain. And they were drawing closer together, starting to build a more dependable and meaningful friendship, one reflecting the ideals they both held dear.

76.

FRIDAY, DUSK. At the end of the hall on the first floor was a corner room assigned to a small woman in her late seventies. This was the best room on the ground floor. It had a huge bay, consisting of three tall windows looking out over the expansive forest behind the hospital.

Soon the spotlights would automatically turn on and put the buildings in glaring prominence, contrasting them against the inky woodland.

The woman sat in a rocking chair with a high ladder-back and thick, padded cushions, waiting for the snow to begin falling. The nurses told her about the impending storm. Watching it drift by the bright floodlights, at the corner of the house, would relax her, put her at peace. She would be able to watch it for hours.

The door to her room eased open and Mary Rabino softly moved inside and approached the lady occupying the rocking chair. Mary stood in front of her and gave her a big smile. "I just came by to find out what you might want for dinner tonight."

The old woman stopped rocking and gazed at the nurse with big, watery eyes. She returned the smile but she didn't return an answer.

Mary bent forward, bringing her head lower and into the woman's level of sight. She tried again. "Tonight we're having broiled chicken, rice and peas. I hope you are hungry because it smells very good to me."

The older woman just kept smiling.

"Does that sound appetizing to you?"

This time there was a nod.

Mary felt satisfied. "All right. I'll see you in a bit. Are you comfortable?"

Again, a nod.

Mary left the room, closing the door behind her, and returned to the night desk.

After the nurse left, the old woman nestled her head back into the soft cushion, looking out the window into the night. Mary had pushed back the curtains so the view of the backyard wouldn't be obscured.

The first delicate flakes were beginning to float down lazily in suspended spirals, one after the other. In the beginning, she could count them individually, but soon they increased in volume and speed, evolving into one white, moving mass, blocking out the woods.

She was slowly rocking again, a smile curling up the corners of her mouth. The damp, still air, moving through the glass panes, began touching her body and enveloping it in a chilly embrace. Deliberately, she gathered the generous folds of her fuchsia mohair shawl, wrapping it snugly around her shoulders. She had all night to watch the snow.

77.

SATURDAY MORNING. It was a few minutes past five o'clock. A Connecticut trucker was the first driver to spot Aline's vehicle. It was upside down in a ditch, running parallel to the southbound lane, covered with snow. The skid marks were buried under a thick, white blanket.

Evidently, she was driving too fast and spun out of control on a sharp curve of the road, greasy with cold slush. She was killed instantly from head trauma when the car flipped over.

The truck driver notified the police on his C.B. radio and was thoughtful enough to wait for their arrival before he left the scene of the accident. He told the police to bring an ambulance with them.

After the officers arrived, he sat in his truck to watch the proceedings. The scene held him spellbound. He made a commitment there on the spot to take better care of himself, to drive more carefully, and to appreciate what he usually took for granted—before he lost it, before it was too late.

Lightning Source UK Ltd.
Milton Keynes UK
UKHW020632170720
366698UK00015B/1935

9 781951 985349